A Gamble in Gozo

An Elspeth Duff Mystery

Ann Crew

A Gamble on Gozo is a work of fiction. Names, characters, and incidents are the products of the author's imagination. Any resemblance to actual persons, living or dead, is entirely coincidental. Existing locations and persons are used fictionally. The Kennington hotels and Magdelena's farmhouse on Gozo do not exist.

Cover photographs of the Azure or Zerka Window at Dwejra Point and Gozitan Landscape near San Lawrenz with Converted Farmhouses and the Mediterranean Sea in the Distance, both on Gozo, by Ann Crew © 2004 and 2017

Author's photograph by Ian Crew

ACE/AC Editions

ISBN-13: 9781548374488
ISBN-10: 1548374482

Library of Congress Control Number: 2017910166
CreateSpace Independent Publishing Platform
North Charleston, South Carolina

anncrew.com

elspethduffmysteries.com

Also by Ann Crew
[In Order of Publication]

A Murder in Malta

A Scandal in Stresa

A Secret in Singapore

A Crisis in Cyprus

Praise for *A Murder in Malta*:

"Each main character has a rich backstory with enough skeletons in closets to provide grist for a number of future novels

An often compelling . . . excursion through exotic locales featuring unusual, complex characters." —*Kirkus Review*

To Joce and Ray
with thanks for all
their kindness and many cups of tea.

Part 1

Magdelena Cassar

Preface

"I can't marry you, Dickie. I just can't. I don't belong here, and you do. Marjorie did, but I don't. Surely you can understand that."

Richard Munro watched the tears run uncontrollably down Elspeth Duff's cheeks and drop off her strong jaw. She did not bother to brush them away when they fell on her silk blouse. His heart was filled with dismay.

"Elspeth, I love you. Try. They're not all that bad. I admit Daphne and Adrian can be a bit pompous, but they'll come round."

"Pompous? Dickie, if they could call out the court executioner and have me dragged out to be hung, drawn and quartered, they would have done so. No, this isn't my world, and I don't want to be a part of it."

She wiped the back of her hand across her chiselled nose and, with disgust, looked down at the mess she had made. He handed her his handkerchief.

Taking it, she said, "You're asking too much of me. Let me go." She blew her nose and wiped her cheeks.

"Do you love me, Elspeth? In Cyprus you said you did."

"I loved you in Cyprus and even before that. I can't deny that. I still love you, but I cannot marry you and become a part of your world. I'm not Lady This or Lady That. I'm a plain Highland lass who has made a major muddle of most of my life, but I've finally managed to come heads up and happily afloat. Now, just as everything seemed to be going right, you came along, made me fall in love with you and then expected me to morph into your life. I couldn't do that when we were young, and I can't now. I don't know why I gave in to you in Nicosia and agreed to marry you at Christmas."

"You said you loved me," he pleaded.

"I do. I love you more than the earth, the moon and the stars. I love you more than I thought it possible to love another human being, but the price of marrying you is too great. Can't we just stay lovers?"

Richard jerked in displeasure at the word 'lovers'. He found it common.

She must have read his mind. "See, that's just it!" she said, tears gone.

"I told them your cousin was the Earl of Tay. That seemed to please them," he said in Daphne and Adrian's defence.

Elspeth snorted unpleasantly. "Have they checked *Debrett's* recently? Or is that dusty tome unlikely to reveal what a joke the whole Tay earldom is, granted in seventeen forty-six by the Duke of Cumberland after the Battle of Culloden to a traitor who turned against his own clan. Nowadays the earldom is probably the most impoverished in all Scotland. I've pleaded with Johnnie to drop the title, but he says he can't, and, besides, it helps him in business. Business, your lofty in-laws would say. Trade?"

"Elspeth, why are you so against titles?"

"I always have been and my mother was before me. A title tells so little about a person, unless they have earned it, as you did. And I don't expect to change my opinion, especially after meeting your in-laws." She raised her voice. "Tell the Higher than the Almighty Earl and Countess of Glenborough that the riffraff has departed, and you have been saved from a descent into hell."

Elspeth spun round and left the room, slamming the door as she did so.

Richard stood there paralysed, unsure how to act. He wanted to grab Elspeth and shake some sense into her, and he also wanted to embrace her and wipe away her anger and tears. Miserable in his indecision, he did neither. He stood and stared at the back of the closed door and hoped no one in the other parts of the building had heard their angry exchange.

1

All afternoon Elspeth knew the storm with Richard was looming, and, with her usual efficiency, she had prepared for it. Before confronting Richard, she had written a stiffly polite letter of regret to her host and hostess, packed her clothes and programmed the number of the local taxi company into her Blackberry. After slamming the door on Richard, she dialled that number. A distant voice assured her that a taxi would be there within ten minutes. Calm now, she waited for a response from the room where she had left Richard, but the door stood unmoving and unrepentant. Elspeth set her jaw, flared her nostrils and carried her own cases to the imposing front door of Glenborough Castle, home of the Earl and Countess of the same name, the insufferable Daphne and Adrian. She hoped her gesture would horrify her hosts. The cold outside air hit her in the face, and she drew in her breath. She was uncertain that she had done the right thing, but she saw no way back.

*

Sir Richard Munro, Her Majesty's High Commissioner to the Republic of Malta, was still standing shell-shocked, when Daphne, Countess of Glenborough, entered the room.

"Richard, I've just received the most extraordinary note from Elspeth Duff, saying she has been called away unexpectedly. Simmons said he saw her leave by taxi a short while ago. What a different sort of woman she is. She sounds slightly American at times. Where did you find her?"

Richard looked at Daphne, knowing full well by her inflection what she meant. Elspeth had not been accepted into the family fold.

"I've known her since I was at Oxford," he said stiffly. "She's a true Scotswoman, fiercely so, although she was educated at Cambridge and has spent her life living around the world, much of the time in California." He was not sure if he was defending Elspeth or merely explaining her.

"At least she dresses beautifully," Daphne said with a condescending look. 'What did you say she does with her life when not traipsing after you?"

"She is one of the security advisors for the Kennington hotel chain," Richard said *sotto voce*, although he immediately regretted his timidity. He clenched his jaw.

"A private investigator in couturier clothing!" Daphne's laughter pealed across the room. "It's just as well she left. I find her uncomfortable. Not quite our sort. Come, let's have a sherry."

Over the years Richard had never liked his sister-in-law, but now he loathed her. Still, he followed her docilely into the drawing room.

Damn Elspeth, Richard thought as he pulled the duvet more closely around his back. Why do I keep chasing her? She has bewitched me for as long as I have known her, as if she had cast a strange spell on me, and now she has taken flight in the most awkward way. But he knew that cursing Elspeth would not stop the pain he was feeling, or the love. Why did I bring her here? And why did she run away? Daphne was being particularly difficult, but, since he and his wife, Lady

Marjorie, who had died four years before, had been childless, he had taken special interest in Fergus, their nephew, Adrian and Daphne's son. Richard could not drop Fergus from his life and, if he were to marry Elspeth, she would get to know the Glenboroughs. Certainly Elspeth should put up with them for Fergus's sake. She had even seemed to like Fergus when they had met the day before. She had showed great interest in his latest electronic device and told him about making films in Hollywood. Fergus had been entranced and really did not want to go off to bed although bidden by his nanny. Why would Elspeth bolt now? In her employment at the Kennington hotels she undoubtedly had dealt with people far more offensive than Daphne.

He turned over in bed and cursed the coldness of the room, thinking of the many times he had spent during the last two years in Kennington hotels, where every luxury was considered and where heat could be adjusted to an individual's liking. He thought about the nights he had spent with Elspeth and missed the warmth of her body next to his and the gentle sounds of her breathing after she fell asleep. Adjusting the duvet and listening to the wind crash against the window was not a substitute.

He came back to Elspeth's parting words before her abrupt departure. Now that Elspeth had gone, he could find no acceptable excuse to stay at Glenborough Castle for the rest of their planned two-day visit. The reason for their stay had been to introduce Elspeth to Marjorie's family and to Fergus, a purpose now gone awry.

For solace, he tried to think of Marjorie, her soft voice and gentle ways, the times they had stayed in this room, and the readiness with which Daphne pandered to her sister-in-law. Yes, Marjorie did belong here. He turned over and banged the pillow. The anguish of Marjorie's death had long since faded. He missed her in quiet times, but Elspeth had replaced Marjorie in his daily thoughts. Elspeth was annoying, strong-minded, opinionated, and filled with fierceness. She pursued life rather than smoothing it over. Richard had seen her face a murderer without flinching; he had held her hand for many days in hospital when she was recovering from an attack by a would-be killer, and now he had seen her run in the most cowardly fashion from his unpleasant but benign sister-in-law. He knew first-hand of Elspeth's courage, but he had rarely confronted her weak side except when she had discovered the murderer of a long-lost love. What was it about Daphne that made Elspeth so sensitive? He could not imagine.

He pounded the bed with his fist. Where did this leave him? Elspeth's impulsive action tore at his need for calmness and order, qualities Marjorie had always provided for him and Elspeth never had. Now Elspeth had made things worse by running off and leaving him stranded and embarrassed to face Marjorie's brother and his harridan wife. For a long moment, he wished Marjorie were still alive, but he also knew he had always loved Elspeth and always would. Marjorie had never said that she loved him more than the earth, the moon and the stars. Marjorie had never made love to him with Elspeth's abandonment. Witch! Witch! Witch! Oh, Elspeth, my damnably beloved witch!

He knew he would follow her in the morning, but where had she gone?

*

Elspeth's final destination caused her much thought as the taxi took her into Aberdeen. The drive took almost an hour, and darkness was falling as they approached the centre of the city. She and Richard were scheduled to go from Glenborough

Castle to Loch Rannoch to see her parents, but Elspeth could not face telling them of her split from Richard. Her father and mother, now in their eighties, had been overjoyed when Elspeth had announced her intention to marry Richard, and she did not want to tell them the news of her flight from him before she had come to terms with it herself. She had the rest of her three weeks' leave of absence from her job to consider her future plans. Her only certainty was that Lord Kennington would welcome her back to her job tomorrow if she asked. He was the only person who had railed against the intended reduction in her workload at the Kennington hotels as she assumed her role as Lady Munro, wife of the British High Commissioner to the Republic of Malta.

Elspeth requested the taxi driver to take her to a hotel where she had stayed before, which was comfortable but not up to Kennington standards. She asked for one of their more expensive rooms and retired into a hot bath, where she made a decision. Rising and wrapping herself in the towelling robe provided in the bathroom and grateful for the central heating after Glenborough Castle, she pecked away at her Blackberry and found there was a direct train to Kings' Cross in London in the morning. She booked on line, found the warm pair of pyjamas she had packed for her parents' home on Loch Rannoch and pulled the duvet more tightly round her shoulders. A long time passed before she slept.

As the express train sped southward, Elspeth watched the late April landscape, still bleak but with promise of the upcoming spring, rush past the window of her first-class coach. She finally rested her head in her hands. She was glad it was Sunday and the coach was partially empty. The only other passenger she could see from her forward-facing seat was an old woman in front of her who was absorbed in knitting something small and pink.

Where now? Elspeth thought. Her question was not about location. She had a flat in London, provided as part of her job, and her own retreat in northern California, both of which could house her. Where now emotionally? She loved Richard; that was not an issue. She enjoyed staying with him in Malta or having him with her in London. They had discussed the divergence of their careers and ways she could gradually take on the role as his wife. They had not settled the details but had agreed they would be able to work things out satisfactorily. Until two days ago, she had been happier than she ever remembered being, even more than the brief interlude at Cambridge with Malcolm Buchanan, which ultimately had ended in tragedy.

Why then had she fled Glenborough Castle? Daphne's rudeness had been the easy reason. Not fitting into Lady Marjorie's circle had been another. But Elspeth knew these were only excuses and not real obstacles in her relationship with Richard. Was it because her marriage to Alistair Craig had failed? After Malcolm's murder, was it her own inability to accept an intimate relationship with a man and once again make herself vulnerable? Partly, perhaps, but not wholly. Was it something about Richard? Did he take her for granted? Did he want her to be a second Lady Marjorie? She could not answer these questions, but she knew she would feel safe asking for help from only one person in the world.

2

Magdelena Cassar wrapped one of her multiple shawls more securely around her large frame and toyed with a Chopin nocturne with the love of long acquaintance. Her eighty-odd years had begun to deform her hands, but her persistent daily exercises at the piano had allowed enough flexibility in her fingers for her still to delight those privileged to be invited to her occasional soirées in San Lawrenz and listen to music that she had once played for prime ministers, presidents, and princes alike. Her mind was not on the music but rather on the phone call she had just received from Elspeth Duff. Magdelena loved Elspeth like a daughter and instantly recognised her distress, although Elspeth did not tell her the reason for it. Elspeth would be arriving by ferry from Malta later that day, and Magdelena knew she must send Giulio in the Mercedes to the dock in Mgarr to fetch her. Had she asked him to do so already? She could not remember, but Giulio was getting on in years as well and would not be upset at being asked twice.

*

Elspeth's Air Malta flight from Gatwick arrived at Luqa Airport outside Valletta in Malta on schedule. She had made the necessary arrangements for a car to take her to the ferry from Valletta across to the nearby island of Gozo and was grateful that Malta's acceptance into the European Union two years before had made clearing customs non-existent. Light rain covered the runway as she walked across to the terminal to collect her bags. Before her departure from London, she had shed her clothes meant for the Highlands and selected lighter-weight ones that she knew set off her fair complexion, light brown hair, and dark blue eyes. Magdelena had taught Elspeth how to dress well, and Elspeth did not want to disappoint her. That morning she selected a light woollen trouser suit and cotton blouse that Aunt Mag had admired on Elspeth's last visit to Gozo. Looking in the mirror in the hallway of her flat before her departure from London, she wished that her face looked less pinched. She had not slept well the night before, despite the comfort of her own bed. She missed Richard being there.

Sitting on top level of the ferry and gazing across at the barren landscape of Malta's second largest island, Elspeth felt its bleakness reflected her mood. A land once rich in forest had for millennia lain dry and almost treeless, victim of the harsh treatment both by humans and the sea. Elspeth tried to put behind her what had happened between her and Richard in Scotland, but her effort failed. Had she been right or stupid? How could she afflict as much pain on another human being as she had on him? She had seen it in his face. But if he did love her, as he claimed he did, why hadn't he come after her? Had it been presumptuous of her to expect that after her last words with him?

Elspeth's spirits picked up as she saw the old Mercedes 600 limousine waiting at the dock. The long car's presence on the island was unique, and Gozitans looked at it with pride, knowing to whom it belonged. Giulio was polishing its bonnet as the ferry approached the landing and looked up to see Elspeth waving from the deck. She knew if she were to make any sense of her life, it would be here in the loving arms of her aunt, who had comforted her so many times before in her life.

*

Magdelena Cassar saw the car approaching from a distance and had chosen the andante theme from Grieg's Piano Sonata in A Minor to play for Elspeth's arrival. Magdelena knew from Elspeth's phone call the night before that Richard Munro would not be arriving as well, and she had chosen music to reflect her sadness. Magdelena loved Elspeth but also was aware of her impulsiveness in affairs of the heart. When Elspeth had declared she would marry Richard, Magdelena had been both delighted and apprehensive at the same time. As much as Magdelena had grown fond of Richard since he had arrived in Malta to take up the post of British High Commissioner, she was not sure he had the character to reign in the worst parts of Elspeth's being. And now this. Magdelena played the Grieg slowly, injecting the pathos she was feeling.

Elspeth flew into the room the way she had as a young teenager. The years of grace and dignity that Magdelena had instilled in her niece fell away her as easily as her bespoke coat, and she ran to Magdelena and burst into tears.

"I've broken off with Richard," she sobbed as she threw herself down on the piano bench next to Magdelena. "I don't know if I'm a fool or not, but I just couldn't take all that snobbery! His and theirs!"

Magdelena said nothing, her caress saying all. Elspeth clung to her. At last, she drew back and said, "I need to pop down to the bathroom. I must look a mess."

"Your looks, *cara,* can be easily repaired. Have a good wash, and I'll have a cold glass of Delicata chardonnay waiting for you when you return."

Elspeth's eyes filled again, not with her anguish but with love for her aunt, and she ran from the room.

When she returned, face and composure restored, Teresa, Magdelena's cook and housekeeper, was pouring out the wine, and Magdelena Cassar was cutting thin slices of cheese. She drew Elspeth to one of the two vast baroque sofas that furnished her Great Room.

Elspeth accepted a glass and took a grateful sip, before launching into her tale.

"I was sitting there having tea, with portraits of Lady Marjorie's long-faced, over-bred ancestors staring down at me with contempt, and everything came crashing down. Richard isn't mine; he still belongs to Marjorie and her world. He was nodding sympathetically at his awful sister-in-law, and she was smiling smugly. That's when I knew I couldn't be a significant part of his life, and he wasn't ready to join in mine. How could I bring him the happiness he had with Marjorie? I can't take her place, and I don't really want to. I'm not sure if he wants anyone but Marjorie as a wife, even though she's dead."

Magdelena took Elspeth's hand. "Have you discussed this with him?"

"We talked about blending careers, generally agreeing it might work, at least until I felt more comfortable in the diplomatic world."

"Did you talk about Marjorie?"

"We have on and off."

"Did you think you could replace her?"

"I thought Richard loved me enough to forget her."

Magdelena kissed her niece's cheek. "Unfortunately, if you do love Richard, you must allow Marjorie to be a part of him. They shared a life for many years together. You can't erase that."

Magdelena sighed deeply and turned from Elspeth. "I'm now an old woman, but I was young once and made a terrible mistake about loving. I've never shared the full story with anyone, not even Frederick, but before I die I want to tell someone about what happened to me and my family during the Second World War and its consequences even now. I'd hoped that 'someone' would be both you and Richard, because there are parallels in my life to yours, Elspeth. I can't heal your heart, *cara*. Sixty-five years ago, I couldn't heal mine, but I learned about life and what was possible and what was not. Come, spend the next few days here with me and let me tell you my story. When I've finished, we will speak again about you and Richard."

3

Up until the time he had become reacquainted with Elspeth Duff two years ago, Richard Munro's life had been orderly and predictable. At the least sign of trouble throughout his career in the Foreign and Commonwealth Office, which thankfully only happened infrequently, he and Lady Marjorie were taken by the High Commission guards to a safe haven, where he confronted the situation from behind a desk and not behind a gun. He had chosen a wife who was well-connected and reasonably wealthy in her own right and a career that assured he could maintain the social status of his and her families, as well as reap the benefits of travel, good housing, and colonial comfort that was no longer available in Britain. He had been granted his title for meritorious and competent service, not brilliance. Until Elspeth Duff appeared back in his life, the only major disruption to his routine had been the death of his wife four years before. Since that time, Elspeth had involved him directly in three murder cases and peripherally in several other ones, and he had fallen in love with her and with life more passionately than he had done when he first met her.

Elspeth's sudden departure had left him at a loss. Marjorie never would have provoked him by leaving a weekend party early and under such a cloud of unpleasantness. He could find no excuse to give his host and hostess for leaving Glenborough Castle early, and therefore gave none, thus allowing them to think the worst. Adrian and Daphne had said nothing that could be construed as unkind, but before the estate car carrying him to Aberdeen departed down the long drive from the castle, Richard could think of no way of apologising other than mumbling, "I am sorry it didn't work out." It sounded lame when he said it. The Glenboroughs had simply waved a perfunctory goodbye, turned their backs and ascended into their fortress-like home.

Much as Elspeth had done the night before, he pondered where he should go. Elspeth's parents expected them Monday, but Richard assumed Elspeth would have called them and told them that he and Elspeth were not coming. Or perhaps she had fled to them, making any move specious on his part to ring them and give their regrets.

By this time, Richard thought he understood how Elspeth's mind worked, but in this instance, he had no idea where she might have chosen to go. Earlier she had told him of her concern for her parents' wellbeing and their thrill when she announced that she was going to marry him, and he suspected she might want to avoid disappointing them and not go directly to their home on Loch Rannoch. She still had time to reconsider her actions and come back to him. Funny, he thought, why do I think she will change her mind and I won't have to change mine?

When they approached Aberdeen, he instructed the driver to take him to the railway station and cursed the fact that he had not hired a car for the weekend, which would have given him easier options. As the estate car left, he felt rootless. Having lived abroad most of his life, he had no permanent abode other than his family's home now owned by his older brother, who had also inherited the Dunsmuir title. He and Marjorie had stayed with friends or family during their home leaves or rented a service flat in London. He, of course, could return to Malta, where he was staying in Marjorie's cousin's house in Sliema, but the emptiness of the over-furnished house would depress him because he would remember the happy times he and Elspeth had spent there together.

He entered the railway station and looked up at the departures board. He had just missed the express to London, and the next train had a change in Edinburgh. He could stay at his club when he got to London, but traveling down there meant he would be distancing himself from Scotland and possibly Elspeth. He bought a single first class ticket and held it in his hand. He stared blankly, reading the destination printed on it, but he was not convinced that this was where he really wanted to go.

Richard's train arrived at King's Cross an hour after Elspeth's, although he did not know it at the time. It was growing dark by then. In Edinburgh he had rung ahead to his club from the first class lounge in the railway station, and a room would be waiting for him. He was hungry, tired, and on the point of irascibility when his taxi deposited him at the discreetly lit doorway near St James's Park. After being shown to his room, he ordered a single malt whisky from the bar, took out his mobile and rang Elspeth's flat. Her brief answerphone greeting came on, and he left a message telling her where he was. He rang her mobile and, getting her voice mail, he repeated the same information. Then he went down to the dining room, hoping to find some old friends who might take his mind off his dilemma, but none appeared. The roast beef he ordered had no taste, and the efforts of the club's chef at a medley of fresh vegetables went unappreciated. He ordered a bottle of claret and drank more of it than he wished he had. Richard could not remember a time when he felt so miserable, even when Marjorie had died. Her death had been slow in coming, and he had been prepared as any person could be for it, but Elspeth's abrupt departure cut through him in a way that he could not fully grasp. Perhaps simply returning to Malta would be best. He would wait and see if she rang in the morning. If not, he would book a seat on British Airways' afternoon flight from Heathrow to Valletta.

As he sat alone in the dining room, he was thinking of the only person in the world in whom he wanted to confide. How odd that this person would be Elspeth's aunt, Magdelena Cassar. Magdelena might be able to shed some understanding of Elspeth's behaviour at Glenborough Castle and might know where she had gone. When he left the dining room and went back to his room, he felt no comfort but at least he had a plan.

4

"In early April nineteen forty-two," Magdelena Cassar said to Elspeth, "I thought my life was over, not my physical life because I survived the air raid, but my emotional life. I didn't want to live, although I did, but the others were gone. That was sixty-five years ago, and thankfully I've lived a fuller and richer life since then than I possibly could have imagined standing among the bombed-out ruins of my home and seeing the destruction of my family. I'm old now but the truth of what happened those many years ago still haunts me. Elspeth, *cara,* before I die, I want you to help me solve a mystery. Then I can go in peace. Now may be the time for you to do this, to put Richard away from your mind for a while and have a way to fill your time before you return to your work. Doing so may also help you discover your true feelings for Richard."

Darkness had stolen the Mediterranean from their view and left only traces of the sea in the cool fingers of the breeze that came in through the French windows that opened on to Magdelena's balcony. Magdelena rose from the sofa and drew the windows closed, but she left the curtains undrawn to allow the rising moon to spill its rays into the Great Room. She left the interior unlit, as if needing only the pale lunar light reflected on the walls to guide her thoughts backwards.

The raid came in daylight, as they sometimes did during the war. Magdelena had left her two children, Robin and Marija, playing on the floor on the upper level of the farmhouse, watched by her widowed father. He sat practicing his cello, as he did every afternoon, and was playing a Bach chaconne, which Magdelena could hear coming from the window. She drew her blue woollen jumper around her shoulders and wished she had brought an umbrella because she could see clouds rising in the distance. The planes came quickly from the direction of Malta, breaking through the clouds in the distance like lightning bolts. Magdelena saw the crooked cross on their tails and knew they were not from the British airbase nearby. Then came the thunder, bombs dropping and hitting the dry earth, the terraced fields, and finally the home where she had spent her summer holidays all through her childhood. She threw herself in a ditch along the roadside. Dust was everywhere. Magdelena choked from it but hoped the desiccated soil would cover her and the pilots of the planes would not see her and make her their target. The Nazis were known to select at random the people and buildings on which to drop their bombs.

How often she and her father had returned to this small Maltese island from England where her father taught voice and music theory at a Roman Catholic college for boys. When war was imminent and the invasion of England seemed inevitable, he had brought Magdelena back to Malta, where his family had lived for thousands of years of recorded time and probably much longer before that, back perhaps to an era when the first settlers had crossed the land bridge from Africa to Europe, before the Maltese islands were left poking up from the sea. During the Second World War, Malta, strategically located between Italy and Africa, had become the focus of first Fascist and then Nazi fury. They bombed the main island of Malta, but by April of nineteen forty-two the raids on that island's smaller sister to the north had become more frequent and deadlier.

Magdelena never knew why they chose the farmhouse that day, why destroying her father and her children helped their invasion plans, nor could she imagine why there could be so much hatred in the world. She huddled the ditch as the planes circled, surveying their desecration of the landscape below, and she looked up only once to see a leather-helmeted pilot sneer down at the damage he had caused and then give a thumbs-up to the pilot of a neighbouring plane.

When the bombers had emptied their payload and the noise of their engines ceased to pierce the sky, Magdelena rose from the trench, wiped her eyes, shook the dust off her clothing and dashed back toward the farmhouse, already knowing that the flames that engulfed it could not sustain any life within. She ran as close to the burning ruins as she could, but the heat, smoke, and stench drove her back.

She never could decide whether she fainted or simply repressed the memory of the next few hours. When she came back to full awareness, the fire brigade, made up of the old men left in San Lawrenz, had exhausted their water tanks, and the farmhouse stood smouldering. Five shrouded figures, two of them very small, lay on the ground. The priest was tending to their last rights, although they clearly were dead. Magdelena moaned, knowing without asking that the charred remains belonged to her children, her father and their two servants. Father Josef rose from those he could not help other than on their path to heaven and came to Magdelena. She looked at him without feeling and followed his lead along the dusty road leading toward San Lawrenz and into the darkness of the church there, which had not been damaged in the raid. She stared at the statue of the Virgin, and she wanted to feel the compassion of the Holy Mother for her Son when he was taken down from the cross. Instead she only felt hatred, anger and emptiness.

Three days later, a British Army officer visited the home of neighbours where Magdelena was staying, introduced himself by rank and name and asked about the bombing raid. She sat in front of him, still in the frock and blue jumper she had worn when the bombers came, not caring if she had washed or if she had combed her untidy hair. The Major was tall, with carrot-coloured hair that stuck up awkwardly when he removed his officers' hat, and he spoke to her in gentle, educated tones.

"Mrs Wells," he said, "there is no way to express my heartfelt condolences for your loss or words to let you know the depth of my sympathy."

Magdelena looked up for the first time in three days and met the blue eyes of Major Frederick Duff. In them she found the compassion that eventually helped to heal her and to hold her life together over the next fifty years.

After his initial visit, he came back many times, telling Magdelena that he was on official business, but almost immediately it became more. One day, however, about three months later he summoned her to the temporary army base housed in tents near the village of San Lawrenz. He had a sergeant with him, and on a table in front of him lay a folder with official looking papers in it. He rose formally and motioned to her to sit down. His right hand was heavily bandaged, she noticed, and he looked exhausted. His severe look made it impossible for her to express concern for his wounds.

He set his jaw and for once evaded her eyes. "Mrs Wells," he began, clearing his throat, "I need to ask you about your husband."

"Frank?" she said, as if his name were a surprise. She had dreaded this moment but knew it must come.

"Francesco Roberto Wells," Frederick said, "born the fourteen of December nineteen thirteen in Milan, Italy."

"Yes," said Magdelena. Her throat constricted.

"Can you tell me where he is?"

She lowered her head and shook it back and forth. "No," she whispered.

Frederick's voice sounded tight. "No, you won't tell me, or no, you don't know."

"I don't know where he is," she said.

"When did you last see him?"

"On his birthday last year. He came home to see the children." She swallowed hard, trying to keep her composure as she mentioned them.

"Do you know where he went after that?"

"He told me he was going on a secret mission and couldn't tell me anything about it. I haven't seen him since."

"Mrs Wells, your husband has a British passport and surname, but his Christian names and place of birth are Italian. We have no record that he entered the British Armed Forces, although he should have been conscripted by this time. Please tell me what you know of his activities here in Malta since the beginning of the war."

"Frederick, or should I say Major," she said, hoping her bitterness was not reflected in her voice, "Frank always told me his work was confidential. I was involved with my young children and did not question him further." She did not mention the terrible rows over the last few years that had estranged her from her husband. Frank had told her he had taken rooms in St. Pawl's Bay on the island of Malta because of his work. He only came to visit his children in Gozo at a rare weekend and on an occasional feast day.

"Did you believe him?"

"I didn't think anything more of it. I tried to be a good Catholic wife. Did I have any choice?"

Several times before he had asked her about her beliefs, saying he feared it might endanger their relationship. He told her that he had been raised in the Scottish Episcopal Church in Perthshire but was now a doubter. During his years in Malta, he confessed, he had tried to reconcile the Roman Catholic Church's influence on the local inhabitants with his own outlook on the world, feeling this was a necessary part of his job. As a result, he did not try to dissuade her from her faith. For this she was grateful because the Church was central to her being.

His voice choked on his next words. "Mrs Wells, we believe your husband has been aiding and abetting the Italians by sending sensitive information to Rome. Our files on him are incomplete, but we suspect he slipped in and out of Malta, possibly with smugglers on their way to Sicily. Can you tell me the circumstances of your first meeting with him and your life together?"

Until now Magdelena had not told Frederick Duff the story of her last few years, as the memories of her father and children stabbed into her too acutely, and she did not want to think about her husband. She knew her relationship with Frederick was a deadly sin, but she desperately needed his comfort and love. Father Josef had not been able to offer that, but Frederick had. She slowly began her narrative.

"My father, Manwel Cassar, was a cellist, and during the summer holidays before the war when he was not teaching in

England, he toted me around to many of the music festivals in France, Germany, Hungary, and Italy. My mother died giving birth to me, and I was my father's only child and therefore very precious to him. In nineteen thirty-six, Father joined a meeting of musicians who were interested in the Baroque music of the Habsburg Empire that was being held in a large inn outside of Budapest. That's where I met Frank. He said that he worked for an Italian recording studio and had been given the job of seeing if the chamber works my father's ensemble were playing could be recorded. As an eighteen-year old, I spent my time preparing for my studies at the Royal College of Music, where I had been accepted to study piano, but in my free time I wandered in and out of the practice chambers where my father's quintet was rehearsing. Frank and I fell into each other's company. We spent a great deal of time together that summer and later he proposed to me. We were married in London at Eastertime the next year. By nineteen thirty-nine I was pregnant, and my father brought me back to Malta when it looked as if war was coming. Frank had an English passport, and there were no questions asked when he came to join us because Malta was still under British control. The twins were born in late July, just five weeks before Hitler invaded Poland."

Frederick moved uneasily in his chair. "If your husband was British, didn't you ever wonder why he didn't volunteer for the Armed Forces or was never conscripted?"

"He told my father and me that he was working for the Secret Service because of his Italian connections."

"Did you believe him?"

"At first."

"Mrs Wells, did you ever have any doubts?"

"Sometimes. Father questioned him about it once or twice, but Frank said he could say nothing because his work was hush-hush. Eventually he and I fought about it. I think that's why he moved away from us."

Frederick wanted to reach out to her in that moment, to hold her, to tell her that no matter what Frank Wells might have been or done, that he, Frederick, had loved her from the moment he had seen her sitting clinging to her soot-stained blue jumper, face dry of tears that still needed to be shed for her loss of family and home. Instead, he swallowed and proceeded with the interrogation.

"Did you meet any of his acquaintances here or on Malta?"

"No," she said. "We first settled in my family's home in Valletta, but Father and I came to our farmhouse here on Gozo when the bombing began in June nineteen forty."

"And your husband?"

"He stayed in Valletta until our home there was partially destroyed by the Axis bombs. Then he told us that he'd found rooms in St. Pawl's Bay."

"Did you ever visit him there?"

"No, Father said it wasn't safe."

"You said he was here in San Lawrenz on his birthday. That would be the fourteenth of December nineteen forty-one. You didn't see him after that?"

"No, we didn't. Not even at Christmas. The twins were too young to ask why." Her voice broke, and she felt tears well up in her eyes. Dismissing the sergeant, Frederick rose and came from behind the table. He pulled her up and put his arms gently around her shoulders.

"Magdelena, he disappeared from Malta on Boxing Day. There is some evidence that he boarded a smuggler's boat for Sicily and went over to the enemy."

She swallowed hard, trying not to cry. "We were no longer man and wife in reality by then," she said, turning and burying her face into his chest. "It didn't matter that he was gone except for the twins. And now that doesn't matter either."

"Magdelena, Magdelena," he whispered into her thick black hair. She tried not to think of his wife back in Scotland.

Magdelena stopped speaking abruptly and moved with the grace of a grande dame to one of her two back-to-back concert grand pianos. Elspeth sat still, not wanting to break Aunt Mag's sorrowful remembrances.

"The next weekend there was a knock at the door of the farmhouse, where I was living in makeshift quarters among the ruins. Two British soldiers took me outside to their army lorry which was carrying an ancient upright piano, much out of tune, which Frederick had sent to me. Luckily, one of the older men in San Lawrenz was the best piano tuner on Gozo. This is the first piece I ever played on it." Magdelena said. She raised her bent hands and picked out the first chords of Beethoven's *Appassionata* sonata, her eyes glistening. Her music grew and filled the Great Room.

5

Elspeth woke the next morning, her head filled with Magdelena Cassar's account of her experiences during the war and felt an acute ache in her heart. She wondered if a great love such as had existed between Magdelena and her uncle could ever be hers. Damn, Dickie, she thought, why do you make it so difficult? But, no, that was not right. Magdelena and Frederick had so much more to overcome than she and Richard did, and theirs was a relationship that lasted a lifetime. They had fallen in love when they both were married to other people, but they had not let this be a barrier to their happiness. According to Elspeth's father, Frederick's younger brother, Frederick's wife Jean had lingered with an unspecified illness up until Elspeth was born in nineteen fifty and died just in time to spoil the news of Elspeth's birth. Elspeth knew that Frederick had never returned to Scotland after the war, except for brief visits when Magdelena was playing in Edinburgh. Magdelena and Frederick had never married although they had stayed together until his death in nineteen ninety-two. Was this lack of legal bonding because Magdelena had not renounced her wedding vows to Frank Wells, or had she never accepted the possibility of his death? Where had he gone? Was he ever found? Was this Aunt Mag's mystery?

*

Richard Munro lay in his bed in Sliema, tossing back and forth, although the mattress was comfortable and on many nights before had lulled him to sleep filled with dreams of Elspeth. Where was Elspeth? Should he call Pamela Crumm, her closest friend as well as one of her employers? No, that would be an admission that he had lost Elspeth, and he could not bear Pamela's sympathy. He turned over again; his clock read 03:45. He rose despite the early hour and pulled on his dressing gown, one which Elspeth had given to him as a gift to celebrate their upcoming marriage. Oddly, she would not call it their 'engagement', which amused Richard. The heavy silk of the robe swaddled him, and he pressed his arms around it as if embracing her presence. The garment warmed him physically but he still felt cold. He walked up the stairs to the open-air terrace overlooking the Mediterranean where he and Elspeth had shared so many breakfasts and looked out at the sea. The moon had risen and in his head he heard the notes of the *Moonlight Sonata,* which Magdelena Cassar had played for them the night they told her they were to be married. The memory gave him no solace. He shivered from the wind blowing off the water.

*

Elspeth drew her dressing gown around her and ventured into the kitchen. Aunt Mag would not yet have risen, but she knew Giulio and Teresa would be up and would have coffee and fresh rolls waiting for Magdelena's breakfast. Teresa grinned as Elspeth entered the kitchen.

"*Signorina* Elspetta," she said, addressing Elspeth as she always had when Elspeth was a child, "eat some of this marmalade. I make it from oranges which Giulio grow in the garden, and it is my best ever."

Elspeth folded the warmth of the kitchen into her robe. "Teresa, you know how precious my aunt is to me. How fragile she seems to have become recently. I can't bear to think of anything happening to her."

"The *signora* is old but she is happy, particularly now you and Sir Richard go to be married. She is happy very much." Despite all her years in Malta, Teresa's English was still rudimentary.

Elspeth did not reply because she had no good way to do so considering the current circumstances. Instead she said, "Teresa, how long have you worked for my aunt?"

"I not remember the date, but I remember she show me a photograph of a young baby in Scotland. It is you."

"Then it has been a long time."

Teresa gave a small smile and started preparing some carrots. "My husband and I, we are very young, just in our early twenty years. We are refugees from Palermo. All our parents are killed in the war. We meet in a camp after the war and get married there. I am sixteen years and Giulio seventeen years. Now we are old, but never I am regretting marrying Giulio or spending our lives working for *signora* Cassar and your uncle. We have a good, very good life."

"Did you ever have children?" Elspeth asked.

Teresa stopped her chopping and looked sadly at Elspeth. "No, God does not want it. It is our great sadness." Her voice became choked. "You understand now, I am hurt by German soldiers during the war. I want always to forget what they do. I try to forgive them, but for redemption God give me my blessed Giulio, and he love me even after what happen to me. He is a good, very good man. Always I love him."

"I'm sorry," Elspeth said. "I mean about the soldiers. Yes, Giulio is a fine man. You are very lucky."

"And you too, *signorina*. You have a good man with Sir Richard, and you, too, be very happy."

Elspeth swallowed her coffee noisily, munched her toast and said nothing. Teresa continued her cooking.

After returning to her room and dressing, Elspeth left the farmhouse, descended the bougainvillea-lined staircase of Magdelena's farmhouse and walked out onto the dusty road winding toward the church in San Lawrenz. This must have been the road Aunt Mag described the night the bombs came and where she took refuge in the ditch. Elspeth looked out over the dry landscape. The sky was clear and the only sound was the wind from the sea and the occasional squawk of a passing gull. The roar of bygone planes, however, rang in Elspeth's ears and unsettled her. Twice in the last twelve hours, women had spoken to her of the unbelievable atrocities of war, but the love of a man delivering them from it. What qualities did they have that she did not? Why could they love and be loved in a way that seemed to elude her? It was not Richard, she knew; it was she. Could she change? She was not sure. In the distance the bells from the church in nearby Gharb rang ten, and Aunt Mag should be rising by now. Elspeth turned and made her way back the way she had come.

*

Magdelena Cassar usually took breakfast at a small table by the French windows looking toward the sea. The table, set with a brightly-coloured tablecloth of deep cadmium yellow and cobalt blue, reminded Elspeth of the happy days of her childhood spent here in Gozo. Elspeth found Aunt Mag sipping a frothy cappuccino and contemplating a grapefruit, which Teresa had sectioned for her. Elspeth poured herself a cup of coffee from a pot on a side table, took a croissant and propped her elbows on the table. She put her fists under her chin and confronted her aunt.

"You told me the beginning of your story last evening," she said, "but you didn't tell me why after all these years you finally want to share it with me."

"Because, *cara,* I am old now, and I wanted someone whom I love to know what happened back then. I also have decided to leave half of my estate to you, and something to Richard as well, because I could die soon, but the recent developments between you two presents a difficulty." she said, eyeing Elspeth disapprovingly from under her thick brows.

"You mean because I've cancelled our wedding?"

"No. Of course that saddens me, but I hope you will find a way to change that soon. No, the reason is that this house belongs to Frank, and it is not mine to bequeath to anyone. My lawyer advised me of this sometime ago, but until now I have done nothing about it."

"Belongs to Frank?"

"To Francesco Roberto Wells, my husband. My father left the farmhouse to him in the old-fashioned belief that a husband should own the family property, not his wife."

"But surely Frank Wells is dead."

"It's never been proven. If he is still alive, he's still my husband. That is why I never married your uncle, although after a short while it no longer mattered. We may not have been husband and wife either in the eyes of the law or the Church, but we were the truest of partners to each other and that, in the end, was what mattered." Elspeth heard the steel in Magdelena's voice.

"Dear Aunt Mag, are you telling me that you want me to find out whether Frank is dead or not?"

"Yes, *cara*. I know no one else with your talents who can help me."

Elspeth rose and went round the table to when Magdelena was sitting. She slid her arms around Magdelena's shoulders and laid her cheek on the heavy grey hair that lay unbound, falling down the grande dame's back.

"You have my word that I'll do everything I can, although you'll need to tell me more, so that I'll know where to begin."

"Let me dress first, and then come and play some music with me, something simple. Do you remember the four-handed piece by Ravel that I taught you as a child?"

"Before you come back, I will see if I can recall it. Dah, dah, dah," Elspeth sang rather off-key.

Magdelena's eyes sparkled. "You have half an hour to practice."

They played together, Magdelena guiding Elspeth in forgotten finger movements, until the notes of master and novice presented a harmony appreciated only by themselves and the walls of the Great Room. As they finished, Magdelena rose and went to the drawer of a vast rococo armoire and drew out a red-roped file.

"I've been gathering all the physical information that I could find concerning my husband Frank, and I've also pencilled in brief notes on these documents in hopes that it might help you. You must forgive an old woman's handwriting. I've not yet been seduced by the computer in the way that Teresa and Giulio have."

Magdelena drew several pieces of paper from the file and handed them to Elspeth. The first was a marriage certificate from a Roman Catholic church in London where Francesco Roberto Wells and Magdelena Marija Cassar were united in holy matrimony on the seventeenth of April in the year of our Lord nineteen thirty-eight. The next were the baptismal certificates of their children Robert Francis and Marija Magdelena, born on the thirty-first of July nineteen thirty-nine, that came from the parish church in San Lawrenz. Elspeth winced because she shared a birth date with them. A photograph of a smiling, dark-haired young man with a baby twin on each knee slipped from among the papers.

Magdelena watched Elspeth studying the photograph and drawing her finger between the two figures.

"There were other photographs of Frank and the twins, but your uncle thought it unhealthy for me to dwell on them and made me put them away in the storage area behind the garage. I did as he said, and later they were lost. This one I found a year ago in an old book of cello scores belonging to my father. When I first looked at it, I almost threw it away too, but at that moment it came to me that you might help me discover what happened to Frank. I've been putting pieces together for you since then."

She handed Elspeth other papers. One was a yellowed piece of newsprint from the *Times of Malta* that contained Manwel Cassar's obituary. Elspeth put it aside for future reading and in doing so became aware she knew almost nothing about Magdelena's family. Next was an official document, written on flimsy paper and headed *On His Majesty's Service,* requesting that Francesco Roberto Wells present himself at the British recruiting office in Valletta on the fifteenth of November nineteen forty-one, and another followed a month later, written on the same letterhead but with more threatening language. Elspeth suspected that Frank Wells had not responded to either one.

Elspeth turned these two letters over, as if they might reveal something on the back. The typed letters were mirrored through the poor-quality stationery but the reverse side gave no further information.

"They came out here from Valletta to find Frank. Frederick told me later that they had found Frank's abandoned quarters in Saint Pawl's Bay and that the authorities had taken everything he owned from his rooms. Frederick later got access to most of Frank's possessions. He gave them to me, but I threw them away in anger because he had deserted me."

"Did you ever have any contact with Frank or hear anything about him afterwards?"

"No, but perhaps that's a blessing. Before the raid, my father, the twins, and I were content here in Gozo. Things were difficult certainly, food was in short supply, but we grew our own food in the garden and raised some chickens. We bartered with the local people for the other things we needed. Father had his cello, and I had my twins and a grand piano. We made do until the bombs fell four months later. Elspeth, you may think me uncaring, but I did not miss Frank. At first I had hoped he might turn into a good father, although I knew he wasn't a good husband, but what kind of father would abandon his children without a word?"

Elspeth thought of her ex-husband Alistair Craig, who, despite his self-centred style of living in Hollywood, had never stopped being in touch with their children. Frank Wells' image darkened in her mind.

"Do you know if any of the official records about his disappearance might still be available?"

"In Valletta perhaps, but probably not. The city was so heavily bombed in the early nineteen-forties that I suspect there is nothing remaining."

"In London? After all, he had a British passport."

"Perhaps, *cara,* but who would have access to files that might record Frank's lack of response to his conscription letters and his disappearance from Malta? Aren't such files sealed?"

Elspeth considered this and first thought 'Dickie' and then 'oh, damn'. She could no longer ask him. She had no idea what records were kept on deserters in the Second World War. Richard would know, but . . . ?

The phone rang and broke their attention. "Aunt Mag, let me go down to my room and get on my computer. Please answer the call; I won't take up your time any longer."

*

Richard Munro rang Magdelena Cassar with his feelings in turmoil. He had not decided what he should say when she picked up the phone and therefore clumsily blurted out, "Magdelena, do you know where Elspeth is?"

He was sufficiently embarrassed by his outburst not to hear the hesitancy in her reply. "Richard, my dear, how nice to hear from you. Elspeth? Why do you ask?"

He composed himself. "We have had a bit of a dustup," he said. "I don't know where she has gone. I thought you might know."

"Oh, dear. I do hope things come round for you."

Considering her reply, Richard wondered if Magdelena was equivocating. "Yes, I do too, but first I must find her. I'm here in Malta. May I come over to Gozo and speak with you. I know I may be presuming, but I wonder if you might advise me on the best way to reach Elspeth."

Richard was not accustomed reveal his feelings so openly, but he had often heard Elspeth say that Magdelena Cassar was a wise and caring person. Richard hoped that she would help him now because he had long since realised that she was fond of him.

"Richard, the line has broken up. I can't hear you clearly? May I ring you back in a short while when the line might be better?"

"Yes, of course, if it's no bother. I'm in Sliema, not at the High Commission. I think you have the number."

"No bother at all, my dear. I do have both numbers. I'm getting used to considering you one of the family."

*

Magdelena sat back and considered what to do. If she had had longer to discuss with Elspeth her current rift with Richard, she might have made her niece see some sense in resuming her relationship with him. Elspeth, when pushed too hard however, could become stubborn, and that would not help. She had shared only a little of what had happened in Scotland. Magdelena suspected that Elspeth had not completely worked out her own feelings, that her reactions at Glenborough Castle had been impetuous, and that she might have begun to regret them. What Elspeth needed now was time to re-examine her current emotions, and therefore Richard's request to visit Gozo presented Magdelena with a dilemma. If he arrived without Elspeth's knowledge, she would feel betrayed, but Magdelena did not want to put off the meeting for too much longer, fearing that Richard would have second thoughts about his ties to Elspeth. The balance was delicate.

Magdelena had just risen from the phone, when Elspeth came back into the room, looking for her reading glasses, which she had left on the breakfast table. "I hope I didn't disturb your call," she said.

"No, not at all. I'd finished. A friend rang to say he had found a new score I might like to see." This was true, although the call had come the day before. "He wants me to go to Valletta, but I think I'll ask him to come at least as far as Mgarr, where we can meet at a fellow musician's home on the outskirts of town. He's only slightly younger than I am, but I pleaded superiority of age. Would you mind terribly, *cara,* if I left you to your own devices this afternoon?"

Elspeth was listening inattentively and agreed without a second thought. Magdelena sighed at her own cleverness. When Elspeth retreated downstairs to her room, saying she wanted to continue reviewing the papers, Magdelena lifted the phone and rang Richard to arrange a private meeting with him in Mgarr.

*

Richard Munro piloted Marjorie's cousin's yacht along Malta's east coast and across the narrow waters between Malta and Gozo. Once in Mgarr he pulled into a mooring that he had booked earlier, secured the yacht and stepped out on to the jetty. He looked for Magdelena's old Mercedes limousine but could not see it. Instead Magdelena stood at the base of the dock, her scarves gently billowing in the breeze off the sea, and she waved to him as he came ashore.

"I took a taxi," she explained. "I think it best that no one knows I'm meeting you. Come, let's find a place for a cup of tea. I know a small café tucked away down a side street here in Mgarr that will suit our purposes."

As they slowly walked up to the town, he took her arm and was impressed by the lightness and ease with which the large woman walked even though she occasionally used a stick. It reminded him of Elspeth, who carried herself with the same dignity and grace.

When they were seated, he said to her. "You look conspiratorial, Magdelena. I hadn't expected you to come this far to meet me."

"Am I so transparent, Richard? Frederick always said so. No, I wanted to meet you where no one would recognise us."

Richard raised his eyebrow. "Am I being too hopeful to believe that Elspeth may be here on Gozo with you at the farmhouse?"

"That," said Magdelena, "is neither here nor there. You may only assume that I've spoken to Elspeth, at least briefly. Now, Richard, I want to hear your side of the story."

He shook his head regretfully. "I've made a terrible mistake. In my joy that I might have finally convinced Elspeth to marry me, I didn't make room for her to get used to my way of living. In the last two days, I've beaten myself up many times for not doing so. I've loved Elspeth most of my life, and I foolishly expected that when she said she loved me and agreed to marry me, I didn't need to change, although I was asking her to do so. If I could go back now and start again, I would. Going to visit Marjorie's relatives was a disaster that I should have anticipated."

Magdelena reached across the table and took his hand in hers. "If you will let me, and it may take time, I believe I can talk Elspeth into seeing you, but I can't make her feel something that she does not. You must understand that you and I have been fortunate to have had someone for most of our lives who stood by us, loved us and cared for us—your Marjorie and my Frederick. You have seen only the best of Elspeth, the bright young Scottish girl, the Hollywood wife, and the successful career woman. Even during the frightening times you've spent together, you probably have only seen her fearless side. Remember, however, that she has never had a long-term, successful, and loving relationship with a man. How long after your met her in Valletta did you have to pursue her in order to break down her emotional defenses and even admit any feelings toward you? Two years, was it?"

"Almost exactly."

"And during that time, you always went to her, isn't that so as well? Did she ever come to seek you out?"

"She asked for help more than once." Richard sounded boyishly happy when he said this.

"But she was always in charge, wasn't she? When you asked her to love you, you asked a bruised person. Elspeth has no fears when tracking down murderers, but she has a strong dread of emotional commitment because of Malcolm's murder and Alistair's indifference. Both wounded her at the very centre of her being."

"I'm not like them, Magdelena. I love Elspeth. I could never harm her in the way they did."

"You may have told her that you love her, but, very deep inside, she can't trust that your love will always be there for her. Surely you can understand."

He lowered his eyes to his teacup and, blowing out his breath, slowly shook his head back and forth.

Magdelena waited quietly and finally spoke. "Elspeth, despite all her fire, passion, and intelligence, is a fragile person and has had difficulty relying on the men she 's chosen to love. If you truly want her to be your wife, you must understand that. The only lasting love she has ever known comes from her immediate family, her children, and me, never from a husband or lover. You know her history sufficiently well to know the circumstances, but don't assume that her sophisticated façade is all there is to her. Underneath she is still frightened."

Richard raised his sad eyes to hers. "Thank you, Magdelena. I should have known this, but, in my happiness, I was thoughtless. What can I do now to make things right between us again?"

"You can't pretend Marjorie did not exist, but Elspeth needs to know that she is first in your heart now."

"She is."

"I know, but she doesn't trust that, and she may never completely. You must tread lightly around Marjorie and your life with her, but you must not avoid it."

"Yes, I see. I was stupid. Will you help me?"

"I'm certain I can get Elspeth to see you again, but beyond that, I can't help. Only you can. Here's my plan."

Richard sailed back to Malta filled with hope for the first time since leaving Glenborough Castle.

6

Elspeth stood up from her computer and stretched her back. Teresa had brought her a cup of coffee, and it had broken her concentration. She looked out into the gardens that Aunt Mag superintended and Giulio tended, and, seeing the profusion of early May blossoms, she smiled. Had Teresa and Giulio really been caring for Aunt Mag for over half a century? She remembered them when she was a child running to and fro in the gardens, much less opulent than they were now, and Giulio shaking his head at her childish destruction of his flowerbeds in pursuit of her ball. She opened the French windows and strolled into the afternoon light and the overwhelming springtime aromas.

The day had been a full one. She had taken notes on the documents Magdelena had given her. They presented only the bare facts of Magdelena's marriage, her motherhood, and the disappearance of her husband. All 'pre-Uncle Frederick', she thought, remembering her lanky, red-headed uncle, who would toss her on his shoulders and tell her outrageous tales of their clansmen rampaging along the burns and through the forests near Loch Rannoch. Uncle Frederick's tales fired her youthful imagination when she explored the countryside around her home, and they filled her with pride at being a Highlander. In the end, however, it was Aunt Mag who had been her strongest supporter and mentor and who had taught her refinement in bearing and dress and the grace and elegance that she needed to be good at her job. Her own mother, dear as she was, had allowed Elspeth free range in her young life.

Elspeth grimaced wryly at her own ability to choose inappropriately and blunder into affairs of the heart that always produced disaster. She had not thought of Richard all day, but he came rushing back into her thoughts. She rubbed her temples and clenched her teeth. Damn, she thought, I'm continually messing things up with Richard. How can he continue to love me?

Turning from the garden, she returned to her laptop, glad of the strong satellite connection. She googled Francesco Roberto Wells and found nothing. Then she tried Frank Wells and found over a hundred thousand possibilities. Next, she typed in 'The Second World War in Malta', with a myriad results. Next 'Deserters/Malta/Second World War' and found nothing. She tapped in 'Deserters in World War Two', which again showed over a million entries.

Aunt Mag had said that records might not still exist documenting Frank's activities in Malta, but Elspeth wanted to be sure. Police records from the time could help, but where would she start? She could call the contacts she had made in the police when investigating the murder of Conan FitzRoy in two thousand and four, but none of them would have been alive in nineteen forty-one. She needed to find someone who could connect her with the Maltese government's archives department. Richard! But that no longer was a possibility.

She heard a car stop at the gates and went to see who was arriving. Magdelena stepped from a taxi and brushed past Giulio, who had come to welcome her home. Elspeth could not remember ever seeing Aunt Mag use a taxi because Giulio always drove her in the Mercedes. Curiosity aroused, Elspeth took the stairs up to the Great Room, where Magdelena was shedding her wrap.

Seeing her niece, Magdelena came over and took her in her arms. Elspeth, in a childlike gesture, laid her head on Magdelena's ample breast.

"Elspeth," said her aunt, "I've lied to you, which I've seldom done before."

Elspeth drew back, ready to be amused by this odd admission. "How?" she said playfully.

"This afternoon I didn't go to fetch a score from my friend. I went and had tea with Richard. Now I've said it."

Elspeth drew back and frowned. "You saw Richard?"

"In Mgarr. He sailed from Ta'Xbiex especially to see me and ask me about you."

"Did you tell him I was here?"

"No, I wouldn't break your confidence, *cara*, but I did say I would try to convince you to see him."

Elspeth looked pained. "Did you ask him here?"

"No, *cara*," she said stroking Elspeth's hair in the way she had when Elspeth was a child. "I'm wiser than that. The time and place must be of your making."

Elspeth set her jaw. "What if I choose not to see him?"

"Elspeth, I love you dearly, but you are as obstinate as Frederick, and when he was stubborn, it was not usually to his benefit."

"Do you think me seeing Richard will be to my benefit?" Elspeth said through her teeth.

"You must decide, but I think you would be foolish not to try."

"Try what?" Elspeth bristled.

"Try again with Richard. What have you to lose?"

"My self-respect."

Magdelena's eyes blazed. "And how far will that get you?"

"Did you and Uncle Frederick disagree often?"

"Frequently. Neither one of us ceased to be ourselves or shed our opinions because we quarrelled. We found ways to live with our disagreements, which often led to deeper understanding between us."

"Oh, Aunt Mag, I'm not made for this. Tell Richard to find someone like Marjorie. That's what he really wants."

"You are wrong, *cara,* and stubborn and wilful, but then again you always have been. I weep for you."

Elspeth flared her nostrils and stomped out. Magdelena waited for a long moment and then, taking the lift, followed Elspeth downstairs to her room. Elspeth lay on her bed staring miserably into space.

"Damn, damn, damn, Aunt Mag. I don't know what to feel."

"Please trust me, Elspeth. See him, maybe not tomorrow or the next day, but soon. He will wait, but not forever."

Having finally agreed to see Richard when he came to dinner the following evening, Elspeth paid special attention to her clothes and brushed on light makeup, hoping it would hide the darkness under her eyes. At Aunt Mag's suggestion, she selected a gold necklace over a cobalt blue blouse, whose colour matched her blue eyes. Her hand shook as she put on a pair of gold enamelled earrings that Richard had given her in Cyprus. What a fool you are, she thought.

Richard arrived ten minutes ahead of schedule. Magdelena was waiting for him at the top of the entrance stairs, and she ushered him into the Great Room, but she did not leave him alone. Instead she went to her piano.

Hearing Aunt Mag playing, Elspeth stood listening before opening the door to the Great Room. Her throat was dry, and she wanted to escape. As she entered the room, bombastic chords from a Liszt etude crashed about her ears. Magdelena had always hated Liszt, calling him pretentious, but this time she had chosen wisely. As Elspeth entered the room, Richard looked up at her, and she walked with dignity to him.

"I am so sorry, Dickie," she said. She knew she meant it.

He pressed her to him and kissed her cheek. "So am I," he whispered.

Magdelena slammed down her fingers at the crescendo. "Liszt must be good for something, and this is it," she cried.

*

Over supper, one of Teresa's triumphs of fresh local fish and vegetables, Magdelena told Richard what she had asked Elspeth to discover, but she wondered if either of her guests were listening.

After they had finished eating, Magdelena moved to the piano. "I shall play the whole *Moonlight Sonata* for you two, and then I shall retire. Richard, I asked Teresa to make up the bed in the spare room downstairs, if you choose to stay and use it. The evening is warm enough for the French windows to stay open at least for now." She drew back her sleeves and, caressing the keys, pulled the beautiful notes from her memory.

Elspeth and Richard strolled on to the balcony and looked out toward the sea in the distance. Stars filled the cloudless sky, and the air was still and filled with the sweet scents of the flowers in the garden below.

"I think, first, we should see what records we can find in Malta," Elspeth said. "Do you know anyone in the archive department of the government here?"

Richard took Elspeth's shoulders and held her at arm's length. "Elspeth," he said, "I love you with all my heart. If the two of us are to follow up on Magdelena's request, you must know that I do so not only because she asked me but also because I want to be with you in every way I can. If this is the best way we can find to be together, you must tell me what is comfortable for you—how close and how far from you I need to stay. I feel like a child beginning to walk. I may be a bit awkward right now, but I want to learn how to be with you so that you are at ease with me. I want us both to be happy."

Elspeth turned from him, tears spilling from her eyes. They glistened in the evening light. He touched them one by one.

"Please trust me. I'm not perfect. I will stumble time and again in everything but my love for you," he said.

"I was a bad wife to Alistair, Dickie."

"I don't think he gave you enough opportunity to be a good one. Let me give you that chance."

"Is the risk worth it on your part?"

"Yes. Is it on yours?"

Elspeth wiped her tears away. "Perhaps I could try, given time," she whispered. "And now where do we start to find the truth about Frank."

"By listening to Beethoven, enjoying the starlight and putting our minds together in the morning."

"Then you plan to stay the night?"

"Only if you want me to."

She looked at him with inviting eyes and slowly wrapped her arms around him. They did not notice that the music had stopped and Magdelena Cassar had already gone to her bed.

The next morning the spare bed lay untouched.

7

"I couldn't find anything on the Internet directly relating to a Francesco Robert Wells in Malta during the Second World War," Elspeth said at an early breakfast they were having in the sitting room of the guest quarters. "The truth about his disappearance in December nineteen forty-one lies buried deep in the mists of time. Do you have any other ideas on where we should start beyond searching the web?" She bit into the crisp toast that Teresa had left for them and on which she had spread a thick application of butter and Teresa's homemade marmalade.

"Possibly in Valletta. I know numerous people who might help. Or in London. I'm sure I could get access to some declassified records from the War Office, as it was called then, or at the FCO."

"But if Frank really was a deserter, or more likely a traitor, wouldn't that be kept secret?"

"After sixty-five years?" he said. "Only if the information was still sensitive. I can't image it would be. But let's see what we can find."

"Where shall we begin?" Elspeth asked, more as if proposing a strategy than asking a question. "I think your suggestion of London is a good one. Do you agree?"

In his current mood, Richard would have agreed to any plan Elspeth put forward.

"We can stay at my flat," she said. "I don't have to report back to work for two more weeks, and by that time we should hopefully be able to dig out something."

Richard smiled in agreement but inside his emotions churned. Had Elspeth contacted her parents and explained their non-arrival at their home? Magdelena had counselled forbearance on his part, but Elspeth's unspoken disregard of any familial obligation to her parents disturbed him. He needed to broach the subject but felt he could only do so clumsily.

"My dearest," he said, "Did you call . . .", but she did not let him finish his thought.

"Who do you know who can get us into the classified files?" she asked, her brow knitted in concentration.

"Elspeth, did you ring your parents to tell them we were not coming to Perthshire?"

"Yes, of course. They understand," she said absently.

"Do they?" He winced inside when he said this. Marjorie would not have been so off-handed about such an important issue. Stop, he thought; Marjorie is not in this relationship.

Elspeth gave a half smile. "Of course. Mother and Daddy are sweethearts. They want us to visit when we can."

Richard thought of his own parents, stern and demanding, but he also knew James and Fiona Duff well enough to know what Elspeth said was true. Where was his lesson in this?

"Dickie, can you alert your contacts in the Maltese government and tell them that we may seek their help if our investigation in London turns up nothing? Two weeks isn't a long time."

No, two weeks with Elspeth was not a long time when he wanted to spend a lifetime with her.

*

They took the afternoon Air Malta flight from Luqa, arriving at Gatwick in the early evening. Elspeth had phoned ahead to her housekeeper, Mrs Brown, and asked her to make up the beds and have milk, bread, eggs, and fresh coffee on hand for them and leave some frozen gourmet dinners in the fridge. Their taxi deposited them at Elspeth's flat in Kensington just after seven.

Richard frequently visited her flat. Every time he entered this place, her inner sanctum, he felt she was inviting him into her private world. He felt no differently this time.

"You know your way around, Dickie. Throw your case in the guest room, and I'll find some wine and glasses. Let me see what I have? Would you like red or white? I have both."

"White, preferably dry."

"I only have dry, red or white. How about a sauvignon blanc? Here's one from New Zealand; I remember it's quite good."

They sipped the wine's silky crispness, and Elspeth lay back on one of her sofas and tossed off her shoes.

"Dickie, we have such a short time. I suggest we lay out our plans tonight and follow up with some phone calls in the morning. Here's what I have in mind. Let's divide the labour. Why don't you get all the information you can from your sources at the FCO, and I'll go to the Imperial War Museum and see what I can find out about secret doings in Malta in late nineteen forty-one."

"What sort of information should I be looking for?" he asked.

"I suggest we try to find out more about Frank Wells' background. If he was born in Milan but had an English surname and British passport, his father was probably English, and most likely registered Frank's birth with the

British Consulate in Milan when he was born. I also want to know why wasn't he in the army. He told Magdelena that he was doing secret work, and, at least at first, she assumed that he was working for us. But, conversely, she also had the letters ordering him to report for duty. Could there be any truth then that he wasn't working for our side? I'm not certain how you could find that out, but you have better access to secret files than I do."

"I can try," he said, regretting that this was not something that she wanted them to do together. "In the morning I'll see if I can find anything in the archives concerning overseas births, and then I'll ask if anyone presently connected with the FCO might have been in Malta in the nineteen forties who could tell us about wartime conditions there. They would be in their late eighties now, even the youngest ones, but might be willing to talk to us if they are still mentally alert."

"If they are like my father, they'll be able to tell you in detail what they remember," she laughed. "Their early memories may still be intact even if yesterday has already faded away. I used to be cynical about such things, but, as I get older, I find myself feeling more sympathetic."

"Me too. Let's hope we age gracefully together with full in retention of our mental faculties." He raised his glass.

"Together?" she said with a seductive half grin. "How do you feel about a gourmet dinner from the fridge. Let's see what Mrs Brown has provided for us."

Elspeth turned over, snuggled more closely to Richard. He held her gently, touching his lips to her hair. She sighed contentedly and reached for his hand, which she placed on her breast, and then fell immediately back sleep. He found the gesture exciting but its casualness concerned him. How many other men had experienced the same sleepy passion from her? Magdelena had only mentioned Malcolm and Alistair. Were there others? He lay awake beside her, his whole being filled with both love and fear—fear that he was only a passing fancy, one of a long list. His physical closeness to Marjorie had always been correctly marital and, on her part, dutiful. In the end, it dwindled to nothing but sisterly love. He wanted to go on holding Elspeth, assuring himself that he was not dreaming and that the woman sleeping beside him was real. Inside he hated the thought that other men might have shared their love with her. But Magdelena had said Elspeth was shy of men, having been wounded deeply by both Malcolm and Alistair. Even with all his diplomatic training, he did not know how he could approach Elspeth on this topic.

As daybreak came through the window of the loft bedroom, she stirred, rolled over and put her head on his shoulder.

"Have you been awake long?" she asked.

"I've been drifting in and out of sleep, dreaming that a beautiful woman was beside me and I was making love to her." He did not share his apprehensions.

She rose on her elbow and looked at him. "Only dreaming? Well, we'll need to do something about that, won't we?"

Later she padded barefoot downstairs and called up to him. "Coffee or tea? I have good coffee, but I must admit only tea bags, decent ones, but, unlike yours, the tea was not specially grown for me in Sri Lanka."

As Elspeth crunched on her breakfast toast, she said, "Dickie, last night we agreed that I should learn more about the history of the war in Malta in December nineteen forty-one. That would have been at the same time as the Japanese attack on Pearl Harbor, but I can't remember anything beyond my cursory history lessons in school about the war in Europe at that time. I could go poke round the Imperial War Museum, but I've a better idea. Daddy was in the war, and he probably would have discussed what happened in Malta with Uncle Frederick. What's today? Thursday? While you are searching the files at the FCO, I could pop up to Scotland and talk to Daddy. I think it would be best if I did this alone, and you could come up on the weekend and tell me what you have unearthed. I can take the noon train, be in Pitlochry by half past six and meet Daddy at his office. He's there Tuesdays and Thursdays. Why don't you come up on Saturday? That will give me time to talk to Daddy."

Richard looked over at Elspeth and tried to avoid noticing that her pyjama top had fallen open slightly, showing the curve of her breast. She seemed to be unaware of how much this roused him, but her words cut into him. She seemed so nonchalant about leaving him to his own devices for two whole days.

"Oh, Dickie," she said at his dismay. "Of course you are to stay on here. It's yours to visit anytime, isn't it, although don't tell the Kennington Organisation. They pay for the flat as part of the compensation for my job. Besides, I assume you will soon be buried in the bowels of the FCO and have no time for me at all."

Richard sipped his tea, which was pleasing but not unique, and helped himself to toast. "No, of course, go ahead," he said, hoping his disappointment did not show.

"Come on the earliest train on Saturday. There are a couple of changes, at Edinburgh and Perth, but I promise to be at the other end of the line, ready to fall into your arms."

Richard was not sure if Elspeth was teasing or not; Marjorie never teased. Then he looked into Elspeth's eyes, which were quizzing him, and burst into laughter. "Elspeth, I believe you will take a bit of getting used to."

"Haven't I warned you about that?" she said cheerfully.

Richard went round to the Foreign and Commonwealth Office after breakfast, and, clearing security, decided to look up an old chum, Jonas Horne, who, he heard, had just returned from New Zealand and taken a desk job in London because his parents were not well.

"Richard, old chap, how grand to see you. I thought you were in Malta," Jonas said, circling the corner of his desk and clapping Richard on the shoulder. "Sorry to hear about Marjorie."

"Thank you. It was rather bad at the end."

"But you look well, glowing, in fact. Another woman?"

"Jonas, you always did suffer from directness," Richard said laughing and reddening slightly. "Yes, there is someone, a childhood friend."

"You must bring her round to our flat. Janey would love to meet her. Tomorrow evening?"

Richard demurred. "She's off to Scotland today, and I follow on Saturday. Perhaps another time."

"Come tonight even if she's not in town."

Richard hedged. "I think not. I have other plans.".

"Where are you staying?"

For the first time, Richard was confronted with having to explain that he was staying with Elspeth in her flat. Did he want this to be common knowledge at the FCO? Rumours spread fast there and tended to escalate.

"At a friend's flat in Kensington," he said.

Jonas winked. "Hers, I hope."

Richard reddened and wished he had not. He changed the topic.

"Jonas, who is the best person here at the FCO who might help me find the records for a British citizen who was born abroad before the Second World War?"

Jonas though a moment and said, "Celia, in Archives. If you need to find anything, she can. Besides, you can look forward to the treat of working closely with her."

Richard remembered that Jonas had always had a wandering eye and wondered how Celia fitted into his relationship with his wife. He did not ask but accepted Jonas's invitation to call Celia and see if she was free.

Celia proved to be a long-legged, short-skirted, raven-haired young woman, who just escaped being beautiful, although her allure was apparent. When Richard entered her office in the basement of the building, she rose from her computer and flashed a broad grin.

"Come in," she said in a deep, provocative voice. "I seldom get such charming visitors."

Richard squirmed even though he felt the compliment was pure flattery. Young people were more forward these days. He cleared his throat and presented his problem.

"I'm looking for a man whose name was Francesco Roberto Wells, born in Milan on the December fourteenth of December nineteen thirteen. From his surname and the fact that he had a British passport, I assume his father, at least, was British. Do you have records that go that far back? Ones that came from the Consulate in Milan, perhaps?"

As she listened to him, Celia stretched out her legs and crossed them and smiled up at him. In the past Richard might not have noticed.

"Lots of records were lost during the Blitz, but I'll see what I can find. Do you have any idea of his parents' names?"

"No, none at all."

"Could he have been a naturalized citizen, or as they called them then a 'subject'?"

"Not unless he changed his name to sound more British. But, then again, one would suppose that most foreigners Anglicised their names in those days."

"Are you sure he was born in Milan?"

"His wife told me he was."

"He could have lied to her and been born in Birmingham as plain Francis Robert Wells. I'll check that out for you too. How soon do you need this?"

"Is tomorrow presumptuous?"

"I've little else to do today. There's not much interest in paper archives these days because so much is available on the Internet and our own website. Ring me in the morning, and I'll let you know what I've found. Would you like a cup of tea?"

"No, thank you," he said stiffly. "I've just had one. Thanks awfully for your help."

"My pleasure," she said and sounded as if it truly was.

*

Richard did not hear the phone call that Celia made after he left the basement.

"Jason, darling, where did you find that dishy man?"

"Dishy? Do you mean Richard Munro?"

"Mmm. Tons of SA."

"Are you sure you mean Richard?"

"Are you jealous, darling?"

"I just never thought of Richard as having sex appeal. Rigid Richard, we used to call him. And his wife, Musty Marjorie, was worse."

"Are you doubting me about the SA?"

"No, but he does seem to have changed. Must be his new girlfriend."

"You may send him down anytime you like," teased Celia, "or come down yourself the way you used to. We can dust off a little space and . . ."

A smile passed over Jason's face. "I just might do that."

*

Having partially accomplished his mission, Richard felt footloose. Elspeth would by now be on the train for Scotland, and he had two days before joining her. He missed her already. He decided to make his way to Malta House, the Maltese High Commission building on Piccadilly, where he might be able to re-establish ties with former colleagues who possibly could lead him to sources relating to Malta in nineteen forty-one. He was a friend of the current Maltese High Commissioner and knew he would help. Then he would go around to his club for lunch, hoping to find some old acquaintances who would not ask about his love life.

8

From the train window, Elspeth watched the countryside go by in a very different frame of mind from the one she had been in five days before. The spring greenery seemed greener, the new blossoms fuller, and the rain more refreshing. She tried not to think of her dilemma with Richard, deciding to postpone its consideration until she took a walk the following day across the braes near her parents' home on Loch Rannoch, where all her life she had gone to confront life's problems.

She had rung ahead to her father in Pitlochry, where he still worked part-time despite his eighty-odd years of age. He said he would wait for her in his office on Bonnet Hill Road. She walked from the railway station, glad of the cool early May air and lingering daylight. She had brought a light overnight bag, which she slung over her shoulder, and made her way up from the station to the premises of the law firm of Duff MacBean and MacRoberts, a short distance off the high street.

As they settled down in the comfortable chairs in his office, James Duff turned to his daughter and said, "I see that you haven't come with Richard. After you not arriving earlier in the week, am I right in thinking there is something wrong?"

Elspeth and her father had always been close, and she never had be able to hold back anything from him.

"Yes and no," she said. "Richard and I had a bit of a spat, but we're on good terms again. He'll be coming up to Scotland at the weekend."

"Elspeth, I detect more in this than just a spat." His daughter never could fool him. "Is the wedding off?"

She bit her lower lip and looked up from under her brows, a trait from her childhood.

"At least for now," she said.

James Duff sat studying her. "What's troubling you, my dear," he said at last.

"I can't make it work in my head, Richard and I being married that is. He wants me to take Lady Marjorie's place. I can't. What's more, I don't want to."

"Do you love him?"

Elspeth shifted in her seat, the way she did as a teenager when uncomfortable, and then sighed. "That's part of the problem. I do. I love him deeply when we are alone together, but we are such a dreadful mismatch in the world out there. I've suggested we stay lovers and not get married."

James Duff smiled lovingly at his daughter, who had never cared for convention, but he knew Richard did. "I assume that Richard will have none of this."

"Daddy, I don't want to be Lady Munro, wife of the British High Commissioner to Malta. What would I do all day long, except perhaps embarrass Richard by my lack of suitability for the post? And how can I ask him to put up with my chaotic life, one day here, a week there, dashing across the world at the mere whim of Lord Kennington."

"Where have you left this discussion with Richard?"

"Rather in limbo, I'm afraid. I'd hoped you could advise me. No, that's unfair; I have to make up my own mind, but I need some of your wisdom."

"In affairs of the heart, I'm not sure I can offer any wisdom. In my fifty-plus years in the practice of law, I've heard too many tales of love gone wrong, particularly when one or the other party took the advice of their families. Your heart is your own, Elspeth, and, wherever it takes you, you must make your own decision. I would be a bad father if I told you otherwise."

Elspeth rose and went to her father, placing her lips on his thick white hair. "I wish I weren't so bad at choosing men to become involved with. It's my nemesis. But I've come to see you for another reason, and I wanted to talk to you about it before we go home to Loch Rannoch to see Mother. It's about Uncle Frederick."

"Frederick? What possibly could you want to know after all these years?"

"I want to know about Uncle Frederick and what happened in Malta during the war." Elspeth explained Magdelena's request.

"Dear Magdelena. What a force she was; no, what a force she still is. I want to drag your mother off to Malta to see her one more time. I'd hoped the wedding would be there, which would have given me a wonderful excuse. Now, tell me specifically what you would like to know."

*

"Frederick was ten years older than I and, when the war came, that made a great deal of difference," her father began. "I was still away at school, but he joined up early. He had always had a flair for languages, speaking German, French and Italian fluently, and he had the ability to pick up new ones with ease. They whisked him to London before Christmas at the beginning of the war, and he kept his whereabouts quiet even during the so-called Phoney War in the winter of thirty-nine/forty.

"Before he left, Jean, his sweetheart of the moment, convinced him to marry her. Many men did that in those days, probably to give them an excuse to sleep with their girlfriends before they left for the front. Things are much more sensible these days than they were then, and girls less guarded. My family could never see what Frederick saw in Jean. She was pretty after a fashion, but rather sickly, unlike the stout-hearted Duffs. She came to live with my family, but I think she always hated Perthshire. She had grown up in Edinburgh but feared the wartime bombings. Frederick never came back to her, not even for her funeral.

"When he first left home, we had an occasional post card, saying he was mouldering in the basement of the War Office, but we all sensed he was not in London.

"In nineteen forty-one we finally had a real letter from him. In a code that passed the censors, we learned that he was in Malta, which caused further anxiety to Jean because she heard that Valletta was being more heavily bombed than London. She soon came down with a condition that defied diagnosis, which did little to endear her further to any of us.

"My father would not let me enlist until I was eighteen and had qualified for university, which was in nineteen forty-three. I joined the army as soon as I could, and, because of my public-school education and my interest in the law, was sent to officer's training and assigned as a sub-lieutenant to the Judge Advocate Generals Division, which eventually followed the troops up through Italy. In Sicily, I made inquiries and discovered that Frederick was still in

Malta, and I requested a pass to go there for a week. My commanding officer, like me, had gone to Fettes College, and he bent the regulations so that I could go to Malta for five days. That was when I first met Magdelena. She was a slip of a girl at the time but had the same intensity about her that she has today. She was living in the ruins of her farmhouse, downstairs in what is now the garage. Frederick had helped her clear out much of the rubble, restored some rudimentary plumbing and electricity and set up her piano by the doors to the back garden. She had begun to clear out the flowerbeds that were destroyed in the bombing and plant the rudiments of a vegetable garden. I stayed there with Frederick and Magdelena and fell half in love with her myself. Mind you, I hadn't married your mother as yet. Magdelena greeted me as a member of the family, and I had no doubt that she and Frederick were lovers by then. Even at my young age I could tell that they would spend their lifetime together and that Frederick would never return to Jean.

"I knew Magdelena had been married previously and that her children and father had been killed in a bombing. Frederick told me that, although she never mentioned it.

"I never discovered what Frederick actually did in the Army in Malta. He had been promoted to Major and always said he was there to help in the reconstruction after the end of the Nazi and Fascist blitzing of the islands. I never believed him. Magdelena shared the fact that he was often away, but he never said why.

"I've seldom spoken to you about some of the things that happened during the war because we all experienced things that will always live in our minds but do not belong beyond them. After the war, when we visited Frederick and Magdelena in Malta or when we met the two of them when

Magdelena was studying at the Royal Academy of Music, or even later when she was on tour in the UK, Frederick and I sometimes would talk about the war, but he never told me anything more about what he was doing there."

*

When they arrived at the Duff's home on Loch Rannoch, Elspeth's mother greeted her with open arms, asked about Richard and seemed delighted he would be arriving on Saturday. She did not question Elspeth about Richard's delay. The Duff's two old labs, who now slept most of the time, snuffled her hand wetly and wagged their tails furiously in welcome.

Friday morning dawned with clear skies and the promise of a cloudless day. Elspeth kept country clothes at Loch Rannoch and rummaged in her cupboard to find sturdy trousers, a pullover, stout shoes, a windcheater and a cast-off tweed hat, all old favourites. Without Richard being there, she did not need to dress other than for her own comfort. As her father was not going into his office that day, she borrowed his vintage Land Rover, promising to be back in time for tea. She pocketed her satellite mobile phone, provided by the Kennington Organisation, filled a rucksack with a pork pie, an apple, a packet of shortbread, and a bottle of water, all provided by her mother. She added a torch as a precaution and set out for a long hike on the moors. Initially she had thought to go to the west of Loch Rannoch, up toward Rannoch Moor, leaving the Land Rover at Rannoch Station, but, as she set out, she changed her mind and turned in the other direction. Fifteen miles on the twisty roads separated the house on Loch Rannoch from Loch Tay and Tay Farm, her mother's family home. Elspeth had decided she wanted to confide in the only family member of her generation who had had a successful long-term marriage—her cousin, Biddy Baillie Shaw. She took out her phone, dialled Biddy's number and waited for the familiar voice to come on the line.

"I suppose your mother and father were as curious as I am as to why you and Richard didn't arrive on Monday, or shouldn't I ask?"

"I need to talk to you, Biddy."

"Are things that bad?"

"Neither bad nor good. I just need to talk to someone about my life."

"Why don't you come over to the farm, 'Peth? I'm baking some scones for the church jumble sale and coffee morning, and you could help."

As she drove across the moors that divided Loch Rannoch and Loch Tay, Elspeth thought about the first time she had met Richard. A hardy fifteen-mile hike in those days meant that if she left Loch Rannoch after an early breakfast, she could arrive at Tay Farm for a late lunch. She usually occupied herself by taking the time to memorise the lines of the latest role assigned to her by her mother, who was the drama teacher at Blair School for Girls. Fiona Duff always cast her daughter in the roles of the young heroes and her cousin Biddy, who was prettier, in the roles of the heroines. Elspeth never minded, as she preferred to hide behind the exaggerated make-up of moustaches, beards, and gaily-coloured pantaloons, while Biddy preferred the flowing frocks of the fairer sex. Elspeth wondered if that had in some way described their two personalities now.

When Elspeth met Richard the first time, she was practicing her lines as Benedict in an abbreviated form of *Much Ado about Nothing*. Doing so put her in a witty mood, and, as she approached the farm, she saw her cousin, Johnnie, the ninth earl of Tay, with a tall, slender, dark-haired man, with square shoulders and a slightly rigid stance. The Duff's two bounding labs, Frolic and Froth, greeted Johnnie and sniffed at Richard's extended hand. He leaned over and patted them tentatively. Later he told Elspeth he had fallen in love with her in that moment, although she was breathless, slightly perspiring from her brisk walk and dressed in a disreputable cast-off kilt and a jumper with holes in it. That was four decades ago. Since then she had had a tragic love affair at Cambridge and a failed marriage in California, and he had been married to a paragon of diplomatic wives for over thirty years.

*

Lady Elisabeth Baillie Shaw, widow of Ivor Baillie Shaw, sister of Johnnie, the Earl of Tay, mistress of Tay Farm, and Elspeth's first cousin, saw the Land Rover coming and was waiting in the drive. Biddy had not seen her cousin since their escapade in Stresa, where Biddy had met her first murderer. She hoped never to meet another.

Elspeth ground the Land Rover to a halt, flew from it and flung her arms around her cousin.

"Biddy, I knew you would be someone who could talk sense into me because I don't seem to be able to do so myself," she said later over a mug of tea. "Ivor and you had such a strong marriage, and I can't even get launched on the path to matrimony with Dickie without getting in a tiff with him. I think Dickie wants a second Marjorie and, no matter how hard I try, I can't see myself in that role. How did you and Ivor solve your differences?"

Biddy watched her cousin as she talked. Before Biddy had become involved in the murder at the Kennington

Stresa, she had idolised Elspeth and considered her life as a security advisor to the Kennington Organisation the ultimate dream job, as it involved jetting around the world and staying at the upmarket Kennington hotels. After the incident in Stresa, Biddy knew that, despite the perks, when on assignment Elspeth was often in danger and seldom had time to indulge in the hotels' many luxuries or even have a full night's sleep. When Biddy returned to Tay Farm from Italy, she re-evaluated her life and felt she had the better end of the stick, a first for her, as she had always been in Elspeth's shadow, even when they were children. Now here was Elspeth, in despair, at her kitchen table.

She asked the same question that Elspeth's father had. "Do you love him, 'Peth?"

Elspeth pressed her eyes together to hold the tears. "That's the damnable part. I do love him. I suppose I'm a fool not to have recognised this earlier, but things finally came together for us in Cyprus last autumn."

"And how do you think he feels toward you, other than wanting you to be like Marjorie, which I don't really believe."

"He is sweet, caring, passionate and almost in awe of what has happened between us."

"Are you lovers?" Biddy had a way of getting to the point.

"Yes," Elspeth said, shyly. "I just wish it could stay that way."

"But he wants you to marry him?"

"Yes."

"And you agreed?"

"In a weak moment last Christmas."

"An intimate one?"

"Well, er, ah, yes. I now regret it. Being married to him wouldn't work. He took me to see Marjorie's brother and his wife at Glenborough Castle last weekend, thinking I would like them and that they would accept me. What a disaster. I ran away, although I'm not proud of that. What a childish thing to do. But I find myself filled with all these silly ideas about pure love and eternal passion, and then, unfortunately, I have to go out in the world and face reality."

The tears finally came. Biddy handed Elspeth a tissue, and Elspeth blew her nose inelegantly.

"You see what I mean," Elspeth said. "I thought if I came here you could talk some sense into me."

"What sort of sense are you looking for?"

"To tell me that once again I'm being stupid attaching myself to a man, that I should go back to my job, forget Dickie and recapture the contentment I had before he came seriously into the picture."

"Is that what you want?'

Elspeth sniffed. "No."

"What would you really like?"

Elspeth smiled wryly. "If I knew, I wouldn't be here asking you to help me."

Biddy had always had a warm nature, and, in later life, had found a way to reach out to others with kindness and compassion, a talent her family would not have guessed she would acquire when she was a pretty but frivolous girl. Her marriage to Ivor Baillie Shaw had changed her earlier coyness. She had learned a certain wisdom from him that now made her a pillar of her community and a willing resource for those needing advice and sympathy.

"All right, let's discuss your options," Biddy said.

"I could simply go back to my job and forget Dickie."

"Could you?'

"No, but I wish I could."

"Next option?"

"I could marry Dickie and become Lady Munro, the lofty wife of the High Commissioner."

"I can't imagine that would work," Biddy said honestly. "You aren't suited for that sort of life. Let's think of other ways. When Ivor and I came to an impasse, we always looked for a third option."

"Other than staying lovers, which Dickie won't agree to do, I can think of none."

"When will you see Dickie next?"

"He's arriving in Pitlochry late tomorrow afternoon."

"Then you have a day and a half to reach a decision that you feel is impossible at the moment."

"That isn't very long for finding a solution to the impossible," said Elspeth, and then she laughed. "Oh, Biddy it's so good to talk to you. I knew you would help."

"I don't think I've helped at all, 'Peth."

"Oh, but you have. If the Red Queen could believe six impossible things before breakfast, surely I can manage to decide on one impossible thing before tomorrow evening." Then Elspeth put her hand on her cheek. "You wouldn't have any suggestions, would you?"

"Mmm," Biddy said, stirring her now cold tea. "I should begin by continuing to love him. Despite your tears, your feelings for him obviously have done wonders for you. After all, he is a known quantity, true and honest, unlike the others." Biddy did not need to speak their names—Malcolm, her murdered fiancé, and Alistair, her ex-husband; Elspeth understood. "Dickie has loved you for a very long time, and, if I'm not mistaken, will do so for a very long time to come. If you had told me you did not love him, things would be different. But I think for the first time in your life, you have fallen in love with a man who will treat you the way you deserve, if you eventually can find a way that works for you both. I can't do that for you, but I think you can do it for yourselves if you give it half a chance."

Elspeth screwed up her face, the way she had all her life when attempting to resolve a difficult issue. "What do you suppose Lizzie and Peter will really think of all this, their mother blethering on about whether or not she wants to marry a man who's her current lover?"

Elspeth's children had been polite but not effusive when she told them she was going to marry Richard. She had not yet told them she had broken it off.

"It doesn't matter what they think."

"But it does."

"It shouldn't. Besides it's not as if you were considering marrying a twenty-one-year-old gigolo."

"That might be easier. He would dote on me and follow me around the world, living off my money. Everyone would feel pity for me, but I would be above it." Elspeth set her jaw.

Biddy burst out laughing. "You haven't changed a mite, have you? Oh, 'Peth, you are so stubborn sometimes!"

"You are not the first person to say that to me this week. In fact, if I count correctly, you are the third. I must look into doing something about it." She arched an eyebrow.

"Do you want to talk more?" Biddy asked.

"No. You've given me a lot to think about."

"Then come, let's have a bite of lunch before I've to have leave for a committee meeting at the kirk in Kenmore," Biddy said.

9

The security guard at Malta House recognised Sir Richard when he came through the door from Piccadilly and immediately contacted the High Commissioner's office. Dominic Fenech came down personally to greet Richard, as they had been friends and colleagues since Richard had arrived at the British High Commission in Malta. Dominic asked his secretary to bring coffee and invited Richard to join him.

After they were settled, Dominic said, "What a delightful surprise. I hadn't expected you to drop in to see me. I understood from my colleagues in Valletta that you are on an extended holiday and perhaps are considering marriage."

Richard hoped the anxiety he was feeling didn't show on his face. "Considering, yes. I still have to get her to agree on a time and place. At our age, we are proceeding slowly."

"Do I know her?"

"She's a childhood friend." Richard did not expand on Elspeth's ties to Malta.

"Ah," Dominic said. "A common occurrence, I understand, childhood sweethearts getting together later in life. But tell me why you have left this lady's side and come to Piccadilly to see me."

"At the request of an old friend, I'm looking for someone who was in Malta during the Second World War. He disappeared, and my friend is now old and would like to know what happened to him. I assured her that the possibilities of finding him are slim, but I told her I would try."

Dominic replenished their coffee and offered Richard another biscuit. He accepted out of politeness although he had no appetite.

"Are you going to remain mysterious or are you going to tell me who this person is. It couldn't be your lady, could it?"

"No, her aunt."

"Oh," said Dominic with a twinkle in his eye. "Her family is using your connections even before the wedding."

Richard shifted in his chair uncomfortably. "Dominic, may the rest of this discussion be in confidence. I hope you may be able to help me, but I'm treading lightly on something very delicate."

Dominic, with the grace of so many of the Maltese, put his finger to his lips and whispered, "Mum's the word."

Richard continued. "You know Magdelena Cassar of course."

"One of Malta's greatest treasures. When I was last on home leave, I had the good fortune to be invited to one of her soirées. She complains that she has slowed down, but I could hear no sign of it."

"My lady, as you call her, is her niece."

"I see," said Dominic, nodding his head. "Then she is Maltese?" Then he stopped. "But you said she was a childhood friend. I didn't know you had been in Malta as a child."

Richard began to realise that, if he and Elspeth did marry, explaining her relationship with Magdelena Cassar might not be as easy as simply saying Elspeth was Magdelena's niece.

"No," he said, "Elspeth is Scottish."

Dominic frowned. "I don't understand. Wait, yes, of course I do. Magdelena Cassar was married to a Scotsman. What was his name? Frederick somebody."

"Frederick Duff. Elspeth is his niece Elspeth Duff. But here's the problem. In her will, Magdelena wants to leave her farmhouse, where you went to the soirée, to Elspeth."

"That won't be a problem. I assume Elspeth is British, and you fear that will affect the transfer of property. Rest assured, I can make arrangements to see that there will be no red tape."

Richard was beginning to feel annoyed at Dominic's presumptions and knew he would have to give a fuller explanation.

"How I wish it were as easy as that. The difficulty is that Magdelena's father bequeathed the farmhouse to her husband and not directly to her."

"When Frederick Duff died, surely he left the farmhouse to his wife."

Richard clenched his teeth and, not for the first time, wondered why he had allowed himself to become entangled in Elspeth's quest to find Frank Wells. Then he thought of the curve of Elspeth's breast at breakfast that morning.

He cleared his throat and plunged into the truth. "Frederick Duff was not Magdelena's husband, although they lived as husband and wife for many years. He died in nineteen ninety-two. Magdelena's husband was Francesco Roberto Wells, who disappeared from Malta sometime after the fourteen of December nineteen forty-one and never resurfaced. Magdelena's concern is that he may still be alive."

"Ah, the skeleton in the cupboard. But sixty-five years have passed. What is the likelihood that this Francesco is still with us?"

"As you know, Dominic, Magdelena is a proud woman. She wouldn't marry Frederick Duff because she felt that in the eyes of the Church and the law she was still married to Wells. I promised Magdelena I would do what I could to establish definitively whether Frank Wells was dead or not."

"But I don't see how I can help."

"I'm not sure how you can either, but I have an idea. Do you know anyone in authority who was in Malta in December nineteen forty-one who might remember what was happening then, particularly someone who was connected to the military's counter-intelligence forces there at the time?"

Dominic beamed. "My grandfather. He is very much alive and mentally alert, although he is almost ninety-five. When will you be returning to Malta? He talks about the war all the time and will relish having a new listener to whom he can tell his tales."

"I'll let you know when I am back in Ta'Xbiex and can meet him. Thank you."

"And will you introduce me to this Elspeth Duff?"

Richard's face did not move. "Yes, of course, when she is in town. She's in Scotland at the moment. I'm going to join her shortly."

When Richard left Malta House, he let out a long breath. From his experience in Malta, he knew how strong family ties were there, even in the twenty-first century. He hoped Magdelena's secret, which he had just revealed to the High Commissioner, would not go beyond the walls of his office, but Richard knew Dominic had not risen to his current position without knowing when to be discreet.

Richard calculated that Elspeth's train would be nearing York by now. He flipped open his mobile to see if she had left a message for him and was disappointed that there was nothing.

In the distance, he heard Big Ben strike two. Where next? He was hungry, but he did not want to eat alone. He walked from Malta House to his club near St. James Park. A lunch tête-à-tête with Elspeth would have been preferable.

Misfortune would have it that one of Marjorie's cousins entered the club at the same moment as Richard. He tried to avoid meeting the man but could not get away with it.

"Richard, well met," he said. "I understand things did not go well at Glenborough Castle."

Richard smiled politely but not warmly. "No," he said, "Daphne was characteristically rude."

"Daphne always is. Bad luck that. A cross to bear for all in our family, I assure you."

Richard suddenly found an unstated reason to leave the club. He found a pasta restaurant close at hand and ate alone, his meal consumed but untasted, but it slaked the little appetite he had.

The afternoon loomed large in front of him. Lack of communication from Elspeth pierced his heart. Why had she put him off for two days? He found his dealings with her more complex than he wished, but at the same time he considered that his relationship with Marjorie might have been overly smooth. Their marriage was for, the most part, uncomplicated and always courteous but, in retrospect, arid. Arid? What a word. Dry. Dearest Elspeth, he thought, these last few days have not been arid, have they? His heart swelled. And then he thought, damn you, you aren't going to make this easy, are you? Up until now, his life had been predictable, but it was no longer. He grinned at the many challenges she gave him. But why was he beholden to any stated arrival time in Scotland?

He was not obliged to take the train to Pitlochry on Saturday morning, was he? Why not earlier?

He rang the railway booking office and found the sleeper north was fully booked for that evening. He hoped to be with Elspeth as early as possible and did not want to take the Friday noon train, which did not get into Pitlochry until well after six in the evening. It was another hour's drive from the railway station the Duff home on Loch Rannoch, and he did not wish to delay their dinner. He found the listing for a well-known car hire firm and booked a large BMW saloon car for the following morning. If he left London early enough, he could be at the Duffs' home by teatime.

He spent a footloose late afternoon in the British Museum, thinking of the times he and Elspeth had wandered through there together, and, afterwards, he returned to Elspeth's flat, letting himself into its emptiness. The lightest touch of her scent lingered in the air, which made him pause, remembering her. He checked his e-mail and found nothing from her; his mobile voice mail only had one message, from someone who had dialled a wrong number. He opened the fridge to find one of the frozen gourmet dinners left by Elspeth's housekeeper, heated it and sat down to eat it alone. Would this be what it would be like if Elspeth continued with her job? How many nights would he be eating by himself, or making arrangements to spend hurried weekends with her? He thought of ringing a friend, but then he would once again have to explain his current circumstances. Instead, he turned on the television and tried to concentrate on an old Dirk Bogarde film on the BBC, but he finally clicked it off and went to bed.

He turned over in the night, but Elspeth was not there.

Richard picked up the car as soon as the car hire agency opened and made his way north, joining the early weekend traffic. He settled in for the long drive. Halfway up the motorway to Scotland, he realised he had not kept his promise to phone Celia with her raven-coloured hair and her long legs. When he stopped for petrol, he pulled out his mobile and found he had forgotten to charge it the night before. The call boxes behind the service station were sprayed with graffiti and were non-functional. If he got to Perthshire early, he would ring Celia, but it was Friday and she probably had better plans for the weekend than to wait for his call. Finding Frank Wells, Richard decided, had waited for over sixty years and undoubtedly could wait until Monday.

10

Turning out of Biddy's farm, Elspeth decided that she was not ready to return to Loch Rannoch. Consequently, she pulled into a lay-by on the way back to her parents' home, shouldered her rucksack and headed along a path that led to a waterfall that had been a magical spot for her in her teenage years. Perhaps the familiarity of the heather and bracken that lined the burn would bring her an answer. The path was longer than she remembered, and it was well after three when she reached her destination. Being early in May, the sun was still high in the sky, but as she made her was down into the narrow, tree-lined glen, she shivered. Digging a pullover out of her rucksack and finding a seat on a rock by the banks by the flowing water, she watched it cascade over the rocks and marvelled at the peace of this secret place. She sat a long time without moving and finally rose, feeling calm, but still no closer to a solution to her conundrum.

She now wished she had brought her windcheater from the car to ward off the rising breeze. She had just started up the steep path when her foot trod on a loose stone and twisted her ankle at an awkward angle, throwing her to her knees. The pain was so sharp that Elspeth knew she had done serious damage to her foot. She pulled her mobile phone from her rucksack and looked at the display. In the cranny of the streambed, no passing satellite picked up her signal.

Elspeth had spent her childhood on the braes and in the glens around Loch Rannoch and knew better than to panic. She looked round and saw a broken sapling with its trunk large enough to support her weight. On hands and knees, she dragged herself to it, and with the paring knife her mother had put in the rucksack to slice the apple, Elspeth began the slow process of cutting through the trunk and shaping a walking stick. It took her almost half an hour. Her ankle was swollen now and was pushing out over the edges of her walking shoe. Clumsily getting to her feet with the help of her makeshift crutch, she looked up at the path ahead and decided that dragging herself along the steep ground up the path was more efficient than trying to negotiate it otherwise, despite the damage it would do to her clothing. It took her until four o'clock to clear the crest of the gorge. She could see her father's Land River but estimated it was at least a quarter mile away over rough terrain.

Thanking modern technology, she pulled out her mobile once again, and this time saw she had a signal. The phone at her parents' home rang ten times but no one came to answer it; they must be in the garden and neither one of them had good hearing anymore. Next she tried Richard's mobile, thinking he could convey a message to them, but she got his voice mail message saying he was not available. She tried Biddy but only got her answerphone. Elspeth was left to her own devices, but she had been so many times before. She thought of dialling 9-9-9 but decided it would be better for her to try to reach the car without rousing the Perthshire constabulary. Setting her jaw, and, now able to stand more easily, she made her way step by painful step toward the distant car, her greenwood stick bending under her weight so that she occasionally landed on her injured foot. About half way to her destination she fainted from pain and struck her head on a boulder. Her last thoughts were 'Oh, damn, why can't I do anything right in my life'.

*

Richard tried ringing the Duffs' home from a call box at the Pitlochry railway station, but neither a person nor an answerphone responded. He remembered Elspeth's assurance that her parents would not notice or even recall the exact time he was due to arrive, so he took a chance and turned west toward Loch Rannoch. Ruing the width of his large car on the narrow, twisting roads, he barely squeezed past several caravans and two tour buses. It had taken him longer to get here from London than he had anticipated, and the winding road out to Loch Rannoch slowed him significantly. James and Fiona Duff were just sitting down to a late tea when he arrived.

Fiona rose, and with obvious pleasure in her eyes, offered Richard her cheek. James put out his hand and shook Richard's heartily.

"Dear Richard, come in, come in," Fiona said. "Was it today you were due to arrive? I thought it was tomorrow, but no matter. Elspeth did say you would be here for the weekend and your room is already made up. Dogs, do settle down! James, help Richard with his case, and I'll get another cup from the kitchen. Or, maybe I don't have to. Elspeth said she would be home for tea, but she hasn't appeared yet. Make yourself at home. Where do you suppose Elspeth has gone? She did say she would be back by four, and we have held tea back for almost an hour. Richard, you must try and instil in her a sense of punctuality. Her head is always filled with a jumble of so many other things."

Richard checked his watch, and it was well past five. In his experience Elspeth was always punctual, despite Fiona's words. Her tardiness distressed him.

"Do you know where she's gone?" he asked.

"Up to Rannoch Moor," James said. "She said she had a great deal to think about and the moors have always offered her a place to collect herself. She's done that most of her life. Is all well between you?"

Richard took a long sip of his tea and considered his answer. "I think we will be able to work everything out eventually, but your daughter has her own ways of doing things. She'll not be rushed."

"Thank goodness she's come to her senses as she has grown older," her mother said somewhat abstractly. "Elspeth always did have an impulsive side, like running off to California with Alistair Craig. That was wrong from the very first and only got worse. But, of course, Lizzie and Peter are wonderful even if we don't see them often enough, which I suppose made the whole thing worthwhile."

Richard nodded politely at Fiona but inwardly grinned. Elspeth had warned him about her mother's run-on thoughts.

The grandfather clock in the hall chimed the half hour. James stirred in his seat. "Elspeth ought to be home by now," he said. "Perhaps I shouldn't worry, but she did go off alone over the moor and, although she still thinks she's as fit as she was at sixteen, she should have returned by now. She said she would leave the Land Rover at Rannoch Station. Would you mind terribly going to see if you could find her? It's about eighteen miles from here and the road is a bit rough."

"I'll be more than pleased to go," Richard said, meaning it. "Give me the directions."

Richard revved the engine of his powerful car and set off west. He followed the narrow country road up to Rannoch Station with anticipation in his heart. Elspeth could not have strayed far from the car park there, even if she had ventured further than she had originally planned. He would wait by James Duff's Land Rover or even set out on one of the paths, at least as far as his London shoes would allow. He motored on cautiously, trying to avoid the bumps and potholes in the road, for which his car was quite unsuitable, but he was filled with contentment. He envisioned her in a kilt and an old jumper coming off the moors, dressed the way he had first seen her many years before, her long hair flying in the wind and two Labradors playing around her. The memory pushed him faster along the road.

Rannoch Station stood at the end of the road with the moorland all around. The main building was a small railway station beside a single line of track, and nearby he saw a car parking area, but no one was about. He pulled up beside one of the cars there and looked around but didn't see any Land Rover there waiting for Elspeth. He got out of his car and stared at the emptiness of the moor with its peat bogs, yellow-blooming broom, and scratchy, low growing heather.

A gated path crossed the railway track and wound out into the empty landscape, known as the bleakest spot in Scotland and edged by a pine forest in the distance. Richard assumed that she had not come this way, or at least no longer was here. Where could she have gone? The act of chasing Elspeth had become all too familiar. He had little choice but to make his way back to Loch Rannoch, trying not to worry about her whereabouts. When he arrived back at the Duff's home, Fiona was starting preparations for dinner, and James was laying a fire in the drawing room. He looked up from his task.

"Did you find her, Richard?" he asked.

"No, I didn't. Would she have gone somewhere other than Rannoch Moor?"

James nodded. "She might have. We always let her go off on her own when she was young, and she always came back safely, if sometimes a little worse for wear and a bit late. But have no fear, she will be here presently."

Richard wished he was as confident as Elspeth's father.

*

As Elspeth slowly came to, she realised she was chilled through. The sun had slid down the sky toward the west, and its paleness was a warning of the coming cold evening. Elspeth realised it might fall below freezing as night came on, and she was not prepared. She raised herself as best she could and looked over at the Land Rover, which stood, solitary, at the end of the path. Her stick, so carefully carved in the glen, lay bent beside her. She knew the cardinal rule of hiking alone was always to tell someone where you are going and when you planned to return, and she rued her spur-of-the-moment decision to seek out Biddy and then to hike down to her magic waterfall rather than going up to Rannoch Moor, as she had told her parents earlier. Had she really thought she was invincible? Not for the first time, unfortunately. She struggled to a cairn nearby and propped herself up against it. All she could do was rest a little more and try to make her way toward the car again. She raised her hand to her face and realised she had cut her cheek in her fall.

She sat down abruptly and leaned her body against the cairn. For the next half hour, she drifted in and out of consciousness. Suddenly she heard the hum of a car coming along the road. How could she attract its attention? Clenching her teeth, she reached into her rucksack and pulled out the torch that she had brought with her. She switched the light on and off. Flash, pause, flash, pause, flash pause, then flash, flash, flash, and finally flash, pause, flash, pause, flash. S-O-S. She repeated the signal again. The vehicle in the distance materialised into a battered van that drew to a halt behind the Land Rover. Squinting, Elspeth could make out a man in kilt and tam who must have seen her plea for help. A few minutes later he arrived at her side.

She looked up at her saviour and recognised him.

"Roy MacPherson," she said, "if ever I needed someone to come along just now, I could not have asked for a better person." And then she lost consciousness again.

*

Roy MacPherson looked at the woman who was leaning against the cairn and wondered how she knew his name. She looked familiar, rather like Lady Biddy Baillie Shaw, but not the same. No matter who she was, here was someone in distress. He and his family before him had served the Earls of Tay and their children since the Battle of Culloden in the April of seventeen forty-six, and the woman in the front of him was clearly a kinswoman. Being short sighted, Roy did not recognise which member of the family was at his feet, but she was a relation, no doubt about it.

He was eighty-four years old and knew he could not get her back to his van without her help. Her rucksack had fallen open by the cairn, and he saw she had a water bottle inside, still half full. He opened it and splashed it on her face.

"Who might ye be, lass?" he asked as she opened her eyes.

Elspeth brought her eyes into focus and grinned. "Do you remember the girl you rescued from the kirk roof when she had gone there to find eggs in a swallow's nest, slipped on the slates and was hanging from the gutter?"

"Ah, lassie, are ye that wee lass who was called Elspeth Duff?"

"Bruised and lamed, I am. Oh, Roy, I need to be rescued again. Can you help me back to my car? I've twisted my ankle rather badly."

"Ye'll never be able to drive back to Loch Rannoch with that foot all twisted. Nae, I shall drive ye there myself, but now we'll have to figure out how to get ye to the road."

"If I can lean on your shoulder, I think I can hobble along."

"There seems no other way as I'm no strong enough to carry ye," he said, "This may take a wee bit of time. Take care ye don't faint on me again."

"Did I faint when I was hanging from the gutter?"

"Nae, but we both were a wee bit younger then, but ye fainted just now after I first saw ye here."

*

The jolting of Roy MacPherson's van sent shocks of pain through Elspeth's foot and heel as she lay on a hessian sack bag among his gardening equipment in the back. She gritted her teeth and was true to her promise not to faint again. He drove slowly and silently, for which she was grateful.

As they drove down the road toward Loch Rannoch, she spoke. "Roy, I don't want to bother my parents. Mother doesn't drive her old Morris Minor at night anymore, and we left Daddy's Land Rover back in the lay-by. Could you take me to Tay Farm instead? Biddy can help me there."

"Nae, lass, ye belong at yer parents, and I know Lady Biddy is at the kirk at a meeting about the jumble sale. I'm taking ye home, where ye should be," he said.

Elspeth smiled at his bossiness, which reminded her of her youth.

"With all yer fancy Hollywood and London connections, ye can call an ambulance when ye get home, for I fear ye will need to go to hospital tonight to get yer foot bound up. But yer parents should know what ye've done."

"Roy, I'm no longer a child!"

"But ye do act a wee bit like one, don't ye?"

Elspeth sniffed but inside felt a flood of relief because she felt she no longer had control of what was best for her.

*

Richard could not remain happy at the Duff's lack of concern for Elspeth. He thought of his own strict days at preparatory school in Edinburgh, the rigours of Merchiston College that were only alleviated when he went to Oxford, the rigidity of his parents, and the tight reins on which they had him held. When Elspeth was in her teens, Richard knew she had rambled across the countryside with abandon, but the rag-tag girl had taken a first in law at Cambridge and was now a sophisticated member of society, more used to the luxurious environs of the Kennington hotels than the Scottish countryside. Besides, she knew enough not to go off on her own without letting others know. Even if her parents were without an answerphone, she would have certainly rung him. Then he remembered he had not charged his mobile and thought, as he often had before, that modern-day devices had their deficiencies. He excused himself from James' company and climbed the stairs to his bedroom. Rummaging through his case, he could not find his mobile charger. He cursed his inattention to the vagaries of twenty-first century technology. Perhaps Elspeth had tried to contact him. She always carried that formidable satellite device with her, and he doubted she had set off earlier without it. He, not she, had broken the communication link between them. He put his forehead in his hands and exhaled. Life around Elspeth was never simple.

The sound of a car brought Richard back down the stairs in the hope that Elspeth had arrived back in the Land Rover. He looked out the window and saw a battered van with one headlamp dimly lit and the other at an odd angle and was disappointed. An elderly man in a kilt opened the door, climbed out and made his way round to the rear doors. He opened them and coaxed a woman from the back. Only as she came fully into view did Richard recognise her.

Elspeth's tweed hat, which had begun the day at a rakish angle, sat squarely on her head with no regard to fashion. The expensive haircut did not stop her hair from being in a muddy tangle. Dirt was caked on her clothing, face, and hands, and her trousers were ripped at the knees. Blood had dried on her cheek. She flinched as the man gingerly helped her out of the rear of the van.

Richard dashed down the stairs to the front door and threw it open. He ran toward Elspeth, picking her up with the strength only a lover can have, and carried her inside. He deposited her on the sofa in the drawing room and took her head in his hands, his whole being filled with concern. He began to laugh. "Oh, Elspeth, dear, sweet Elspeth, for all your worldly ways you still are a tomboy at heart. You look worse than I've ever seen you, but I love you the more for it. I wouldn't change you one bit, but you have given us a scare."

Elspeth looked out from under her brows at Richard, her expression halfway between a scowl and a piteous plea. "I am rather hurt," she said and passed out again.

Richard's mood turned from merriment to fright. He turned to the man who had brought her home. "I'm Richard

Munro," he said, "Elspeth's . . ." He hesitated, not knowing how to describe their relationship.

"I know who ye are, Sir Richard," the man said. "I'm Roy MacPherson. The Tay/Robertson family and I go a long way back. I remember when ye first came to the farm with Lord Johnnie. Now I'll leave ye to take care of Miss Elspeth, for she's very precious to us all, but she always has been too foolhardy for her own good."

*

The Atholl Clinic in Pitlochry was small but efficient and signed Elspeth in immediately, although it was late and she was not a registered patient. The doctor who was taking the evening surgery hours was young and handled Elspeth with kind respect.

"Mrs Duff," he said, "you have pulled your Achilles tendon, which must be painful, but I'm pleased to tell you that I don't think you have any broken bones. I'm sending you to A&E at the Perth Royal Infirmary, where they can diagnose you further and probably put your foot in a walking cast. At your age, it should take about three weeks to heal. Stay off it as much as possible. A crutch would be best if you do need to walk. Or PRI can provide you with a wheel chair. Unfortunately, I can't give you any medication other than paracetamol, but they may give you a stronger pain-killer in Perth."

Richard cleared his throat and assumed his most pompous posture, practiced over his years of diplomatic negotiating. "Dr Anderson," he said, reading the name badge on the doctor's lapel, "in your training you undoubtedly learned how to treat pulled tendons. Here in the Highlands, I'm sure, you see them as a matter of course with hikers and send them on to Perth on a regular basis. However, you have not addressed

Ms Duff's fainting spells. She has lost consciousness by my count at least five times since her fall."

The young doctor's face reddened. "And you, sir, are a relative?"

Richard did not answer directly, as his relationship with Elspeth kept shifting. Instead he said, "A year ago, Ms Duff was attacked and suffered massive head injuries. She was hospitalised for almost a month and spent over four months recuperating. I'm concerned that her accident today may have exacerbated her old injury."

"Where was she treated?" the doctor asked.

"Privately, in London."

"Sir," the doctor said. "After her Achilles tendon is treated, I suggest that she is taken back to London as soon as possible because we don't deal with head trauma here. I would suggest that she has an MRI scan when you get there. In the meantime, I'll recommend that she stays overnight in Perth for observation, and she should follow their instructions. I'll give you a letter stating my report."

11

Lying alone in his bed at the Duff's home, Richard thought of how he might approach Elspeth in the morning when he returned to visit her in the hospital in Perth. He suspected that Elspeth would object to the expense of him hiring a private plane, and he felt uncomfortable asking Lord Kennington for the services of his personal one. His family had left him only enough money for him to get through Oxford and start his career. The family title and home in Aberdeenshire had been left to his older brother, David, now Lord Dunsmuir, whom Elspeth had not yet met, thanks to her flight from Glenborough Castle. Marjorie's wealth, however, had eased the way to his success throughout his career. When she died, she had willed everything to him, which, although not a fortune, this, with the money he had invested from his remuneration from the FCO, had left him comfortably off and easily able to afford a plane to convey Elspeth to London. He also knew suggesting such a thing would raise a howl of protest.

His thoughts returned to the scene in the Duff's drawing room when he laid Elspeth down on the chintz-covered sofa the evening before, and to Roy MacPherson's appeal to him to care for Elspeth. Roy had spoken so plainly about Elspeth being precious to them all. Richard began to understand how this affection must have formed a part of Elspeth's character. As she had grown up, the people around her loved and cared for her, gave her free rein to be herself, but they were there for her when she needed them. Richard had watched Elspeth in her job, often fearless, doggedly independent, and usually stretching her mind into places others dared not go. These qualities assured that she excelled at her job, but also made her a complicated, if always exciting, companion. He would have to come to terms with this, he knew.

How often had he made comparisons between Marjorie and Elspeth? As a child, Elspeth had rambled across the highlands, savouring all the wild and open spaces offered there, while Marjorie had been educated in the confines of Glenborough Castle, the British High Commissioner's residence in New Delhi, and privileged schools that mainly taught the arts of polite society. Marjorie was everything Elspeth was not. Marjorie was politely witty, but, in retrospect, not terribly bright. She could make appropriate conversation with anyone, although generally it stayed superficial. She charmed people but did not stimulate them. Little had ever threatened Marjorie's adult life other than her last fatal disease. She had never injured herself severely; she had never been coshed by a would-be murderer, nor shot at, nor been threatened with strangulation. She had never confronted anything more menacing than an angry houseboy, except for a brief incident during an uprising in Zimbabwe, when she simply ignored what was going on about her. And, unlike Elspeth, Marjorie had no sense of rebellion, particularly in matters of social correctness.

Marjorie had seldom defied Richard and never embarrassed him. Their relationship had been symbiotic. She gave him status with her title, and he gave her a reason to be in the world. She had money, and he had come from an aristocratic family, although he was a second son and did not bear the family title. Their partnership worked because they both had accepted it as one that functioned for them without excessive demands. They did not have children, but neither took extraordinary measures when none appeared; they accepted the lack without exploring options to do otherwise. They fell into an easy life that their money and status offered them and, with one exception, lived an uneventful life together for over thirty years without questioning its dullness. What little physical intimacy they had soon faded away, and they became supportive companions, not husband and wife other than in name. Richard was devastated when Marjorie died because he never expected their cossetted existence to end.

On the other hand, his relationship with Elspeth had embarrassed him on more than one occasion. She could be outspoken. She frequently became engaged in lively conversations over a vast range of topics without any thought of ladylike reserve. She was always up for a debate and had an easy acquaintance with things intellectual. She was passionate about music, perhaps because of Magdelena Cassar, although she neither sang nor played an instrument. Unlike Marjorie, who tended to look dowdy, Elspeth always dressed exquisitely and with understated flair, except when roaming across the Highlands, when she reverted to the scruffy dress of her youth. Elspeth often turned men's heads but was more interested in their minds than their romantic advances. She was tough when circumstances required it, although she also could be generous and tender. Marjorie had had a hidden snobbish unkindness underneath her exterior, but Elspeth had none. Elspeth thought nothing of following a case across the world to its often-dangerous conclusion. Being with Elspeth always produced the unexpected, and she aroused in Richard both passions and joys he did not know he could feel until now. He was as likely to be as enthralled by her as irritated, but she always stimulated him, and moments without her filled him with longing. Marjorie would never have asked to be lovers rather than husband and wife; to Elspeth this seemed a logical solution to the disparity in their lives. Richard grinned and shook his head. Dear, dear, dear Elspeth. He never imagined anyone could enchant him so. He turned over, thought of making love to her and how warm her responses would be and then fell into happy sleep despite her absence.

*

Elspeth's night had been neither restful nor comfortable. The doctor came in regularly to check her neurological signs, making her perform long rows of mathematical subtraction, and asking her to follow his fingers up, down and to both sides, denying her sleep until he was satisfied she would not fall into unconsciousness again. Consequently, when Richard returned to Perth the next morning, she was tired and in a tetchy mood.

"No, Dickie," Elspeth said from her hospital bed, "I won't have you go to the expense of hiring a plane to London. "It's a foolish waste of your money and Marjorie's, and one Marjorie would not condone if she were here."

Elspeth seldom mentioned Marjorie, and her words shook him. Patience, he thought.

"The money is mine. She left it to me, trusting my instincts to use it well."

"To hire a private plane for your lover?"

Richard ground his teeth at the term. He wished Elspeth would stop using it to describe their relationship.

"Besides," Elspeth lied, "I feel perfectly well this morning except for my heel, and even that doesn't hurt unless I put weight on it. I'll soon be on the mend and back tripping along the burns, over the braes or on city pavements with you wherever we happen to be."

Richard was glad to be included in her plans despite disagreeing with her optimistic prognosis.

"Roy MacPherson charged me with your care, and I took that seriously. How many days did I sit by your bedside in hospital last year? Far too many, my dear. Can we compromise?"

"How?" she asked before agreeing.

"Let me drive you back to London then. I will hire a larger car. But you must agree to go to the head trauma clinic as soon as we arrive."

"Must?"

"Must, if you want me to drive you back," he said, looking down his long nose.

"You are harsh, Dickie."

"Roy put you my care. I can't ignore that."

"All right," she said with a laugh. "You win this round."

Oh dear, Richard thought.

*

On Monday, after a long but uneventful trip south the day before, they sat in the reception area of the head trauma clinic waiting to hear the results of Elspeth's MRI scan, which had been performed earlier that morning. Elspeth's headaches had decreased in intensity since their arrival back in London, and her Achilles tendon was less painful than it had been when she stumbled two days before. Despite her condition, Elspeth was suddenly filled with mirth, her eyes twinkling, and she was unsuccessful in chocking back her laughter. Richard turned a puzzled eye.

She snorted in an undignified manner. "Here we are, dear Dickie," she whispered, "with the heads of everyone around us swathed in bandages, figuratively if not literally and all I have to show is a cumbersome walking cast and a cut on my cheek. Do you think the other patients might wonder if my brain is lodged inside of the cast rather than in my skull?"

Richard grinned at Elspeth's absurdity. Only she could have made such a comparison, and he loved her for it.

Several of the others in the waiting room looked across at the middle-aged couple who seemed so amused at something she had said. Certainly they looked respectable enough, both dressed expensively and more formally than most modern-day Londoners, and one onlooker secretly thought they might have had a tipple or two before coming to the clinic, although it was only half past ten in the morning.

Elspeth's merriment however was sobered as the doctor, who had seen her through her therapy a year earlier, gave his opinion of her condition.

"Richard, Elspeth, delightful to see you again. Do I hear rumours of an impending marriage?" The doctor had witnessed Richard's dutiful attendance when Elspeth was recovering from head wounds suffered after being attacked at the Kennington Singapore.

Before Richard could answer, Elspeth said, "Never believe rumours. Now, tell Richard that his concerns are foolish."

"Not completely foolish, I'm afraid," the doctor replied. "You have to realise, Elspeth, that the blow you suffered in Singapore was life threatening, and there were times when I wondered if we would pull you through at all. Your recovery has progressed well, but you will always be prone to recurring problems if you exacerbate the healing by falling and hitting your head. Luckily, your life is no longer in danger, and your MRI scan shows you only suffered a minor concussion this time. Part of your fainting may have come from the pain of pulling your tendon. I recommend you take it easy for a month or so. Are you still with the Kennington Organisation? I can contact Lord Kennington if necessary."

"I am, but in the middle of three weeks' holiday. There's no need to bother him."

"And you, Richard, still in Malta?"

"Yes, I return the week after next."

"Well then," the doctor said, "my diagnosis is this. If I remember correctly, Elspeth, you have an aunt in Malta, on the island of Gozo. I recommend that you go to Malta, spend the rest of your holiday with her and see Richard as often as possible." The doctor winked and smiled. "Love has a wonderful way of curing all ills. I'll send the appropriate paperwork to Lord Kennington, in case you need to extend your stay."

As they left, Richard said to Elspeth, "Are we so obvious?"

"You are, dear Dickie," she responded, "and perhaps I am too. I'm not sure we should be seen in public together if our sinning is becoming so apparent."

Richard winced at her words and was glad they were out of hearing range of the other patients.

12

Magdelena Cassar brushed the keys of one of the two grand pianos in her Great Room, and pleasure spread through her large body not only for the music but also because Elspeth was coming back, and so soon after leaving. Richard had warned Magdelena that Elspeth had injured her tendon and had a minor head wound, but Magdelena trusted Elspeth's resilience and needed to continue speaking with her about Frank Wells. Since sharing her story with Elspeth six days before, her mind had been filled with the years of her marriage and the war, and these reflections would not leave her in peace. She hoped Richard and Elspeth had discovered something in London that would help put her mind at rest.

From habit her fingers flew up and down the keyboard in her daily exercises, which were no longer simple scale progressions but the rhythm of her life. Richard had said they would be on the afternoon plane to Luqa, which should get them to the farmhouse for dinner. Magdelena had sent Teresa off to get fresh fish, and Giulio had taken the Mercedes to Mgarr to meet the ferry. The late afternoon was warm, carrying the hint of the hot summer to come, and she had left open the French windows to her balcony. The wind had shifted, and she could hear the rolling of the sea. Magdelena thought of Frederick, which she did so often at this time of day, and loneliness filled her. She was glad that Elspeth and Richard would be here soon.

As they ate dinner, Magdelena expressed her disappointment at Elspeth and Richard's lack of progress. She was now in her eighty-sixth year and her health was deteriorating. No one knew this but her doctor, and she especially did not want Elspeth to become aware of it. Magdelena hoped this would be a time for Elspeth to rejoice in her love for Richard and not grieve for a dying aunt.

Elspeth must have sensed Magdelena's anxiety and put her hand gently over the old woman's hand.

"Aunt Mag, for the last few days I've been more immobile than usual, and consequently I've had masses of time to think about you and Frank and Uncle Frederick. The small amount you shared with me last week was more than I had ever heard about your early life. I think the answer to the mystery of Frank's disappearance may be hidden in your memory. Since I've made myself an uninvited guest for the next few weeks and dragged Richard along too, will you take the time to tell me as much as you can remember about Frank, particularly all the little things?"

"What good would that do, *cara*?'

"Please trust me. This is what I do for Lord Kennington, and he pays me vast sums of money for doing so. All I will require from you is bed and board for us, a daily recital from you, and as much detailed information as you can recall."

Magdelena raised her famous hands to her temples and rubbed them up and down several times. She sighed and said, "I will tell you all I can. The guest quarters are yours for as long as you need them, and, Richard, you know you're always welcome here too. I'll let you sort out your own arrangements. But my bedtime approaches. Let's begin in the morning before the day gets too warm."

*

Despite the awkwardness of Elspeth's injury, they had chosen to share the guestroom with the larger bed. When she awoke in the morning, she opened her eyes sleepily and found him kneeling at her side of the bed, studying her face. He leaned over and kissed her.

"Awakened with the promise of a kiss," she said lazily. "If that promise is real, then help me up, so that I may take care of the necessaries. And when I return, you may ravish me."

At first Richard was taken back. He had not yet reached a level of comfort with Elspeth's humorous protestations of love for him to accept them easily. She watched his face and then smiled with understanding. "I love you, Dickie, and I won't mind being ravished by you. In fact, I think I shall enjoy it."

*

In deference to her advancing years, Magdelena had installed air conditioning in the farmhouse and, several years later, a lift, which she took to the ground floor after her breakfast. She found Richard and Elspeth in the garden. Elspeth was propped on a chaise-longue with her Velcro–strapped cast settled on a cushion, and Richard was sitting cross-legged on a pillow on the path beside her. He seemed delighted with something she had said because he threw back his head and laughed. As Magdelena, supported by her cane, hobbled into the garden, her mind flashed back to the day when she had first promised herself to Frederick Duff, and they had sat in the same spot, in love with each other and oblivious to the rest of the war-torn world. Magdelena prayed that Elspeth would be as happy with Richard as she had been with Frederick.

They turned toward her as she came up to them. Richard rose and pulled round the chair that Magdelena always claimed fo. r herself.

"I'm not sure where to begin, but I think I will start with my childhood," she said, lowering her large frame into the seat.

She hesitantly began relating her latest memories.

"Both my mother and father were Maltese and both from old families. At that time, arranged marriages were still common among families living here, but my father always told me that he and my mother had married for love. Sadly, however, most of both their families died in the Spanish flu epidemic of nineteen-eighteen and nineteen-nineteen, and my parents were left with no immediate family, an unusual thing in Malta. I was born in nineteen-twenty, but my mother died in the process of childbirth. As I grew up, my father was everything to me, and he reciprocated by saying I was the world to him. Saddened by my mother's death, he decided to leave Malta and work in England. He was a proficient cellist and music theorist and found a job teaching music and directing the choir at one of the larger Roman Catholic colleges in London. I was brought up there and educated by nuns in a nearby convent, but we usually spent summers here on Gozo, therefore I always considered this farmhouse my home. My father had inherited the farmhouse from one of his relatives, who had a Gozitan wife, and, when we were here, we spent the days playing music and socialising with my father's musical friends. The conditions were much more rustic in those days but, as a girl who spent much of her life at a religious boarding school, I found being here delightfully liberating. My father had started giving me piano lessons when I was four, and by the time I was ten years old, I'd decided I would be a world-famous pianist."

Magdelena smiled as she said this because she had achieved success beyond her wildest childhood dreams.

"My father kept a grand piano here, not a very good one, but he always had it tuned before we came home for the summer holidays. I loved Gozo because here I was not the odd, dark-haired girl with an olive complexion in the lily-white world of England in those days. Even in the Roman Catholic community, which had its share of prejudice directed against it, I was singled out for being different. In London my father never stopped playing the cello, even though much of his time was spent teaching, and by the time I was in my teens, he had joined a chamber music group made up of fellow teachers who sometimes joined us in Gozo during the summers, although they usually gathered in Central Europe. At first they met in Germany, but, as the political situation there worsened, they moved their meetings to Budapest. I went there with my father, and on rare occasions he would ask me to accompany his group on the piano. It was at one of these events that I met Frank."

Magdelena shifted in her chair. "Am I going too far back?" she asked.

Elspeth looked up at her aunt and shook her head. As Magdelena unfolded her story, Elspeth imagined her as a girl and young woman. She had seen the photographs of Magdelena and Frederick when they both were young, he in his army uniform and she in an ill-fitting frock and with a small, precariously perched hat. The grainy black and white images hung among the myriad photographs on the Great Room's walls. Most of these photographs showed Magdelena with princes, presidents and public personalities, all recognisable. The ones with Frederick, however, were the most precious to Magdelena.

"No, not too far back at all," Elspeth said. "But tell us everything you can remember about the day you met Frank."

"I was nervous playing for my father's colleagues and felt I had tripped clumsily over several the notes in the piece his group was practicing. Father must have felt my distress because he called a halt to the session and suggested we all have an early lunch. In those days, I was slender and always hungry. Lunches at the inn where we were staying were simple: bread, fruit, cheese, cold meats, sometimes soup, and always delicious cakes afterwards. We were sitting out on the terrace when a young man approached. He, like me, was dark-haired and olive-skinned, although when he spoke, we knew he was English."

"English? Why?' Elspeth asked.

"Unlike now, in the era of ubiquitous blue jeans, in those days one wore one's country of origin openly. Each nationality wore their own sort of clothing and shoes, had their hair cut differently and even walked in a distinct way. We have become so homogenous in dress and manner these days, that we sometimes forget how formal it was then."

"Did he approach you directly?"

"No, he spoke to Father first."

"How did he introduce himself?"

*

Richard watched Elspeth as she gently led Magdelena back to her life before the war. The old woman had seemed at first halting, but as Elspeth asked her questions, Magdelena relaxed and seemed to return to her younger self. Elspeth had slipped effortlessly into her professional manner, which he had seen her use so many times before at the Kennington hotels. Seeing her artful manipulation, he tried to work out how over the last few days this same woman could also be so tender, needy, headstrong, exacerbating, and seductive all at the same time. He wondered where she was leading Magdelena. He was certain that Elspeth had a plan in mind.

"He said he was working for an Italian recording studio."

"What name did he use?"

Magdelena thought for a moment, "Frank Wells, I think; no, I'm sure of it."

"When did you find out his full name? Didn't you tell me it was Francesco Roberto Wells?"

"It was, but I didn't know that until we were about to be married. I always assumed Frank was his real name, but he told the priest when we were preparing for our wedding that his Christian names were Francesco Roberto. He explained to me later that when he was in England or speaking English, he always used the Anglicised version.

"You said you were married in London. Do you remember which church or the name of the priest?"

Magdelena smiled into the distance. "Saint Stephen's and the priest was Father Michael McCormick."

"Frank was Roman Catholic then?"

"Yes. Before the wedding he said his mother was Italian and he had been born in Milan. As a child, he'd been raised in Italy, but he said he was sent to boarding school in England when he was ten, and he spoke flawless English."

"Although he had grown up in Italy and told your father he was working for an Italian firm, did he give you the impression that he considered himself an Englishman?" Elspeth asked.

Magdelena frowned. "He did. He must have lived in England for a long time. He definitely appeared to be English."

"Did he have a regional accent? You spent much of your childhood in England. Would you have noticed?"

"His accent was educated; I knew that because the nuns taught us to speak the Queen's English with perfect diction."

"He had no trace of an accent?

"None."

Elspeth did not further question Magdelena's assurances.

"Now," Elspeth said, changing tack, "tell me what led up to your marriage."

"From what I've told you about my childhood, you can imagine that I was extremely shy around boys and men. I went to a convent school and spent summers with my father and his older friends. Frank was the first man I ever knew who looked at me as a grown woman. I remember going back to the inn that night and looking in the mirror to see if I was pretty."

Elspeth's eyes softened with understanding. She had done the same thing the night she had met Malcolm Buchanan at Cambridge.

"The next day," Magdelena said, "he came round to one of the practice sessions. Fortunately I was not playing that day, so when he motioned me to come outside, I slipped from the room without my father noticing. We walked by the Danube, which was nearby, and he asked me about my life. I spoke about my music, which was the most sophisticated thing I could think of. He listened and asked me to play for him later. For the next fortnight, he would come every afternoon after the practice sessions and ask me to perform. My father was more indulgent than I could have imagined but insisted that I come home after immediately I'd finished playing."

"But it sounds as if you were left alone long enough for Frank to propose marriage. Did he do that in Hungary?"

"No, Father and I left after the fortnight was over and returned to Gozo. One day, Frank arrived on our doorstep with a large bouquet of roses. He asked me to marry him, saying he had talked my father into agreeing to it."

"Did your father show any reluctance?"

"He made Frank promise to support me when I entered the Royal College of Music in the autumn. That's why we were married in London. After our wedding, we moved into a small flat near the school, and I spent a term at the college before I became pregnant. In those days married women were shunned in conservatories, but I had entered without telling them I was married. In the end, I could not hide my morning sickness and later my expanding body."

"What was Frank doing during that time?"

"He travelled a great deal. He had quit his job with the Italian recording company, saying he could no longer support Italian industry because of Mussolini's policies. He found jobs in sales when they were offered, although none of them were permanent. Father helped support us during that time because he wanted me to continue my studies. In the summer of nineteen thirty-nine, when war was so obviously imminent, Father brought me back to Malta, thinking it would be safer here for me and my expected child rather than staying in London, but he had not foreseen the extensive bombings of Malta by the Axis powers."

Magdelena paused.

"Frank joined us in Malta shortly after we arrived in nineteen thirty-nine. Although we stayed most of the time in Valletta, the twins were born here in San Lawrenz at the end of July, five weeks before Britain declared war on Nazi Germany." Magdelena's face was filled with sorrow.

"I think, dear Aunt Mag, I've grilled you enough for one morning, with regrets that I've brought up painful memories," Elspeth said.

Magdelena nodded her head. "You, *cara,* are good at your craft."

"But I never wanted to be cruel."

"The pain is not of your doing. The war was of man's making, and we often wondered where God was during that time."

After lunch Magdelena retired to her room, leaving Richard and Elspeth to their own resources, but she promised to return at teatime and continue with her story.

Richard rose and came to Elspeth, who was stretched out on the sofa in the guest sitting room with her laptop propped on her knees.

"Where are you going with your questioning?" he asked.

She bit her lip and frowned. "I'm not sure, but I'm trying to find out as much about Frank Wells as I can. I want to get the names of as many sources as possible to check here in Malta, and in London as well. Gathering fresh information about Frank's activities in the war will be difficult because so much was destroyed, particularly in Valletta. But, in the end, Francesco Roberto Wells doesn't ring true to me."

"So I gathered when you probed Magdelena about his origins. I wonder if . . ." He stopped in mid-sentence.

"What, Dickie?"

". . . if what Celia's idea might be valid."

"Celia? Do I've a rival?"

"A raven-haired one with long, slender legs in black tights," Richard said and suddenly realised he was teasing Elspeth.

"Then how about we have a lie down, and I will obliterate her from your mind. But seriously, who is this Celia?"

"A woman at the FCO who works in the archives and sets her cap on any approaching male."

"That doesn't help me," Elspeth said.

"When I went down into the basement file rooms, where she holds out, Celia suggested that Francesco Roberto Wells might be plain Frank Wells from Birmingham."

"Did she suggest anything else?"

"Yes, but with you in the wings I didn't take her up on it. I scurried up to Scotland instead. However, I should have followed up with her, which in my haste to see you, I didn't do."

"Not when you have something better here," said Elspeth, raising her eyebrows suggestively.

13

Visions of the days leading up to the war in Malta disturbed Magdelena's rest. Her labour was long and painful, producing the twins, who were small but healthy. As the last days of summer brought war to Europe, it also brought the joy of the babies into Magdelena's life. It also took Frank from her. He was open in his feelings of impatience with the twins, their tears, messes, and needs, as well as their smiles and gurgles. She, her father, and the children moved permanently from the Cassar palazzo in Valletta to the farmhouse in Gozo. Frank did not follow. He came on an occasional weekend, almost dutifully, but said he was engaged in secret war work and needed to be on the island of Malta, not its smaller sister, Gozo.

Magdelena rose from her afternoon nap, unrested, and walked to the window of her bedroom to see if Elspeth and Richard were in the garden. She saw them emerge from the door of the guest quarters, Elspeth with her crutch, brushing away Richard's help. He pulled the chairs round so that they were in the shade and caught the afternoon breeze off the sea. They laughed at something and touched each other lightly, as only lovers can do. *Cara,* do not let this man go, Magdelena whispered to herself. He will give you what you have always wanted and needed. Magdelena loved Elspeth as if she were her own and chuckled at how much Elspeth was like her uncle, not in appearance for she took after her mother's side of the family, but in temperament. Magdelena also knew that part of that temperament included a passionate and loving side, which Elspeth was only now discovering but probably still did not yet trust.

Magdelena slipped into her shoes and wrapped her shawl across her body. She took the lift to the ground floor, and, calling into the kitchen to ask Teresa to bring them some tea and biscuits, made her way to the garden.

*

Richard rose to greet Magdelena and took her over to where Elspeth sat, her foot propped up on another chair. He noticed the shadows under the grande dame's eyes.

Elspeth looked up at her aunt. "Aunt Mag," she said, "I wish I could come over there and hug you the way you always hug me when things aren't right in my life."

Magdelena smiled and drew herself up. "I'll consider myself hugged, and now I'll act appropriately for my advancing years, not moaning about my relationship with Frank but instead continuing to answer your questions as unemotionally as possible. After all, it was I who instigated this investigation. Where did we leave off, *cara*?"

"With the start of the war. I think if Richard and I are going to get to the bottom of why Frank Wells vanished, we will need to find out something about his so-called secret war work. Did he ever talk about it?"

Magdelena shook her head. "After the war began, Frank was away most of the time. At first, he came to Gozo at the weekends, but this soon tapered off to once every two or three weeks. When he came for the last time, on his birthday in December nineteen forty-one, we had not seen him for six weeks."

"Did he seem different?"

"When he arrived here at the farmhouse, even at the beginning of the war, he spent most of his time sleeping. Father, the twins, and I were living upstairs, but we had the room downstairs where you are staying made into a bedroom for Frank, where he could rest quietly without the children bothering him. It originally was a tool room, but we moved the things stored there into the garage with our old Ford, which was useless because ordinary civilians in those days could not get petrol. Frank would come on Friday night and stay through Sunday lunch. Sometimes he would bring us small gifts, but most times he was empty-handed. He was always uncommunicative both about his work and his life in San Pawl's, where he said he was living, and he basically ignored the children and me."

"What sort of gifts did he bring?"

"The one present I do remember was a box of Italian chocolates. Chocolate, particularly good chocolate, was one of the many things we saw little of in those days. These were delicate dark chocolates, each individually decorated and wrapped in foil. I asked him where they had come from, and he said that he had 'taken them off' an Italian soldier. My father thought it an odd turn of phrase."

Richard had several times read Conan FitzRoy's great novel set in Malta in the war and had devoured all Churchill's books on the Second World War. He tried to recall what was going on in Malta in December of nineteen forty-one. The Afrika Corps was racing across Tunisia toward Egypt, and the Germans and Italians were bombing Malta heavily. But Malta never capitulated. The stories were legion about the many sacrifices the Maltese made and the deprivations they suffered. A box of handmade Italian chocolates did not fit into historical reality because the Italians had never invaded

Malta, and the Maltese and British forces had defended the island almost exclusively from the air and not on the ground. A box of chocolates was hardly something a shot-down Italian pilot would have carried on a mission, or that would have remained unscathed in a plane crash. How had Frank obtained the chocolates?

"How did you survive in those years," Richard asked.

"We were among the lucky ones, living so far from a large town. We had a garden where we grew vegetables, and we raised a few chickens. We traded eggs for fish, bread, and milk. We had no coffee, and only occasionally tea, and we learned to live without any luxuries. Then Frank brought the gift of chocolates. I ate several and their richness gave me terrible indigestion. I've never liked Italian chocolates since."

"Did he say or bring anything else that might give a hint of where he had been?" Elspeth asked.

"He said living in Valletta had become too dangerous, and he had moved to St. Pawl's Bay. I never visited him there, so that may not have been true."

"Was he ever in uniform?"

"No, which I suppose I should have questioned more fully. Almost all the young British men and many of the Maltese, both here in Gozo and on Malta, were in uniform. Frank said his work was hush-hush, and he did not have any official rank. When he did talk, he boasted how important his work was, but never the nature of it."

"What about the conscription letters?"

"I never understood why they were sent if he was working for the British."

"Aunt Mag, when Uncle Frederick first came to see you, what did he tell you about Frank's activities after his disappearance?"

Magdelena shifted in her chair. Richard rose and asked if he could move it round under the shade.

"No, I like the sun," she said and continued with her dialogue. "In the beginning your uncle told me nothing. He said he had come to help with the rehabilitation and resettlement of the people in San Lawrenz and the other small villages nearby."

"Did you suspect Frank was dead, particularly since he didn't contact you after the bombing that destroyed the farmhouse? You said the raid was in April nineteen forty-two. That was four months after his so-called disappearance. Surely, he would have sent his sympathies at your loss and the loss of his children, if nothing else, had he been alive."

"Even now I don't know what had happened to Frank after December, but by the time I met your uncle, I didn't care. I felt I'd been abandoned and, even before then, after the children came, I'd ceased having any feelings for him. The marriage had been a mistake almost from the first." Magdelena lifted her jaw with the dignity of a thousand years of Maltese ancestry.

"If you don't want to answer my next question, I'll understand, but it would help if you would. Had you and Uncle Frederick become . . ." Elspeth paused for the right word, "intimate before he came to interview you officially about Frank's wartime activities?"

"Had we become lovers? Don't be afraid to ask. Yes, we did almost immediately after we met. I'd lost everything, and I clung on to him in those first days. He became my salvation and the core of my life. We never stopped loving one another, and I still love him today."

She pulled a handkerchief from a hidden pocket and wiped tears from her eyes.

"Thank you, Aunt Mag," Elspeth said softly. "Knowing that puts things in a different light. Now tell me again about the day Uncle Frederick summoned you and interrogated you about Frank."

Magdelena repeated what she had told Elspeth earlier.

"You said Uncle Frederick told you that he suspected Frank might have boarded a smuggler's boat for Italy for the purpose of passing on information to the Fascists. Did he actually say that Frank had gone over to the enemy?"

"He didn't need to say it. Frank was half Italian, had been a boy in Italy and obviously was evading his military duty to the British. That he was involved in smuggling, whether goods or information, made the most sense. The smugglers in those days were stealing from the Maltese, who had so little, and carrying things of value into Sicily. Frank's participation in these activities seemed the only logical explanation for the way he acted. That he could actually change his allegiance did not surprise me, that is, if he had been loyal to the King in the first place."

Elspeth frowned. "You said that when you met Frank, you thought that he was English. Did you ever hear him speak Italian?"

"What a silly question, *cara*! He was half Italian." Magdelena laughed and then her face fell. "But on second thoughts, I don't remember that I ever did. In those days, my Italian was limited to musical notations and that doesn't get one very far in conversation. We never went to Italy together, so I wouldn't have heard him speak Italian. Before our wedding, he said his parents were dead, so they couldn't attend, and therefore I never met them."

"Did he speak other languages?"

"A bit of German, I think, only because he could read the signs in German in Budapest, and he had learned some Hungarian. Not much though. Just enough to order a meal or buy a concert ticket. He also picked up a smattering of Maltese while he was living here."

"Did you ever discuss Frank's disappearance with anyone other than Uncle Frederick?"

"No, Frederick had authority over this area, and I assumed, despite our personal relationship, it would have been his duty to give me any information he had learned about Frank. Besides I didn't want anyone else to know."

"Did Uncle Frederick ever say that Frank had died?"

Magdelena thought for a long while. "No, because after the war, when the ownership of the farmhouse was questioned, Frederick said it would be best if I said nothing about Frank's last days on Malta. Frederick also advised that since Frank became the legal owner of the property after my father's death, it would be wise to maintain that he had disappeared but was not known to be dead, and that, as his wife, I could continue to live here. Had the British Government let it be known that Frank was a traitor, they might have confiscated the property.

"You said Uncle Frederick was the British authority here."

"He was until nineteen forty-three. Later he was assigned to Valletta. Unlike Frank, he returned home as often as possible despite the danger of crossing between the two islands. By now he thought of the farmhouse as his home, and together we had restored the downstairs bedroom and a small kitchen and bathroom. It was only at the very end, when the Allied Forces were entering Germany that he left for any length of time. He was gone from January until June nineteen forty-five. He resigned his commission as soon as possible after the war and returned here. He lived here until he died."

"But you travelled widely."

"Oh, yes. In the autumn nineteen of forty-seven we went to London, where I finished my musical education, and, of course, we travelled all over Europe and even to North America during my professional career. But in the first two years after the war, we didn't leave Malta at all, even with all the hardships here, and they were the best years of my life."

Elspeth cautiously asked about Frederick's wife. "Did Uncle Frederick tell you about Jean?"

"Oh, yes, even on the very first day."

"I'm glad," Elspeth said.

"You see, Elspeth, neither one of us was able to remarry, but it didn't matter. For fifty years we lived without the blessing of the Church and outside the Law, but we were husband and wife to each other, and that was all that counted. Now, because I can think of nothing more to tell you today, I will go and play for you, something joyous, for you have lifted a terrible burden off my shoulders. I'm so relieved someone else now knows the truth about what happened here all those years ago."

*

Elspeth woke during the night, her foot hurting. She had left her pain killers and a glass of water on the bedside table and reached for them, fumbling to get the tablets out of the foil. Richard turned and murmured something like "Are you all right?".

"Fine," she said, although she was not. "Go back to sleep." He mumbled some unintelligible words and rolled over away from her.

Something that Magdelena had said bothered Elspeth, but she could not put her finger on it. Something about Frank Wells that did not ring true. In fact, there was a great deal about Frank Wells that did not ring true, but this was something very specific. Had she been alone, she would have turned on the light, and opened her laptop, or found some paper on which to write her thoughts, but she did not want to disturb Richard. Instead she turned toward him and put her arm round his shoulder. He grunted contentedly but gave no other response. So much for continuing bliss, Elspeth thought, but the comfort of his body next to hers did not send her to sleep immediately. Something in the documents Aunt Mag had showed her contradicted her memory of the events, Elspeth thought. She must ask to see them again in the morning. Her pain tablets now had begun to work, and she adjusted the position of her foot so that she would not knock it into Richard's leg. She pulled up their duvet and drifted into sleep.

14

"I suggest we spend the day in Mdina," Richard said when he was shaving the next morning. "Do you think you are up to the ferry ride to Malta? I'll call ahead and make sure we have a car when we arrive in Valletta."

Because of her proclivity to seasickness, Elspeth was thankful that he had not suggested they take his sailing boat back to the yacht club at Ta'Xbiex, where he usually moored it. She turned over in bed and raised herself on her elbows so she could see him in the mirror.

"With your help, I think I can manage. Do you want to speak with Dominic Fenech's grandfather? Doesn't he live in Mdina?"

"Yes, and today seems a good time. I expect Magdelena has shared with us all she can emotionally for the moment, and the old general may be helpful in giving us information about the military conter-intelligence services in Malta in nineteen forty-one."

"Good idea," Elspeth said, admiring his shaving skills. "But I had a thought in the night."

"So that was what all that tossing was about," he said, rinsing off his chin. "What was it?"

"I'm not sure."

"That's a good thought," he said, the corner of his lips trembling in a suppressed laugh. Having finished his task, he came back into the bedroom. "Do you have many of those in the middle of the night and does it always cause you to trash about so?"

She threw a pillow at him. Was this really stiff old Dickie? He had thawed, and she wondered how much she had to do with that. She could not imagine Marjorie in a battle with Richard, using pillows as a weapon.

"I won't throw one back," he said with mock dignity. "I shall never be accused of attacking an injured woman."

"You didn't treat me as if I were injured earlier."

"And we weren't in a pillow fight either," he said with a big grin.

They left the farmhouse before Magdelena had risen, and Elspeth was able to retrieve the folder Magdelena had shown her earlier. She felt it might jog her memory about her concerns during the night. Giulio drove them sedately to the ferry and took a wheelchair out of the boot of the limousine for Elspeth's use when boarding. Giulio explained that it was stored there in case Magdelena needed it, but Elspeth had never seen her use it.

Elspeth brushed it away. "Thank you, but no. I'm getting on quite well on my own now, Giulio, and Sir Richard can help me, if necessary. I'll ring you to let you know when we'll be back. If it's late, we'll get a taxi."

"*Sì, signora* Elspetta."

Elspeth noted he had dropped the *'signorina'* of the past. Neither he nor Teresa could be ignorant of her cohabitation with Richard and had changed from the single to the marital form of address. When she pointed this out to Richard, he frowned uncomfortably.

"Elspeth, since you insist on keeping the status of our relationship in permanent limbo," he said to her as they were sitting on the deck of the ferry, "how shall I introduce you to the General?"

Elspeth thought a moment and said, "Perhaps as Magdelena Cassar's niece. There is no sense announcing our illicit relationship to a man who is probably of the old school and a Roman Catholic to boot."

Richard had dressed in a dark suit with his Oxford college tie, which Elspeth patted with an approving glance before they left the farmhouse. She had chosen a pair of dark trousers, thankful that the current fashion was for loose fitting legs, because it partially covered her cast, and she put on a simple white top and a blue and green Thai silk over-shirt that she had bought in Singapore before she was attacked. Its colours particularly flattered the depth of the blue in her eyes. She added a gold necklace of delicate workmanship that she had found in a shop along the Arno in Florence. Rather than use her crutch, she had found a silver-headed cane in Magdelena's umbrella stand and purloined it for the day.

They made a fine-looking couple as they approached the General's home in the old capital of Malta. Several tourists in shorts, tee shirts, and baseball caps stopped and audibly admired them, wondering what the formal occasion might be. One even took a photograph.

They found General Rafel Fenech's house on the main square and knocked at the pair of ancient wooden doors. An older woman dressed in black answered and told them the General was waiting for them in the drawing room on the first floor. They climbed a wide staircase lined with mediaeval armour and flags from past Maltese campaigns.

The General was standing erectly by a brocaded chair, wearing his wartime uniform with his medals proudly pinned on his chest. As they entered, he was checking the medals in the mirror and straightening his jacket, although the uniform noticeably hung on his ageing shoulders.

Grasping his walking frame, the General approached them and offered them seats on the stiff wooden chairs that surrounded an overwhelming stone-carved mantelpiece.

"It looks grand," he said, pointing to the fireplace, "but it smokes terribly and hasn't been used since the time of Napoleon. And the chairs are hard, but that is what one must endure living in in one of these grand old houses. Now, Sir Richard and *sinjura*, how may I help you? Dominic telephoned from London saying the British High Commissioner would be paying me a call and had some questions about the war." He nodded toward Richard. "I was delighted when I received your call this morning. I seldom get a chance to recount what I remember about the war. Young people are no longer interested."

The General turned toward Elspeth. "And who may this beautiful lady be? Is she interested in the war as well?"

"General, may I present Mrs Elspeth Duff, who is presently staying on Gozo with her aunt, Magdelena Cassar."

"I'm charmed, Mrs Duff," he said, "particularly because I've always been enchanted by your aunt's playing. I trust she is well."

"As well as can be expected," Elspeth replied. "Thank you for asking. I shall tell her you did so. And thank you for letting me come with Sir Richard."

"What may I do for you, Sir Richard?" the General asked.

Richard was not sure how to begin, but Elspeth jumped to his rescue.

"General, I'm afraid I've imposed on Sir Richard's kindness. I'm doing some research into the history of Malta during the Second World War for my cousin, the Earl of Tay. He's writing a paper that he hopes to publish in the *Oxford Journal of History*. He and Sir Richard were friends at university, you know. I recently had a nasty turn and tore my Achilles' tendon while walking on my cousin's estate in Scotland, and have come to recuperate my aunt on Gozo."

She coyly stuck out her foot as if to verify what she said. The old man smiled sympathetically and seemed to enjoy eyeing a lady's ankle, although it was wrapped in stiff cloth and secured with Velcro.

Richard frowned both at the General's glance and Elspeth's words. He did not like Elspeth's habit of prevarication when she felt it was needed. Wouldn't a simple explanation have done?

Elspeth continued. "I told the earl that I would help him gather some data while I am here. My cousin is focusing on the role of the Secret Services in Malta in late nineteen forty-one. I thought that whilst I was here in Malta I could be of assistance to him. I asked Sir Richard to make inquiries as to who might be most able to help." She leaned over and put her hand over the General's. "Richard was so good as to set up this appointment with you through your nephew in London, knowing of my cousin's research."

The General beamed. "Dominic has done well in the Commonwealth and Foreign Office, but that was to be expected. He's a bright young man. May I offer you some sherry? You will have to pour it yourselves, I'm afraid, because my hands are rather shaky these days. And now, *sinjura*, what would you like to know."

Once started, the General seemed transported back to nineteen forty-one. Richard and Elspeth sipped the sherry, which was old and fine, but declined a second glass as it still was early in the day. As the General rambled on, Richard watched Elspeth and wondered what questions she would ask and how she would formulate them. He suspected that she might be devious after shamelessly using Johnnie Tay's name.

"General," she said, finding a convenient lead in, "during nineteen forty-one were there, I am not sure of the right term, 'irregular soldiers' here in Malta. British officers or service men not in uniform who might have been involved in undercover work?"

"In every war there are people who work undercover, usually behind enemy lines."

"Does that mean there might have been German or Italian agents here in Malta during the war? Did the British forces have a counter-intelligence branch here?"

"A small one, yes."

"Tell me, how did this work?"

"I worked under the command of Air Commodore Hugh Lloyd, who oversaw all the military forces here, and I wasn't directly involved in counter-espionage, other than in the most general way. I do know that we used local informants to flush out any of the spies that Mussolini or Hitler sent here."

The General went off on another rant, this time about how ineffective Mussolini's submarines were, to which Elspeth and Richard listened politely.

When he finished his tirade, she asked, "Did you know my uncle, Major Frederick Duff?"

"Major Duff?"

"My uncle was extremely tall, well over six feet, and redheaded. You might have met him."

"Let me think. Yes, we did meet on several occasions. He was stationed in Gozo."

"Was he in counter-intelligence, or are you allowed to tell me?"

"I suppose after all this time it doesn't matter if we talk about what was secret then. I must be declassified by now. Few of us are still here who were directly involved during the war." He paused. "Yes, now I remember. Major Duff was assigned to Gozo specifically to ferret out any insurgency or subversive activity that might have developed there. In his public role, he was an administrator representing the government, which of course was British at the time. His position allowed him to come into contact with much of the local population, and, in that capacity, he had the ability to move freely among the people without arousing suspicion. As the war progressed, we were worried that Hitler and Mussolini seemed to be winning, and the local people would turn their loyalties to the Axis powers, particularly to Italy, and help them in the hope of future rewards after their victory. I understand Major Duff was quite clever at finding out what was going on behind closed doors and had a group of local people who cooperated with him."

"Did he uncover any traitors?"

"I think he found several."

"Do you remember their names?"

"I'm not too sure I ever knew. That wasn't my department."

"Could you put us in contact with someone who might know?"

"I think most of the people involved have long since passed on to their heavenly maker, but, if I remember any, I'll let you know."

Elspeth looked up at Richard and nodded almost imperceptibly, acknowledging that she had found out the information for which she had come. Out of courtesy, they stayed another half hour. Richard revelled in the old man's stories, but eventually even he grew restless.

"We must impose no further," Richard said. "I do need to get back to the High Commission, and I think Mrs Duff is tiring."

Having made their excuses, they left the General, who seemed delighted that someone had sought him out, and bothered to listen to what he had to say.

"Elspeth," Richard said as they got back in their car. "You were incorrigible in there. Johnnie doing a paper for the *Oxford Journal of History*? I don't think he has had his nose in a book since he left Oxford."

"Only in financial ones, Dickie dear, and I believe he is doing quite well these days in his business. I did extract some good information from the General, didn't I?"

"Where did you learn your role as an interrogator—in Hollywood?"

"No," she said laughing. "Dramatics at Blair School for Girls and from my mother's knee. Mother would have been delighted at my performance just now. She always said 'when in doubt, improvise'. I rely on that advice all the time in my work. And I acted the role of 'a helpful relative to titled people' quite well, didn't I?"

"I thought you disdained your aristocratic connections."

"I do, unless they are useful."

Richard suppressed a smile but began to doubt if he could safely turn Elspeth loose on the diplomatic community.

15

"Malta being such a small place," Richard said, "I fear that if I don't at least put in a brief appearance at the High Commission, word may get back to my staff about my return to Malta. Will you come with me?"

"I can't very well run off, can I?" she said taking his hand and rubbing her thumb gently across the back of his hand, "but won't your sudden arrival cause a bit of a stir?"

"Stir? In what way?"

"Weren't you supposed to be in Scotland introducing me to your family and friends? No one here knows the wedding has been called off."

"Has it really, Elspeth? You know well enough I want it to be otherwise."

Richard was glad that his chauffeur-driven hire car had a window between the driver's compartment and the back seat where they were sitting.

"I can't make it work, Dickie. As much as I love you, and I do, I can't see how we could manage our separate lives once we were married. When I went to Perthshire, I spoke to both my father and Biddy about this. I hope you don't mind."

"I do mind, Elspeth," he said gravely, "not that you talked to your father or Biddy, but that you have called off the wedding. Will you tell me what they advised you to do?'

"My father said I should make my own decision. He's done that since I was a child."

"And Biddy?"

"Biddy said I should find a third option."

Richard looked puzzled. "A third option? What were the first two?"

"The first was that I forget you and return to my job full time. The other was that I become your wife, assume all the duties that would entail and leave my job entirely. Neither would work for me. I love you too much to forget you, but I don't have the skills or temperament to be a diplomatic wife."

"Have you found a third option?"

Elspeth looked miserable. "No, and these last few days we've had together has made everything seem even more impossible."

Richard thought over the last week with the warmest of recollections and could not understand Elspeth's logic. "But surely that would make you want to marry me even more."

"It has made me love you even more."

"But not enough to reconsider marriage?"

"I can't take Marjorie's place, Dickie. I would be a miserable failure at it and would probably pull more stunts like the one just now with the General. I'm better fitted for my job with the Kennington Organisation."

"I always assumed you would return to work at least during the transition. In fact, Lord Kennington made me promise that I wouldn't carry you off before he had found a replacement for you."

"Eric? When did you talk to him?"

"Right after you said you would marry me. Actually I talked to Pamela Crumm first, and then to Eric Kennington."

Elspeth let go his hand and turned away from him. She clenched her jaw. "That's why it won't work," she said.

"I don't understand," he said, so soulfully that Elspeth turned back to him.

"You're talking to Pamela and Eric and not mentioning it to me. I've been accused of being both obstinate and independent, and perhaps I am, but at least you could have told me."

"I only wanted to tell them our news. You said you had mentioned it to them earlier."

"Only in an off-hand way."

"How does one mention that one is planning to be married and say it in an off-hand way?"

"I told them that you had asked me."

"Did you tell them what your reply was?"

"I said I'd agreed in general terms but that we hadn't worked out the details," she said in a small voice. "We haven't, have we?"

"Don't you think this is something we need to discuss in more depth, my dearest? I want you to marry me, not in a general way, but in a very specific way. I want the world to know that I love you and that you love me, and we have agreed to be husband and wife. We may not have worked out the details, but that doesn't change how I feel us getting married."

"I'm more trouble than you need, Dickie," she said stubbornly.

Magdelena's words a week before in Mgarr came back to Richard. *When you asked her to love you, you asked a bruised person. Elspeth despite all her fire, passion, and intelligence is a fragile person. . . If you love her, you must understand that.*

His voice softened. "My dearest one," he said, "the only trouble I can see is that because I love you so much I shall become your lap dog."

Elspeth looked over at him and grinned, fighting back the tears. "There's a strict hotel policy that no dogs are allowed. In some of the larger hotels we have luxury kennel facilities in the basement, which will cost you more than your little squeaker did in the first place," she said in a falsetto voice and then became serious again. "Is there a third option, Dickie? I can't find one."

"It's a problem worth working out together," he said.

"I have a feeling that I'm not what you originally bargained for, that I'm not really the person you imagine me to be."

"You are more tender than I imagined you would be, but I love you better for it."

She put her hand into his and leaned over to kiss his cheek.

He cursed that they arrived at the British High Commission in Ta'Xbiex so quickly. He directed the driver to take them round to the side entrance reserved for the High Commissioner and his private staff and hustled Elspeth into the lift before he could be confronted by anyone in the building. They reached the top floor and as he unlocked the lift gates he leaned over and kissed the top of Elspeth's head without saying anything.

When he opened his office doors, Margaret, his PA, was there sorting some papers.

"Oh, Sir Richard," she said, jumping back in surprise, "I hadn't expected you back until next week, but I'm glad you came as I've been trying to reach you. They need you in Brussels first thing Monday morning. I didn't realise you were back in Malta. Shall I book the flight from here? I've arranged for one from Edinburgh, but I can change it to Luqa, if you wish."

"Thank you, but I'll book my own flight because I'm not sure where I shall be leaving from or when," he said. "Is my presence in Brussels so necessary? I'm supposed to be on holiday."

"They didn't say. Perhaps you should call Brussels directly. It was Hans Becker who rang."

Margaret came round the desk and took Elspeth's hand. "How nice to see you again, Mrs Duff. I understand that congratulations are in order. Have you two set a date?"

Elspeth smiled her most diplomatic smile. "Thank you, Margaret. No, we haven't. At Richard's age and mine, these things don't need to be rushed."

"Margaret, I only stopped in to say hello, but we need to get back to Gozo, where we are staying. Don't worry about Hans Becker. I'll take care of the matter," Richard said.

As their car left the High Commission, Richard turned a puzzled eye toward Elspeth. "Did your comment to Margaret mean you might reconsider my offer?"

Elspeth said, "I was trying my hardest not to embarrass you. Did I succeed? Do you really need to go to Brussels?"

"I'm afraid so, worse luck. I was hoping to stay in Malta until your tendon was fully mended. I shouldn't be gone more than a week. But we have four more days before then. Is that long enough, do you think, at least to try and discuss a third option?"

"If you can think of one," she said with a small twist of a smile. "Now, can we have a bite of lunch? I'm ravenously hungry and a little heady from the General's sherry, good as it was."

Dared by Elspeth to find a third option, on their return to Gozo Richard decided to leave Elspeth and her aunt at the piano. He hiked toward the sea, which was a short distance away, and walked along the cliff that edged on the Mediterranean. He thought best on the water and wished he had not left Marjorie's cousin's launch in Mgarr, but its retrieval would require a ride across the island, and he did not want to ask Magdelena for the use of her car again or to bother Giulio.

He made his way along the dusty road, deep in thought. When he came back from Brussels, where would he live? At first he supposed he would return to Marjorie's cousin's house in Sliema, and come over to Gozo to see Magdelena when he had a chance. He walked on, deep in thought. Marjorie's cousin's launch and Marjorie's cousin's house, he mused. The house would not be a suitable place for Elspeth to live. Moreover, he had not cut his ties with Marjorie's relatives as surgically as Elspeth had severed her life from Alistair Craig in California and from the ghost of Malcolm Buchanan after she found out the truth about his murder in Singapore. This, however, presented a dilemma for him. If or when he and Elspeth did marry, they could find a place of their own, of course. If they didn't, where could he go? He would find a flat or a small house near the High Commission, he supposed. Perhaps it was time he bought his own boat as well. He had enough money and could well afford to buy a suitable yacht. But he knew Elspeth dislike sailing, and he was not inclined to leave the house in Sliema if Elspeth did return to London alone to resume her job.

What had Elspeth said in the car? "I can't take Marjorie's place." Had he made room for her to come to grips with her feelings about Marjorie—and with his as well? The first step in the third option might involve him divesting himself of his dependence on Marjorie's family, but he was not sure he could do so easily.

*

Elspeth's eyes followed the music, and she turned the pages with the precision of long practice. Aunt Mag seemed joyful today and had chosen a Chopin waltz, which she said she had forgotten but played with such dexterity that it suggested a strong latent memory. She came to the end of the piece and sat for a moment, her hands resting on the keys.

"Why won't you marry him, *cara*? He wants you to. Is it because you're having doubts about your love for him?"

"No, not that."

"What then?"

"I don't know how to live with him and fit into his life."

"That's a dilemma for most couples at first, but it's something that evolves over time. Have you discussed this with him?"

"Yes, a little. We had a bit of a tiff about it."

"Do you want to tell me about it?"

"What's to say, Aunt Mag? He's going to Brussels on Monday. As soon as my tendon is healed, I'll be going back to London, and Eric Kennington will be sending me off to Timbuktu or somewhere else on assignment. If we're here together in Malta, where would we stay? I certainly can't move into Marjorie's cousin's house in Sliema. Richard can stay at my flat in London, but he can't very well live there and carry on with his job in Malta. What would be the point of being married when we should see each other just as often as we do now, enjoying our love without any complications or sense of marital duty? You and Uncle Frederick lived all those years together without marriage and certainly you were happy."

"We were, but we couldn't legally marry. We made our own partnership work as if we had been. Had I known if Frank was dead, I would have married your uncle in an instant after Jean died. We had many more problems to overcome than you and Richard have, but we learned that when a relationship grows from love most difficulties can be worked out."

"Tell me about Uncle Frederick," Elspeth said, purposely changing the topic. "I came here so often when he was alive, but I never really knew who he was. How did you manage financially, for example? My father's parents were highly respectable but never rich. Did Uncle Frederick have a pension from the British Army?"

"A small one, yes, as well as some money from his father, your grandfather, but we didn't worry. Although my family lost a great deal of property during the war because of the bombings, my father was a cautious man and had put part of the family money in Swiss bank accounts before the war came, with instructions that if anything happened to him, I could draw on them without Frank's signature, a precaution since Frank might be in the Armed Forces and unavailable. It was the closest thing my father ever did to give me independence, and over the years I've been very grateful. After the war, I brought some of the capital back to Malta and rebuilt the Cassar palazzo in Valletta as well as the farmhouse here. Your uncle oversaw the layout and plantings of the gardens, and I was responsible for the refurbishment of the houses. After the renovation of the palazzo was complete, I let it out on a sixty-year lease. That brings in a good income even now.

"Frederick was clever with money. He took an advanced degree in accounting at the London School of Economics while I was finishing at the Royal College of Music. He invested his money and mine wisely, and we lived well once the horrors of war were replaced by better times. When I became established in my career, he became my business manager and handled our financial affairs. To the world, we were husband and wife, but we also were business partners. Frederick didn't have old fashioned ideas about women not being able to handle money, the way my father had. I would have married your uncle if I could, but you *can* marry Richard. Don't make excuses as to why you can't. Nothing is standing in your way but your own doubts."

"Am I making excuses? I hadn't thought of it that way. I'm trying to be realistic, not silly just because we are having rather a wonderful love affair."

"Do you think of it only as that, *cara*, a love affair?"

Elspeth lowered her head on to Magdelena's shoulder. "I don't want what Richard and I have together to change or disappear. Marriage is too complex for what we share now. I've put Richard through enough the last few years, and he still seems to love me. I don't want to press my luck beyond that."

"You'll have to make a commitment to him if you want to keep him."

"Is his love that fragile?"

"I think not, but I think yours may be. To love and live with someone, you must make yourself open to change, and also to the possibility of loss."

"Did you feel that open with Uncle Frederick? I never did with Alistair."

"Always. I met him at the most vulnerable moment of my life, and I knew with certainty he wouldn't ever violate that trust I had in him. He never did. If you genuinely love Richard, you'll have to give him that same trust."

"I'm not certain I can."

Magdelena leaned over and kissed Elspeth's cheek. "You must try," she said, "for both your sakes."

Part 2

Frank Wells

16

"I'm working on a theory about Frank Wells," Elspeth said to Richard, "but I need more information. I'm trying to think of the best way to find it, and I think your raven-haired beauty at the FCO can help, long legs notwithstanding."

They were sitting in the garden outside their rooms and enjoying their breakfast. Neither had spoken of what had been uppermost in their minds since Richard had returned from his walk the previous evening.

"Is there any chance you could be in London next week and go to the FCO to see Celia?" she asked.

"I doubt I can because normally the committee meetings in Brussels run on endlessly and the chances of getting back to the FCO in London during Celia's working hours are slim."

"You've never told me what you do in Brussels. You just keep running off there."

"Currently I am chairman of one of those EU committees devised by the President of the European Commission. This one concerns immigrants' rights. The topic is rather explosive right now, and every country seems to have a different way of approaching the problem. I think they appointed me chair because of my reputation for a cool head."

"How much longer are you in the chair?"

"Only until the end of the year, thank goodness," he said, blowing out his breath.

"And how much longer are you here in Malta as High Commissioner?"

"Probably as long as I like. Two more years, anyway."

"I see," said Elspeth. "So, you returning to London permanently isn't part of the third option, is it?"

"If I chose to leave Malta," he said, trying to follow her gist, "I should probably be assigned somewhere else much less accessible to London. Vanuatu or the Maldives perhaps."

"Never tease me over geography, Dickie. As you know, *The Times Atlas of the World* sits on my coffee table in London and, when I am not otherwise distracted, I have my nose in it, finding places new to me. My grandfather taught me geography using his early twentieth-century atlas in the library at Tay Farm and instilled in me a fascination for far-off lands," she said with a huff. "Besides Lord Kennington might send me to either place on the least whim."

"If he had a hotel there, but your assignment would last a week and mine four to six years."

"Is that true?" she said. "Hmm. Malta does seem a good alternative. But if you do stay here, where would you live? Will you continue to stay on in the house in Sliema? Don't you find it a bit bizarre?"

"Until yesterday, I didn't think of it at all except as a place to stay with a nice balcony over the Mediterranean where I could share breakfast with you."

"And yesterday?"

"Yesterday, after we got back from Malta, I called Margaret and asked her to make an appointment with an estate agent during the week I get back. If I am to stay in Malta, I'll need a home that will be ours, not just mine and not in any way connected to Marjorie. It's a first step toward a third option, my dear one, small though it may be."

Elspeth looked up into the love in his eyes and smiled in return.

"Does that I mean I can come here and live with you when I'm in Malta?"

"It's my first step," he said. "The next is to buy my own boat, then I may . . ."

She did not let him finish. "Dickie, may I be honest for a moment?"

"I hope you always are and not only for a moment."

"I love you but I loathe sailing."

He reached for her cheek and brushed it lightly. "I already know that, my dearest. The boat is for me when I have to flee from your stubborn, obstinate, and infuriating ways."

Elspeth's whole body seized inside. "Am I really so awful?" she asked.

"No," he said. "I want nothing to come between us, but I know there will be times."

"Yes," she said, pressing her lips together in dismay. "Unfortunately, but I will try to keep things in check."

"Then you will come live with me?"

She looked at him and bit her lower lip. "Aunt Mag says I should trust you in all things."

"Your aunt is a wise woman."

"Dickie, how can it work for us?"

"I haven't figured that out yet. The only thing I know is that being together can work both for you and for me."

Elspeth turned from him and said, swallowing. "Yes, together would be lovely, just not marriage."

Without waiting for his reaction, she reached for her coffee cup and stared into it for a long time. "Is it all right to get back to the subject of Frank Wells?"

"Of course, since you have just given me more hope than I've had since the great disaster at Glenborough Castle. Tell me your theory?"

"I think Frank may not have been who Aunt Mag believes he was."

"In what way?"

"Do you remember me saying that something was bothering me, but I didn't know what it was?"

"I still bear the scars where you hit me with your cast as you were thrashing about during the night." He wondered how she would react to his teasing.

"Fiend," she said, grinning. "You may need that new boat sooner than you think. No, I'm serious. Think back to what Aunt Mag told us. Frank Wells proposed to her here in Gozo after they returned from Hungary, or rather approached her father to ask permission to marry her before he approached her. If you were someone who wanted an excuse to come to Malta in the late nineteen thirties, what might be an easy way?"

"By marrying into a Maltese family?" he suggested.

"Exactly. From the first moment they met, Aunt Mag made a number of assumptions about Frank: that he was at least half-British, that he was born in Milan, that he had an Italian mother, and, perhaps incorrectly, that he loved her, at least in the beginning. She had grown up with a doting father and been educated in a convent school. Frank told her he was a Roman Catholic and married her in a Catholic church. He also said his parents were dead. She took his word for it, but was it true? You were there when I asked her if he spoke any foreign languages other than Italian and English. She said a bit of German. Does this suggest anything to you?'

"Are you implying that he might have been a Nazi or a Fascist spy?"

"I haven't gone that far—yet. But I think he may have been trying to find a way to get to Malta without attracting undue suspicion from the British authorities. When he got here, he wanted to appear to be British, not Italian.

"Poor Magdelena," Richard said. "Do you really think she was used as a pawn?

"Possibly. In nineteen thirty-six, Hitler already had designs for a greater world order. You are a lover of history; I don't have to tell you that. Even before the war began, Malta was viewed as a strategic location in the Mediterranean, so why not put an agent in place here? The only problem I can't grasp is who was Frank working for, if he was not in the British Secret Service. The Nazis? Mussolini? The Allies? Or himself?"

"For himself?"

"He sounded a bit of an opportunist, didn't he? By setting himself up here, he could sell his services to the highest bidder. Early in the war, didn't it seem as if Hitler and Mussolini would win?"

"Yes, in fact most people thought they would. It wasn't until Hitler invaded Russia and was turned back that Allies' expectations rose. We were also given hope when Rommel's second offensive was turned back at El Alamein in the autumn of nineteen forty-two and never reached Cairo," Richard said.

"What was it Uncle Frederick told Aunt Mag, something about Frank interacting with the Italians? She told the story of Frank bringing her Italian chocolates and telling her how he had got them from an Italian soldier. Did she say 'stolen' from the soldier or was it 'took them off him"? The implication is that Frank had been to Italy, where he might have got the chocolates. The only Italian military in Malta would have been the fighter pilots or their crewmembers shot down by the

RAF and who were in captivity. I'm not sure where I'm going with this, but I want to find a way that we could find out more about what Frank Wells was doing in Malta when he wasn't here at the farmhouse on Gozo?"

"Magdelena might know if there's anyone still here in San Lawrenz now who was also alive then and might have known Frank," Richard suggested.

"Mmm, yes, at least let's ask her. I wonder if there's any way to discover if he actually lived in St. Pawls Bay, or if he was lying. We only have Magdelena's version of the facts, or rather the ones Frank told her. He could have been anywhere, including Italy or even Africa. Could he have been engaged in smuggling or selling information to the Fascists or was he an outright spy for the Axis powers? I want pull this all together and make some sense out of it, which it doesn't right now."

"Do you have any alternative theories?" Richard asked.

"Yes, that he may have been doing something quite different altogether. Let's say he sold his services to the highest bidder. It could be the Italians, for sure, but it also could be the Germans. It even could be the Allies."

"The Allies? What makes you think that?"

"Because, for all we know, Frank Wells was a bit like a weasel, particularly in the way he treated Aunt Mag, and that probably was indicative of his personality. Why would he take so little interest in the twins? They were his children after all. Were they an accident that was not part of his design, a mere inconvenience? Even Alistair did not desert Peter and Lizzie after our divorce and remains close to them to this day. Paternity is such a strong force that it's hard to imagine that Frank had no feelings toward his children. We need to know a great deal more about Frank. That is where your raven-haired beauty might come in."

"Please explain more." Richard said, trying to follow Elspeth's path of reasoning.

"We need to know if Frank really was English, or his father for that matter."

"Do you think he might not have been?"

"We have no proof that he was, unless your Celia can turn up a record of his birth and parentage. If the English were so easily identifiable in those days, they could also be easily impersonated, and might easily fool people like Magdelena and her father. Or, Frank could have been a consummate actor."

"You are motivating me to slip away from my meeting next week and slide into the basement of the FCO to see Celia, not just for her long legs."

"Only if your motives are genuine. Is there any chance a phone call would do?"

"Are you jealous?"

"Should I be?" she asked, quizzing him.

"Do I need to answer that?" he said with a broad smile.

The question of Frank's real identity continued to dog Elspeth. She could not grasp who he was or what he was like even after all that Magdelena had told them. As they enjoyed their breakfast in the garden, they heard scale progressions coming from the Great Room and knew Magdelena was up and had finished her morning repast.

"Dickie," Elspeth said, "Aunt Mag seems so relieved to have shared her recollections of the war with us, the details of her marriage to Frank Wells, the bombing of San Lawrenz, and meeting Uncle Frederick, but I suspect she has more she could tell us. There must be hidden memories, and we need to find a way to persuade her to pull these things out of the fog of her past. We have one photograph of Frank with the twins. Does she have others? They might prove useful if we want to find people who were here at the time and who might know something about him."

*

Richard had often seen Elspeth working and recognised that her mind was at work now, and this was not a time to impose his personal feelings on her. Could it a part of the third option, a way he could give her space at what she excelled? But how could she continue to work for Lord Kennington and maintain a life with him? He watched her knitting her well-shaped eyebrows and knew her mind was concentrated on Frank Wells and not him. Did that feel uncomfortable? Strangely it did not. How odd that he should be the first to have a professional reason to break into their time together. When he was in Brussels, he knew he would have little chance to interact with her, his time devoted to the incessant demands of the members of his committee. Would he be able to call her even once a day? Perhaps, but only at odd hours in the early morning, or late at night.

He watched Elspeth puzzling over the problem of Frank Wells and knew that, if she kept her job with the Kennington Organisation in the coming years, she might be as occupied as he would be during the next week. Elspeth had challenged him, saying she did not think that keeping their separate careers would work for them. But on what did she base her premise? He would miss her desperately when he was in Brussels, but he would not stop loving her. His work sessions there were always intense. At the end of them he fell into bed exhausted, but he knew he would dream of her being at his side. And when they met afterwards, he fantasised that their meeting would be better for the absence.

Elspeth broke his reverie. "Perhaps if you went to see Aunt Mag while I have a bath, she might tell you things she would leave out when speaking to me."

"It's certainly worth a try. What did you have in mind?"

"Try asking her about the war itself, and the people here, not Uncle Frederick or Frank Wells, but rather how the local population in San Lawrenz survived during that time. She has told me personal things but might tell you what was going on in Gozo and Malta in a more general way. She knows you are interested in history. And then I have plenty of time for a good soak without someone making suggestions about . . ."

He looked at her with mock innocence. "Suggestions about what?"

"Just about things that have little to do with either cleanliness or godliness."

Richard had first met Magdelena when she had played at a benefit concert for a children's home in Valletta when he had first become the British High Commissioner to Malta. He had introduced himself and, knowing Elspeth's connection to Magdelena, made his acquaintance with Elspeth known. Magdelena had invited him to one of her soirées, but their friendship had been cemented when Elspeth returned to Malta shortly before Conan FitzRoy's death. When Magdelena became aware of Richard's attraction to Elspeth, she encouraged him in his pursuit but was always disappointed when Elspeth brushed him off like a crumb from a sleeve. As a result, Magdelena had been elated when Elspeth had rung her several months before to tell her that she had accepted Richard's proposal. Richard imagined how irritated and saddened she must have been when Elspeth had arrived on her doorstep saying that the marriage was off. As much as she loved Elspeth, he remembered how in Mgarr Magdelena had portrayed her niece as someone emotionally unwilling to accept how much he had to offer her. Magdelena's own failure to marry had always meant she considered lawful wedlock as one of the highest achievements in life, or so she said.

Magdelena stopped her scales as Richard came into the room. "Come sit by me," she said, "and turn the pages."

"I don't read music with any ease," he said.

"I'll tell you when it's time, but you must get Elspeth to teach you. If she ever practiced, she would play reasonably well, for her own enjoyment if nothing else. But I'll nod when I need a paged turned, so watch closely."

Richard settle on the bench beside the grande dame and thought how full her life must have been, even without being able to marry Frederick Duff. How many concert halls had she filled with the joy of her music and how many young pianists had she inspired to reach her dizzy heights?

As she played, more from memory than reading the pages, Richard dutifully turned, he asked, "What was it like here during the war? Here in Gozo?"

She looked out beyond her piano but continued playing. "We felt that every day might be our last, and therefore we grasped at all the happiness that we could find in small things. The losses were so great that most of us became numb to them; the few who could not sometimes took their own lives, although it was against the Church's teachings. Others became foolhardy and, rather than seeking shelter, would rush out during the raids in the hope they would be killed and join those they had lost. Many people thought it strange that I should choose to come back to live at this farmhouse after what happened, but I felt close to my father and children here, and Frederick came to stay with me when he could. When we first met, he brought me small gifts, a flower, an orange, or bits of food he had taken from his own rations. I remember one day an old piano arrived at the farmhouse. I laughed because it was so dreadfully out of tune when I first played it. But one of the men in the village, who was the best piano tuner in Malta and who had been born in San Lawrenz, had come here to escape the bombings of Grand Harbour in Valletta. I gave him eggs and vegetables, and he kept the old piano in tune. We played duets together, and he shared pieces of sheet music with me and his unrealised dream of becoming a concert pianist. His family had been unable to afford the lessons when he was young, and he had to support them as he got older. He died perhaps twenty years ago, but his son still tunes my pianos. When he comes, we talk about his father and as often as not about those years of the war. He, the son that is, is married and has saved enough for his daughter to go to the conservatory at the university." Magdelena smiled into the distance. 'I've helped a bit, of course. She is good but never will be great, but she will please many of her friends and family, and she already plays the church organ."

"What about the British officers and men who were stationed here?"

"Frederick brought them here sometimes, to rest and listen to music. One had a viola, and sometimes we played together. He was killed during the invasion of Sicily, and afterwards his commanding officer sent the viola to me. I gave it to the local school, and one student adopted it. He still plays it in a local chamber music group, although not very well, but the airman didn't either."

In the last few days Richard had seen that Magdelena's life was completely centred around her music and on an impulse asked, "Did Frank like music?"

"No, sadly he didn't. When we first met in Hungary, he took me to concerts and recitals, but after we were married, I discovered he was tone deaf. I was disappointed at first, but that was the least of our problems."

"Did he ever sing in the shower or hum under his breath?"

"He whistled. Terribly, and off-key. He seemed to prefer the old music hall tunes from the London Palladium."

"Not Italian arias?"

"No, not even Italian popular tunes."

"Magdelena, Elspeth has asked me to find out more about the people here during the war. Do you have any friends from that time who are still alive today?"

"I am old Richard, so old that I now admit my age. Few of us are left. But if you go to see the son of my piano tuner, he may help you. Go alone. I think Elspeth would overpower him; he's a gentle soul."

"I never know what you think of Elspeth," Richard said, turning another page.

"Don't you know or can't you guess? She means everything to me, but I'm not fooled by her faults. I've known her too long and loved her too much."

"Am I to take that as advice on how to manage her?"

Magdelena nodded and ran her fingers up the keyboard in a perfect progression. "Yes, *caro,* if you are wise, which I think you are."

17

"Elspeth, I'm just going down to the village," Richard called through the bathroom door. Balancing on one foot, she opened door, letting the steam pour out, kissed him briefly on the lips and said, "Do you have a reason to desert me?"

He laughed at her. "You are wet and unclad."

"Ah," she said, arching an eyebrow, "so I am. Well, hurry back, I promise to be dry when you return." She said nothing about being clad.

Richard sought out the address Magdelena had given him, first finding the street and then the intricately painted ceramic house number. He raised the polished brass knocker, which was in the shape of a Maltese cross, and struck it against the metal plate on the door. An old woman with a much-lined face answered his knock. Richard judged she was Magdelena's age but had been weighed down with the harsh reality of Gozitan widowhood.

Richard did not give his name but simply asked for the piano tuner, who must be her son.

"He is out but he will return soon. *Sinjur,* will you come inside?"

"Thank you, *sinjura.*"

The old woman looked at him. "You are a guest of *Sinjura* Cassar. I've seen you there with the *sinjura* who is her niece."

Small things did not go unnoticed in a village the size of San Lawrenz.

"Yes," Richard said. "I hope to marry her soon."

"That is good news," The piano tuner's mother said. "Everyone here in San Lawrenz is proud of Sinjura Cassar. She brings music to the entire village. She invites all the notables from Valletta and beyond to her soirées, but then she asks us to come as well. Do you know her story?"

"Tell me, *sinjura*."

"*Sinjura* Cassar's family is from Malta, descendants of the great architect, Girolamo Cassar, but her great uncle married a Gozitan and inherited the farmhouse. Her great uncle, his wife, and their children died in the Spanish flu epidemic, and the *sinjura's* father took over ownership of the farmhouse. She has made it very grand, hasn't she? During the war, it was almost completely destroyed."

"Yes, very grand, indeed." Richard said.

"It wasn't always that way. Before the British officer, Major Duff, came to help us, it was ruined by the bombs, and we never expected it would become what it is today. But after she became famous, she had plenty of money."

"So I understand," Richard said. The old woman did not refer to Frederick Duff as Magdelena's husband. Was their secret so open in the village?

"She came here with her father just before the start of the war. She was very pregnant and gave birth to the babies. My mother was the midwife. The *sinjura* was terrified at the birth because her mother had died when she was born, but the babies, twins, a boy and a girl, were strong and my mother said that they were beautiful. The *sinjura* wept at their birth."

"And the twins' father?" Richard asked.

"He was not there. The *sinjura's* father was waiting outside the room where they were born and afterwards cared for the babies like they were his own. His branch of the Cassar family was dying out and the thought of twins delighted him."

"What do you know about the twins' father?"

"Very little. He seldom came here."

"Do you know his name?"

"I don't remember, but it will be listed at the Parish Centre near the church in the baptismal records kept there. You can ask Father Lucca. He can show you the records. They were hidden there when the bombings came."

"Do you remember anything about *Sinjura* Cassar during the war?"

"Yes, it was sad for her. First her husband deserted her and then her father and babies died in the bombings."

"Her husband deserted her? Is that true?"

"Yes, *sinjur*. He went to live in Marsalforn where he stayed with a family who were killed in the bombings later that summer."

"Was *Sinjura* Cassar's husband killed with them?'

"No, he was in Marsalforn until June nineteen forty-two. My husband, who went there to tune the piano of an old friend, saw him once or twice on the streets. We talked about mentioning it to *Sinjura* Cassar, but we decided it was better if she weren't told. She had enough sadness to bear."

"Do you know when her husband was last seen?"

"Yes, it was on the feast of Saint Peter and Saint Paul in June nineteen forty-two."

"Why do you remember that so clearly?"

"Because my husband was in Marsalforn that day and saw a Red Cross ambulance come and take the *sinjura's* husband away. Someone said he had attacked a British officer, others that the officer had beaten up the *sinjura's* husband. My husband, God rest his soul, said he did not think that *Sinjura* Cassar's husband could have survived. And then when the *sinjura* married the Major from Scotland, we knew her first husband must have died."

"But *Sinjura* Cassar did not marry here?"

"No, in London after the war when she went to study there."

Richard knew this was not true. How much else had the old woman fabricated, and how much of what she said might be only half-truths that had been magnified by local gossip?

"Elspeth," he called, as he came into their bedroom, "I think I finally have something new for you."

Elspeth was sitting on the bed, her foot up on a cushion and her back supported by a pile of pillows. As he entered, she slid her small, round reading glasses down her nose and looked over the large tome propped on her knees.

"I've finally decided to read Conan FitzRoy's book on the war in Malta. Aunt Mag had an autographed copy upstairs. You are quite right; it is totally absorbing."

He came around to her, took the book from her hands and said, "Did you hear me?'

"You said you have something new. A present for me?" she said with a quick smile.

"Better," he said, kissing her freshly-washed hair that was now dry but still smelled of shampoo. "A lead on Frank."

Elspeth took off her glasses and laid them alongside the book on the bedside table where Richard had put it.

"Really," she said excitedly, "tell me."

Richard repeated what the old woman had told him.

"Do you think she was telling the truth, that in late June Frank was in Marsalforn? That's near here on the northern side of Gozo, not on Malta, which means Frank was in Gozo well after the raid that killed Aunt Mag's father and her children. Why wouldn't he return here to console her after all that happened? Tell me again about him being taken off in an ambulance?"

"She said Frank had been in a fight with a British officer and got the worst of it. Then she added that Frank must have died because your uncle had married Magdelena in London after the end of the war when she went to study there. Didn't Magdelena say they went there two years after the end of the war?"

"But little of what the old woman said makes any sense. Even if Frank were dead, Jean was still alive in nineteen forty-seven. I know for certain that Uncle Frederick never divorced Jean, and I also don't think Aunt Mag would marry a divorced man while his wife was still alive. Do you suppose Uncle Frederick told people in San Lawrenz that he had married Aunt Mag? I don't think Aunt Mag would have lied to them somehow. Dickie, help me up, and let's go out in the garden to talk this through."

After they had settled themselves alongside Giulio's flowerbeds, Elspeth said, "The thing I don't understand about the old woman's story is the involvement of the RAF ambulance. Surely if Frank had died in their custody, the authorities would have informed Aunt Mag, or at least Uncle Frederick, who was nominally in administrative charge of this region, and asked him to tell her. Do you suppose that Frank was living under an assumed name, and no one but the old piano tuner recognised him as Aunt Mag's husband? The piano tuner could have been one of the few people in San

Lawrenz who knew Frank's connection with Aunt Mag, since he must have visited the farmhouse when Frank was there. Where else might we look for a record of this fight with the British officer?"

"I expect the military would want to cover up that sort of thing, particularly if the officer did kill Frank."

Elspeth bit the side of her lip. Richard watched with amusement. "You did that when you were a girl," he said.

"Did what?"

"Bite your lip like that when you were thinking."

"You've known me too long, Dickie. Can I hide nothing from you?"

"Do you want to?"

She laughed. "If I did have something to hide, I wouldn't tell you that I wanted to hide it. That way you wouldn't know I had a secret. But, wait, maybe I have something there."

"I'm not following you."

"Why was Aunt Mag not told the truth about Frank Wells still being in Gozo in June, or his possible death in Marsalforn?"

"Do you suppose someone wanted to keep it from her?"

"Exactly, and probably that someone was . . . "

"Frederick," Richard said, finishing her thought.

"Yes, he had every reason to want to conceal Frank Wells' existence in Gozo. By the end of June nineteen forty-two, Uncle Frederick and Aunt Mag had been lovers for several months. Dickie, I believe that their love for each other was as real as ours. I once asked Magdelena if she knew about Jean, and she said she did. Did it suit Uncle Frederick's purposes to have Aunt Mag think he was as unable to marry as she was?"

"The other possibility could be that Frank Wells did not die, and Frederick knew it."

"That also could be so. Do you remember what Uncle Frederick told Aunt Mag when he questioned her about Frank? Let's go back to what she said. If I'm correct, that would have been about the time Frank got into the fight with the officer."

"I wasn't there when Magdelena told you about Frederick's interrogation of her. Try to remember because I think you're on to something."

"Aunt Mag told me that Uncle Frederick said, 'we think he', meaning Frank, "is abetting the Italians'. I assume the 'we' was the British authorities. Aunt Mag said that Uncle Frederick became very official during the interrogation, but why would he mislead her?"

"Because he loved her?"

"Would you mislead me, Dickie, and keep such a secret from me?"

He wondered, if he had been in Frederick Duff's position, whether he would have lied to Magdelena or not. "I honestly don't know. War tests people beyond limits that those of us who grew up in peacetime will never know."

She looked up at him, and in her eyes he saw the sadness that had been there before she had discovered the truth about Malcolm's murder, the kind of deep despair that comes from lost love and hope. He rose and came to where she was stretched out. "Under those circumstances, if I had loved you the way I do now, I think I might have done what your uncle did, assuming it's true." And then he took her in his arms. "How thankful I am that I can love you without deceit."

She pressed her head into his shoulder. "So am I. How lucky we are," she whispered.

Elspeth sat straight up in bed, waking Dickie. "Why didn't he tell her after Jean died?"

Richard, who was getting accustomed to Elspeth's sudden night-time bursts of inspiration, turned over and pulled her to him. "Can we talk about it tomorrow?"

"Sorry," she said, snuggling against him, "but I do my best thinking during the night."

"So I gather," he said, "but let's discuss it in the morning. I can think of better things to do in the night."

"She gave a short grunt in protest but did not object.

19

Elspeth was leaning against her pillows, reading Conan FitzRoy's book when Richard woke at her side. Her body, clad in red Chinese silk pyjamas, was silhouetted against the morning light coming through the glass doors.

She looked at him over her reading glasses and said, "I had no idea how bad it was here during the war. As you know, Daddy came to Gozo then and visited Uncle Frederick and Aunt Mag, but he said Uncle Frederick never spoke about what his real job was, even at the end of his life. When you spoke to Aunt Mag, you said she talked about her music and the village and exchanging eggs and vegetables for piano tuning, not about Frank Wells or Uncle Frederick. Can we be so unfeeling as to ask her more about Uncle Frederick, because I think he, not Frank, may hold the key to our mystery. If our assumption is correct, Uncle Frederick knew what really happened to Frank, but his love for her was the reason he didn't tell her the truth."

"We should be able to think of a better way than asking her again," Richard said, turning toward her and raising himself up on one elbow.

She frowned and twisted her mouth sideways. "Do you suppose anyone in Marsalforn who is still alive who might have seen what happened the night of the fight? It was a small fishing village then, though rather a tourist trap nowadays with holiday villas and boat hires. But sixty-five years is a long time for anyone to remember the incident, if it did happen."

"Do you have a plan concocted about how to find someone who might?" Richard asked.

"That's my current conundrum. I've this damned tendon to deal with. Otherwise, I should go down there in a flash and start asking around. Dickie, you wouldn't mind going in my place, would you?'

He started to protest but lay back instead, not answering. Was this the promise of their future together? Would she be constantly consumed with prying and probing, which was a part of her very existence? In good faith, he could not ask her to be different from what she was. The thought was not reassuring. Was it simply comfort that he wanted from her when she demanded so much more? Elspeth, despite the sensual pleasure that she gave him, did not give him peace of mind. He expected that she was totally unaware of this, and, in the end, he would have to come to terms with it.

"May we talk about it after breakfast?" he asked.

She smiled down at him, kissed the bridge of his nose, and said, "Of course."

Magdelena Cassar was not an early riser, perhaps because she had lived for so many years performing concerts in the evening, but as Elspeth and Richard settled in the garden to have their breakfast, Magdelena descended in the lift and joined them. Richard rose to greet her.

"My dearest ones," she said, "I'm going into Valletta today to see my doctor, a task I have to perform far too frequently these days. Will you come with me? I want to show you my family's palazzo there. The tenants who live there now are elderly, even older than I am, and their lease has already expired. They have told me that they wish to move to a care home. Initially I found this a great vexation, but now it's become a blessing. Richard, you must move in there after you two are married so Elspeth will have a home when she comes to Malta."

Elspeth was taken aback. "But Aunt Mag!" she protested.

Magdelena Cassar gave them a smile that had charmed prime ministers and kings and said, "I'm an old and rich woman and, consequently, may do as I please. If you don't marry Richard, Elspeth, then you must allow me to offer some respectability to your liaison with him. Richard, if you agree to my plan, you will stay in the palazzo as my guest. One wing of the building was set up as separate living quarters for an ever-so-great, great uncle of mine, who was a Cardinal, and frequently visited from Rome. These rooms should suit you perfectly, and, Elspeth, you, of course, will always be welcome in 'your aunt's home' when you're in Malta. I've not lived in the same house with you over the last week without noticing the strong feelings of affection between you two, and this will be my small gift of celebration to you both."

Elspeth protested again. "This is too much."

"I have few things that delight me these days, but this past week has brought back all the joy I once had with Frederick. How could I deny you the same happiness? Besides, I'd planned to give the palazzo to you and Richard as a wedding gift anyway. When the twins were born, it was bequeathed to me by a distant cousin who had more liberated ideas than my father on property rights for women. Unfortunately, my cousin was killed during the siege of Malta in the early nineteen forties and I became the owner."

Elspeth set her jaw with determination. "No, Aunt Mag, it's too much," she said again.

"Then I shall turn the palazzo over to the Maltese Government, and they can make small offices out of the grand rooms that have housed my family since the sixteenth century. They've done that with other palaces in Valletta, you know, but that would break my heart."

"You are a harridan, Aunt Mag."

"I learned stubbornness from two members of the Duff family," Magdelena Cassar said, raising her carefully darkened eyebrows and looking down her long, aristocratic nose at Elspeth. "At least come and see the palazzo. I've asked Giulio to bring the car round at ten."

Richard said nothing but, as Magdelena rose to go, he went over to her, put an arm around her shoulders and whispered in her ear. "Thank you," he said. She gave Richard a conspiratorial smile and turned her back to Elspeth.

After helping Magdelena to the lift, he returned to their breakfast table and found Elspeth kneading a ball of bread in her fingers.

"She can't do that. Besides, what would they say at the FCO? The British High Commissioner to Malta requests the pleasure of your company for dinner at the home of his lover's aunt who wasn't really married to her uncle. Dickie, I don't think that would be acceptable in the diplomatic community, even in the twenty-first century."

"If I decide to accept her offer, I would agree to pay a fair rent. I believe Magdelena would agree to my request. But isn't this another reason why we should get married?"

"I won't marry you, Dickie, just so that you can have a place to live in Valletta. I would only marry you if . . ." She suddenly stopped.

"If?" he asked.

She looked at him with sudden confusion. "Oh, damn," she said hastily, "it's almost ten, and I must get ready if we're going to Valletta. It takes me ages to get ready with this cast." She rushed from the garden as quickly as someone could with an injured foot.

After her departure, Richard sat without moving. If what? Why was she so resistant to his proposal? Did she think she would have to come permanently to Valletta if they accepted Magdelena's offer? He still did not understand what she envisioned their marriage would be like, and in truth, neither did he. His whole idea of Elspeth and his earlier perception of what their life together would be like had changed radically over the last week. He loved her more, if that was possible, but also found her endlessly more perplexing. He looked at his watch, saw it was shortly before ten, and he, too, needed to dress for their excursion.

*

While Magdelena was consulting with her doctor, Elspeth and Richard walked along the bastions at the edge of the Lower Barracca Gardens and turned toward the neo-classical monument to Sir Alexander Bell, the first British Governor of Malta. Neither spoke, but Elspeth was aware that Richard had not taken her hand or even her arm. He had his hands shoved into the pockets of his trousers and did not look at her.

"I . . ." she started, ". . . I'm being difficult again, aren't I?"

"I don't understand you, Elspeth. I have nothing else to give you. You know how much I love you, and you know I want to marry you. What's lacking in that formula? I thought you loved me too."

She walked along beside him, not being able to find the right words.

They stopped near the monument as a large cruise ship entered Grand Harbour and stood silently watching it pass.

"Nothing is wrong at your end, Dickie. It's me," she said finally.

"But I love you, isn't that enough? And after this week I thought you might have changed your mind."

"Me marrying you won't work for you—or for me."

"Tell me why you think that."

"I'm not good at commitment." The words sounded weak as she said them. "I've never been able to make a success of things like marriage."

"Am I correct, or not, in thinking that you were only married once, to Alistair Craig?"

"Yes, but I wanted to marry Malcolm, and you know what a mistake that would have been. If you remember, I went forward with my plans to do so even after you warned me against him."

"That was very presumptuous of me, although in the end I was right. I was jealous."

"And you married Marjorie and had a long and successful marriage. I can't promise the same to you."

She closed her eyes and swallowed hard. They stood without speaking, letting the wind off the sea touch their faces. Damn it, Dickie, she thought, can't you say something that will make everything better?

"When I was married to Marjorie," he said, "I thought I had all that a man could want. I was comfortable and content, and I never doubted that she was too."

"You won't find that with me," Elspeth said.

He turned toward her and took her face firmly in his hands. "Let me finish, Elspeth," he said with more ferocity than she had ever heard him use before. "I thought I had all a man could want with Marjorie, but I was wrong. I had comfort and contentment, yes, but I had no passion, no real joy, and no thunderous love of the kind that rocks me every time I look at you. I don't want contentment. I want you, Elspeth, everything you are, every new thing I'm discovering about you day by day, and everything I will learn about you in future. I want you, no matter what it takes. Just tell me what you want."

"I don't know," she said in a whisper, shaking her head. "Can I just keep on loving you and not change things from what we have now?"

"My God, Elspeth, you are quite exasperating and try a man's soul!"

*

Magdelena Cassar noted the coolness between Elspeth and Richard as they lingered over coffee at a tiny restaurant on St George's Street, one of Magdelena's favourite places for lunch. Both were extraordinarily polite to her and to each other, but Magdelena noticed that the previous loving gestures between them were missing. Had she gone too far in offering them the palazzo? Was she just a doddering old fool and an interfering busybody?

Elspeth spoke first. "I think, Aunt Mag, that today would not be the best time to see the palazzo."

Magdelena nodded slowly. "Yes, I thought that too," she said.

Richard rose from the table. "Magdelena, I must be in Brussels on Monday, and I need to go round to the High Commission this afternoon to make final arrangements, so I am going to refuse on your offer of a ride back to San Lawrenz. I'll come over to Gozo before I leave and say goodbye."

"And what, *cara*," Magdelena Cassar asked her niece once they were back at the farmhouse, "brought that on."

Elspeth clenched her jaw. "I told him again I wouldn't marry him because it won't work."

"Are you going to let him go off to Brussels on that note? Do you really mean it or are you merely playing with him? You mustn't do that if you are seriously in love with him. His patience won't last forever. Men are funny that way. I think you need to do a great deal of soul searching right now, Elspeth, my dear."

"What would you advise me to do?"

"Tell him how you feel now, not how you view the future with him. That can be resolved between you later. But first you must make up your mind if you want to make your marriage to him work. If the answer is yes, you need to commit to him with a full heart. In the meantime, I suggest you ring him and apologise."

"Apologise? For what?"

"For being an idiot, *cara*. I've never talked to you this way before, but you are about to lose the best thing that ever happened to you. Why can't you see that?" Magdelena let out a sharp breath of disappointment.

"I don't know how to apologise."

"Call him and ask him for dinner at eight, and he is expected to stay the night. Tell him you will give him an answer in a week, when his meeting is over in Brussels."

"How can I be certain that I can make my decision by then?"

"You are a highly intelligent woman, Elspeth. This is surely something you can decide in a week."

*

That night they lay close to each other, speaking little. Finally, she pulled away from him. "Thank you for coming back," she said hoarsely. "Aunt Mag told me I was an idiot and I have been. Dickie, will you give me yet another week to get all this sorted out? To decide what will work for me and not presume what won't work for us?"

"Of course," he said quietly. "Oh, my darling, darling, most precious, Elspeth. How could I ever have been so angry with you?"

20

"Elspeth?"

She opened one eye and looked at him. Judging by the length of the sun's rays coming through the French windows, she knew it was late in the morning.

"I have to leave Malta early before noon to be in Brussels for the late Sunday opening dinner of the conference. Today is Friday, and we still have not finished our investigation here. I suggest we spend the rest of the time I have remaining attempting to discover what happened to Frank Wells in Marsalforn, if anything did. How is your tendon feeling? Are you comfortable enough to undertake an excursion?" He smiled happily. "I've decided that, if you are up to it, we should follow up on one of your madcap hunches. Why not start this morning?"

"I hadn't thought any of my hunches were madcap," she said archly.

He beamed at her without comment. "Any excursion today with you would seems madcap to me, and I'm fully intending to enjoy every minute of it. Marsalforn, anyone?"

Elspeth had never seen Richard in a such giddy mood before, not even when they were young. She burst out laughing and kissed him on the tip of his long nose.

"All right," she said. "Is all forgiven?"

"If you stay on your best behaviour," he teased.

"I promise," she countered, not sure she could spend the entire day with him being totally good or even if he would want that. Inside she felt elated that things had not changed significantly between them despite their falling out. The decision that she had to make in the week ahead presented a great and frightening challenge for her, and she wanted to savour the enjoyment of being with him without commitment while the opportunity presented itself.

*

Instead of allowing Giulio to drive them in the Mercedes, Richard asked if they might borrow the old Renault that Teresa kept for running about. Grappling at first with the gear-lever, he gradually felt comfortable synchronizing the gears. When they set off on their excursion to Marsalforn, she clutched the strap by the door as he negotiated the narrow roads and blind curves at a considerably faster speed than the small car was designed to be driven. His high spirits soon spread to her, and they were laughing merrily as they came into the resort town nestled around a narrow bay. He found a place to park near the marina and then turned to her.

"Elspeth, have you devised a way for us to proceed?"

"This excursion was your idea, Dickie, and I thought you might have one, but I do have an inkling of an idea. Let's find somewhere for lunch and give me a moment to work things out. Preferably a place near the marina, particularly one where old men are sitting and talking together. If we're lucky, we might come upon someone who was here in June nineteen forty-two. It would be a start anyway."

Richard thought Elspeth's suggestion a good one. Marsalforn had grown into a tourist destination for both Gozitans, Maltese and foreign visitors, and the streets were lined with restaurants and holiday accommodations. The marina was now filled with yachts and sailboats, most of them expensive and new, but interspersed among these were several traditional brightly-coloured Maltese fishing boats, called *luzzu* or *dghajsa* in Maltese, whose design went back to Phoenician times. On their prows were brightly painted pictograms of the eye of Osiris, the Egyptian god, a symbol that was supposed to ward off evil, a pre-Christian superstition carried on despite Gozo's Roman Catholic population. On the waterfront were a number of cafés with outdoor tables and chairs, few of which were occupied as there was a stiff breeze coming off the sea.

Richard helped Elspeth from the car. He noticed she was dressed in a plain grey, baggy dress, which did not suit her. He wondered why. She had pulled her hair back from her face in an unattractive manner, had not applied any makeup and was wearing what looked like a wedding ring. He could not avoid seeing it.

"It's an old prop," she said in response to his look, "when I need to appear to be married."

"Had you considered making it permanent? I can help."

She frowned. "Dickie, you said you would give me a week."

He took her hand and squeezed it. "I did promise. Now, lead on, Lady MacDuff. Where do you want to try first?"

Over the last week, Elspeth had mastered walking with her crutch and used it with dexterity as the centre of Marsalforn was concentrated around the water and the car park flat and devoid of impediments. The first café they found proved unsuitable for their task, but one of the waiters suggested another place further down the quayside that was patronised by locals. They walked toward it and found several old men sitting there and playing backgammon with their pints of ale beside them.

They approached the group, and Richard spoke to them. The oldest man appeared not to have seen or heard them, but he turned toward them when Richard spoke again, this time in Maltese.

The old man's face broke into a grin, showing the gaps between his remaining teeth. "You speak Malti well for an Englishman," he said.

Richard did not correct the old man's mistake about his country of origin, but said, "We are looking for anyone who was here in Marsalforn in June nineteen forty-two. Would you know if there is anyone still alive from that time?

"You have a beautiful wife," the old man said, chuckling. "For her sake I will tell you."

Elspeth spoke less Maltese than Richard but understood enough to smile at the compliment, despite her dowdy disguise.

"Does she speak Malti, too?" the old man asked.

"She speaks only a little, so be careful what you say. She may understand. One never knows with woman," Richard responded.

The old man laughed and took a long drink from his glass.

"I was here," he said, "and my brother as well."

"Were you in the Armed Forces?" he asked.

"Of course. Every brave Gozitan man wanted to fight Hitler and Mussolini."

"Were you stationed near here?"

"I had a bad knee, so they didn't send me to Africa to fight Rommel, but I worked alongside your airmen as one of the aeroplane mechanics on the airbase here on Gozo. We had to patch the broken-down heaps of metal that were based here because no new ones were sent out from Britain. I don't suppose they had enough of them to spare."

"Do you remember anything about that time?" Richard asked, following most but not all of what the old man said. "Here, let me buy you another drink. My wife and I were about to have something ourselves and would like you to join us and have you tell us more," he said, without consulting Elspeth. She seemed puzzled by much of the conversation but nodded politely when Richard gave her a gentle nudge.

"*Iva*," she said. "Yes."

"Let ask my brother and my wife to join us," the old man said. "They remember too."

Richard, amused, suspected he was financing drinks for more people than was absolutely necessary in order to get the information they wanted, but he bowed toward the old man. "It will be my pleasure," he said. "May we sit down? My wife has hurt her leg." He could not think of the Maltese word for 'foot' or 'tendon'. "She would be glad to rest it."

The old man winked at Elspeth and said, "Please ask her to come and sit by me."

Elspeth knew enough Malti to laugh. "*Nifhem xi ftit.* I understand a little."

The old man put his hand on hers and said in English. "You are beautiful, *sinjura*. I hope your husband is good to you."

"*Dejjum*. Always. But you speak English!" Elspeth said.

"Of course, *sinjura*. I was a sergeant in the Royal Malta Artillery during the war and worked with the Royal Air Force here repairing planes that had been damaged by the *Luffwaffe* and *Regina Aeronautica*, the Italian Air Force. They often attacked us from their bases in Sicily. Most able-bodied men over sixteen years of age were conscripted in Malta, but I volunteered early in the war. Fishing continued here, of course, with the young lads and grandfathers doing their bit. They often took their catch to Valletta where food was more scarse than here on Gozo, although one of our boats was blown up by a mine in Grand Harbour."

Richard loved stories about the history of Malta but had never heard a Gozitan tell his version of what happened on the island during the war. He could see, however, that Elspeth was growing impatient with the man's long-winded discourse.

She interrupted him. "Then perhaps you can help me and my husband," she said, the word 'husband' rolling off her lips as easily as if they had been true.

"Sinjura," he said, nodding his balding head, which was covered with only a few strands of unwashed grey hair, "Tell me what you want to know."

"I'm trying to find out about my uncle who was here in Malta during the war. His name was Frank Wells." Elspeth smiled a radiant smile, her blue eyes flirting with the old man. He grinned again, exposing the few tobacco-stained teeth that he still had left.

Richard choked. He had seen Elspeth question people before, but he had never seen her embellish her enquiries with such flagrant falsehoods and with such alluring eyes. She looked up at him innocently. In Mdina she had skirted round the truth when they spoke to General Fenech. But now, he thought, she was devising a story that had only a modicum of truth. Elspeth's many sides continually amazed him. He remembered that when he had first met her, she and her cousin Johnnie were filled with mischief, but Richard had hoped this was a thing of the past. Apparently, it was not, but he could see that the old man was captivated.

"We know he was here in Marsalforn in June of nineteen forty-two," Elspeth continued.

"Was he in the Royal Navy or RAF?"

"Neither, at least not openly. He told my aunt that he was doing secret work. She didn't know what that meant, but I don't think he was in uniform. We have heard that when he was last seen here, he had been in a fight with a British Army officer and was beaten so badly that he may have died. Do you remember anything like that?"

"There were many brawls between servicemen," the old man said. "We were all tensed up much of the time and even small disagreements led to fisticuffs."

"Do you know anyone who might remember that night?"

"What did your uncle look like?"

"Here," Elspeth said, "I have a photograph." She pulled out a sheet of paper from a folder in her large shoulder bag. it showed the head of Frank Wells in grainy detail. She had scanned the photograph of Frank and the twins on Teresa's copier, cropped it and printed out the portion showing Frank alone. Richard was glad that she had thought to bring it.

The old man reached in his pocket and drew out his reading glasses, that were held together with a paper clip at the temple and duct tape along the bridge.

"Do you recognise him?" Elspeth asked.

The old man called his brother over. They spoke in Malti that was so rapid that even Richard could not follow them. The man's brother interrupted. "It is better you do not ask about this man."

"Why?" Elspeth said, her eyes widening innocently.

"It is better you do not ask," he reiterated fiercely.

"All right, but do you know anything about him getting into a fight in June nineteen forty-two and being taken to a military hospital? Someone we spoke to thought he might not have survived, but my aunt never knew for sure whether he was killed or not. She would like to know before she dies," Elspeth said half-truthfully.

The old man turned away and shook his head, but his brother answered. "Our sister may know. She was a nursing sister at the RAF field hospital on Gozo during the war. Today she lives in Victoria, although now she's housebound. She likes company and may remember if the man in your photograph was treated there. I don't know about him or the officer, but another drink would be appreciated."

As they sipped their ale, the old men ran on about their war experiences but refused to give any details about what happened between two British men on the night of the feast of Saint Peter and Saint Paul in nineteen forty-two. Had they seen the fight or heard about it? It began to seem unlikely. Richard watched Elspeth and saw that she had ceased to follow the men's chatter once the subject of Frank was dropped. Seeing her dismay, he said he and 'his wife' should go.

As Richard and Elspeth left the cafe, he turned to her. "You were quite despicable to play up to that old man; he positively drooled over you. And how did you come up with your story?"

"Dickie, you were quite as bad as I was. You were the first to call me your wife, so you're not completely exonerated."

"You wore the ring."

"You didn't need to notice."

"But your 'Uncle Frank'?"

"I did change things around, didn't I? But, if Aunt Mag were really my aunt, which she technically isn't, and because she was married to Frank Wells, wouldn't he have been my uncle?"

Richard burst out laughing. "In the Mad Hatter's world perhaps, but seriously what do you suppose all that meant? About it being better to not ask about Frank?"

"I'm not sure, but I think we may find out more from the old man's sister. Shall we be off to Victoria?"

"Lead on, fair lady!" he cried, suddenly glad to be a part of their escapade. "But before we meet his sister, let's have some lunch."

They motored up the hill from Marsalforn to Victoria, the capital city of Gozo. Searching along the narrow streets, they finally found a parking space near the *Pjazza Indipendenza*, in the centre of the city. Because they were unfamiliar with the restaurants in Victoria, they decided to risk a sandwich from a kiosk bordering the open seating on the square itself. They found an empty table in the shade of an umbrella and settled themselves on the orange and blue plastic seats.

After they had selected sandwiches from a menu on the table, Richard went to order them and joined a short queue for service. He looked back at Elspeth and shook his head in disbelief. For all the old man in Marsalforn had flattered her, she did look dowdy in her dusty clothes and without the benefit of makeup or jewellery. He found her beautiful, not conventionally, as her face was too chiselled, but for her liveliness, intelligence and graceful bearing. Her present guise reflected none of this. She looked up at him, smiled and winked, reminding him of all he loved about her, even when she had donned such an unfashionable disguise.

Richard ordered their lunch at the kiosk and took the holder with the number they assigned to it. He sat beside her and took her hand with happiness. "My dear Lady MacDuff, you do look a sight," he said. She grinned back at him and giggled wickedly.

"I borrowed the dress from Teresa because I thought my usual garb would be intimidating when and if we met with Second World War survivors in a bar in Marsalforn. Do you like it?"

"Not particularly," he said dryly.

As the sandwiches arrived, he happened to glance across the square and saw two faces he recognised from his past. He gulped because there was no way the advancing couple could be ignored. Kenneth Lambert had served under him in Zambia and would not have forgotten him. He groaned inwardly, because he had never liked Kenneth and because he knew he would have to introduce Elspeth in her present unfashionable state. He chided himself, thinking that he should not judge her by her unsightly clothing, but when he was with her he normally felt proud of her stylishness and her self-possession.

"Richard," Kenneth said, shaking his hand up and down. "I heard you were the HC here now. When my wife and I came here on holiday I'd hoped we might meet you. Fancy bumping into you here in Gozo."

Kenneth's wife, whose name Richard could not remember, held out her plump hand. "Richard," she said, "I was sorry to hear about Marjorie." Then she looked over expectantly at Elspeth.

Not turning to Richard for guidance, Elspeth looked up at the dumpling that was Kenneth's wife and said with the deepest Scottish burr, "I am Elspeth Craig, an auld friend of Richard's since we were *wee bairns*."

Richard looked over at Elspeth with both embarrassment and amazement, but she avoided his eyes.

"I met Richard," she rolled his name over her tongue, "here in Malta and we have rekindled our *lang* acquaintance."

Richard wanted to put his head in his hands, as he knew Kenneth Lambert was one of the worst gossips in the FCO, and the word must have already circulated that he was going to marry an old friend from Scotland. Instead, he ignored Elspeth and withdrew his hand from Kenneth's.

"A chance meeting," Richard said, annoyed at her prank, which too readily reminded him of Elspeth and her cousin Johnnie's devilishness during the summers he spent with them in Perthshire while he was at Oxford.

"We had thought to pop round to the High Commission next week to say hello," Kenneth said.

Richard became his most pompous. "Unfortunately, I will be in Brussels all next week. Perhaps another time."

As they left, Richard turned to Elspeth. "You know they'll spread the word at the FCO that you are my intended."

"Wee Elspeth wearin' your wedding ring," she said, her eyes dancing.

"Elspeth, you will be my undoing."

"Mmm, perhaps," she said, her lips quivering in suppressed merriment.

They both burst out laughing.

Kenneth and his wife looked back as they left, and both shook their heads in disbelief that Richard would choose replaced Marjorie with someone the likes of 'Wee Elspeth Craig'. But then again, Lady Marjorie had been dowdy herself, but she spoke beautiful English, a result of her Scottish aristocratic upbringing. Wee Elspeth did not. Had Richard gone mad?

"You know you may pay for this charade someday, don't you?" Richard said.

Elspeth looked askance at him and started to laugh again. "I most assuredly will, but I couldn't resist. They were so obsequious."

"Unfortunately, false courtesy is sometimes part of the diplomatic game," he admitted.

Elspeth raised her eyebrows but could not supress a gleeful smile.

"Oh?" she said.

*

After lunch, Richard and Elspeth sought out the house where the old man's sister lived, which they found on a side street off the steep hill up to the Citadel. They pressed the bell push beside the ancient door. Soon they heard the padding of feet. The door was answered by a woman who could have been anywhere between forty and sixty but definitely not old enough to have been a nurse in the Second World War.

"We are looking for *Sinjura* Monsarrat," Richard said, reading from the scrap of paper the old man had given him. "Her brother told us we might find her here."

"My mother lives here, yes, but she is not well. May I ask why you wish to see her? Are you from the government?"

They could see her trying to assess who this British couple might be. Elspeth had put on lipstick and shaken out her hair, which had taken on the shape that her London hairstylist had intended, and although her clothes were still dull, she no longer looked drab, just respectable although badly turned out.

"Forgive me, *sinjura,*" Richard said, "my wife and I are trying to find information about her uncle who was here in Gozo during the Second World War. Our name is Munro. Her brother in Marsalforn thought your mother might have useful information."

Elspeth noted the glibness with which he now reeled off these fabrications and thought he might be coming down from his lofty tower, the way he often had back in the Highlands during their teenage years.

"My mother is having her afternoon nap, but I'll see if she's awake and willing to see you. She has little to occupy her mind these days, but her memories of the war are as sharp as if it were yesterday. I've heard the stories many times, but, if she is willing to see you, I'm sure she would love to tell them again. Please come in and wait out of the sun."

As in many Maltese homes, the main door led into a hallway with a stone-tiled floor and benches along the sides. The woman showed them into a side reception room that smelled of age-old dampness and was filled overstuffed chairs adorned with antimacassars of fine Maltese lace.

"Let me get you some tea, and then I'll see if my mother is up."

Both Richard and Elspeth nodded gratefully at the traditional kindness of the Gozitan woman, accepted the offer of tea and took seats in the armchairs. Several minutes later she brought the tea on a silver-plated tray with a lace teacloth.

"*Sinjur, sinjura,* please."

As they sat waiting, Richard said, "How many times do you suppose this same ritual had gone on in this house? For two or three centuries or more? I regret how many of the old ways have been lost these days, but some traditions still linger on," He sighed contentedly.

"And how much has changed, too, Dickie. A hundred years ago would we have been here together, you and I?"

He paused before answering. "No, not a hundred years ago, but perhaps in the war, even in the First World War, when social barriers were starting to break down."

"Isn't it better that today we can be ourselves and not be so tied to strict rules of propriety? Even sixty years ago Cambridge would not have granted me a degree, I would have been considered a blue stocking if I wanted to pursue a career, have become a writer of turgid fiction and probably would have become an embittered, sexless spinster because I refused to conform to society's expectation for women."

"I cannot imagine you being sexless," Richard said with a straight face.

"Could you have said that a hundred years ago in polite society? Probably not in London, certainly not in Perthshire and definitely not in Malta."

"Not being a scholar of social etiquette," he said, "I'm glad I don't need to know. Elspeth, did I ever tell you that I love you?"

"Frequently, in a most twenty-first century way," she said, raising an eyebrow. "I think I'm bringing you into the new century."

They heard shuffling footsteps approaching. An old woman, who was wearing a faded navy blue dress and carpet slippers, and wheeling a walking frame, entered the room.

"Mr and Mrs Moore," she said, "my daughter tells me my reprobate brother has sent you to me here to ask about the war. He is always taken in by a pretty face," she said, nodding toward Elspeth. "But, if I can be of help, I will try. I remember the war, of course. All our generation do."

Elspeth glanced in Richard's direction. He took the lead.

"Sinjura," Richard said by way of introduction, "my wife has always been told that her uncle was here in Gozo during the war, but he never returned to Britain. She is trying to find out what may have happened to him. Her family think he may have died, but they have never had confirmation of this.

We've been enquiring about him for my wife's aunt's sake and, from what we have learned, he could have been in the Secret Service because he was out of uniform when he was here during the war. We know he was a linguist, speaking in German, Hungarian and Italian, and he may have been here to detect any pro-Axis sentiment in Malta. We've traced him to Marsalforn, where he was last seen at the end of June in nineteen forty-two."

"There were many British forces here then, mostly from the Royal Air Force or the Royal Navy," the old *sinjura* said.

Richard continued. "We have heard that he was in a fight with a British officer in Marsalforn and was severely injured. It would have happened on the Feast of Saint Peter and Saint Paul, on June twenty-ninth. According to witnesses, he was taken away in a military ambulance, and we heard he was so badly hurt that he might well have not survived. Your brother told us you were a nursing sister working at the military hospital in those days. By any chance do you remember such a man?"

Elspeth pulled the photograph of Frank from her handbag and showed it to the old woman.

The woman sat back, gently rocking to and fro. "Do I remember?" She did not speak for a moment, seeming to return to the war in her mind. "In those days we patched up many members of the forces who had fought with each other," she said. "Tensions were always high and brought out the worst in some, even if they were fighting on the same side. All the sailors and airmen, both British and Maltese, knew they might die at any moment; it only was a matter of when. They would drink too much to hide their fear and fight with each other to quell their panic. But, yes, I remember the man in that fight, the one you are speaking of, because this case was unique. They brought many men who were attacked into the hospital, many of them victims of the stab wounds and blows from a fist, but when they brought this one in, I knew something was different. The matron told me the man should be kept in a separate room, away from the others. Because he was not in uniform, I assumed he was a prisoner of war, although he appeared to be English. Later a Naval Commander from the Air Commodore's Office in Valletta came and asked the hospital staff to destroy the man's medical records, as if he never had been there. The Commander told me that I was not to mention him to anyone, no matter how high their military rank or position in the government. Later we heard from several sources that the man had attacked a tall, red-headed officer in a British Army uniform, yelling at him and insulting him, and that in retaliation the officer smashed his face and nearly killed him. I found this unusual because there were so few members of the British Army here. Most of the British men were in the Royal Navy or the RAF."

"Nearly killed him?" said Elspeth.

"Nearly, yes, but the man miraculously survived. I cared for him personally. He said his name was Frank, but he never mentioned his surname. I suppose it no longer matters, but the Commander told me I must tell no one that Frank had survived."

"Didn't you find that strange?" Elspeth asked.

"In the war we didn't question such things," the old woman said. "On the doctors' orders, the hospital released Frank in August. I remember the date because it was when the convoy bringing desperately needed supplies to us finally got through to Grand Harbour, a day of great celebration because the people of Malta were saved from starvation. Frank was badly battered and still had multiple lacerations, but by that time he was recovering his health. I remember he left the hospital in the dead of night, dressed in a borrowed suit and carrying only the few things we had given him—dressings mainly. I don't know where he went. I suppose after all these years it's all right for me to tell you these things."

Elspeth leaned over and covered the old woman's hand with her own. "Thank you," she said. "You have helped a great deal. It's a relief to know that he did not die from the wounds."

Their mood was less jubilant as Richard steered the Renault back toward San Lawrenz.

"So Frank was alive after December nineteen forty-one," Richard mused.

"It seems that way," Elspeth said. "And the officer was tall, red-headed and in a British Army officer's uniform. Who does that remind you of?" She blew out her breath. "This certainly puts a twist in the tale. Uncle Frederick told Aunt Mag that Frank had disappeared in December, but we just have spoken to two people who said he had not. What's the truth, Dickie?"

"I don't know," he said, and noisily changed into a higher gear

.

21

Richard woke the next morning to see Elspeth wrapped in a light blanket, sitting on a bench near the glass doors, and writing on a pad of paper. She did not turn when he rose, and he padded barefoot across the room to where she was perched. He bent down beside her and kissed her.

Not looking up, she kissed his cheek absently and said, "Scratchy." Then she turned back to her task.

"I'll go and take care of that," he replied, but she did not seem to notice his departure. When he returned ten minutes later, he kissed her again.

"Better," she said absently but did not reciprocate. She clenched her biro in her teeth and read over what she had written. "I think I'm beginning to understand what might have happened, but I'm not quite there yet. Dickie, be a love and get me some more coffee. Teresa always leaves the coffee maker on when she and Giulio have a day off." She held out her mug and went back to her writing.

He was puzzled at her distance. Normally she was affectionate when they woke. Why was he being put off now? She hardly seemed to notice that he was there. He made his way to the kitchen, switched on the kettle for his tea and took an orange from the bowl of fruit that Teresa had set out for their breakfast. He slowly peeled it while the water boiled. He had performed the same task many times before when

Marjorie lay dying in Cumbria four years before. He had not thought of Marjorie since deciding to move from her cousin's house and dispose of her cousin's boat. He looked at the calendar recording the Saints' Days hanging on the kitchen wall and frowned. Had it only been twelve days since he had followed Elspeth from Glenborough Castle? He put slices of bread in the toaster, found butter and strawberry jam in the fridge. And prepared his teapot. After arranging the toast in the rack, he filled Elspeth's mug with hot coffee and returned to their room.

"Dickie, how wonderful!" she said, eyeing the tray. "I'm starved. You have domestic talents that I didn't know about." She buttered a piece of toast, spread it thickly with jam and took a large bite. "Mmm. That's better. I have this idea," she explained, "and I must get it down. Give me ten more minutes."

He sipped his tea and watched her. She continued writing, oblivious of him, although she looked up several times and smiled at him. If Elspeth consented to marry him in the future, is this what the mornings would be like? She had retreated into another world, one where he did not belong. He hoped the last ten days had not been only a dalliance on her part to fill her time before she went back to work. Was she cooling toward him? He could not fathom it. He did not want to lose what they had found together over the last eight months since Cyprus. This would be their last full day together before he left for a week, and here she was scribbling away at something that she could just as well have done after he had gone.

"No," she said to herself, addressing her notepad. "That isn't right. It couldn't be." But she did not explain. She ran her hand through her hair, which fell back across her forehead. "No," she said again, her whole face grimacing. "That can't be the answer."

She looked up at him in confusion.

"Could you share your ideas with me?"

"Dickie, I'm so sorry, but not yet. I thought I understood what happened here in nineteen forty-two, but my reasoning can't be right. No . . . I must find another explanation."

"Do you want to talk about it?"

"Not yet, because I don't like the conclusion I've just reached. I'll leave it for the moment. Now come here and let me show you how I feel about you."

He had her attention now and took full advantage of it. She left her notes behind on the bench and made all his earlier doubts disappear.

He watched her dress and realised he had seldom seen a woman dress herself before. His mother had her own apartments and Marjorie her own bedroom and dressing room, but Elspeth seemed happy to shed her nightwear and don her clothes in front of him. It delighted him. He knew her appearance was her one vanity. She selected her clothing from the wardrobe, looking critically at each piece, matching colours, checking for wrinkles and then hanging it on the door near the full-length mirror. She had chosen tan, loose-fitting gabardine trousers, an open-necked crisply starched cotton blouse, with bold navy and green stripes, and a light jacket that fell almost to her knees. She carefully adjusted each item as she put it on, opening the blouse one button lower after winking at him, and then she looked at herself in the glass to make sure that all hung perfectly. She turned to her shoe collection and chose a pair of sandals that he knew she had bought in Paris and which probably cost more than the annual income of the average person in many countries where he had served. He had seen them before, on the day they went to

Kantara Castle in Cyprus. She put one on and scowled at the chunky walking cast on her other foot. Then she opened her jewellery box and ran her fingers over the earrings, brooches, and bracelets inside. She selected a pair of gold earrings that he had given her and three simple gold slave bangles.

After brushing her hair and applying light makeup, she looked at herself and sighed. "That will have to do," she said.

"Elspeth, except when you are playing Wee Elspeth or crawling helplessly on the braes in Scotland on your hands and knees, you are always perfection."

She brushed away his compliment. "Now, we have a task to do. When I'm here on Teresa's day off, I always bring Aunt Mag's breakfast up to her. Will you help me take the tray because I don't trust myself with this horrid thing on my foot? I'll go up and make sure she knows you'll be coming, but don't be long. I don't want to her asking too many questions about what we have been doing."

"I won't tell if you don't," he teased.

"Dickie! Not about that. Really!" She huffed and began to laugh. "No, I mean about Frank."

*

Elspeth found Magdelena sitting up in bed, studying a score.

"Elspeth, *cara,* good morning. You haven't forgotten me. But where is my tray?"

"Richard will be bringing it up shortly," she said. "I didn't think I could balance it with the cast on my foot, even in the lift."

Magdelena turned to Elspeth. "While we wait for him, do you have news for me?"

"News, Aunt Mag?"

"News about you and Richard?"

"No, I asked him for a week to decide. That was only two days ago."

"What is so hard, *cara*?"

"I don't know if he will accept me, particularly if I ask for any conditions."

"Accept you? Conditions? Elspeth, do you have a mind of straw? Richard dotes on everything about you."

"Me, or his idea of me?"

"I'm old enough and wise enough to know the two of you are not leading a strictly chaste existence downstairs. Come, *cara,* do you still doubt him?'

"That he loves me, no, not at all. That he loves me for who I really am, not just during this stolen interlude in Gozo, but in everyday life, yes."

"But he has seen you at work."

"True, but he sees me as an illusion, not as a real human being. I watch him look at me. Does he see all the doubt and all the fear I sometimes have? I think he considers me the 'brave Elspeth', who has survived three murder attempts. Admittedly he was there to help all three occasions, but he didn't know how terrified I was each time. He sees me as someone who has the determination to crawl across the braes with a damaged Achilles tendon, but can he know the incredible pain I was in at the time? Does he know how much it hurt to learn the truth about Malcolm or to drift out of what I thought was love for Alistair? Does he know what it took for me to rearrange my entire life after my divorce, and finally make my new situation a happy one? Does he know how much he has upset my chosen direction in life? And, does he know how much I'm risking if I marry him?" Elspeth pleaded.

"Elspeth, *cara,* how many risks have you taken in your life? Isn't this the one that will make you the happiest?"

"I can't answer that yet. How many days do I've left? Five? He said he would give me the time to decide."

"No one can understand the full extent of another's doubts or fears, but I know love is an emotion that can be trusted when it is truly felt by both parties. I shared it with Frederick for fifty years. You may not have that many years with Richard, but do seize all the ones you can."

*

As Richard put the warm toast for Magdelena's breakfast on the tray, he wondered what had disturbed Elspeth that morning, particularly what she felt could not 'be right' when she looked at the notes she had written. She had ripped the written sheet off the pad and folded the pages together before putting them into her laptop computer case, shaking her head as she did so. Wanting to respect her feelings, he could not press her to tell him what she had written or the thought that had gone into it.

He took the tray up the stairs and knocked discreetly on the door to Magdelena's bedroom. On Magdelena's command, he entered with a bow.

"Sir Richard," she said, "today you have given me a first in my life. I've never before been served breakfast in bed by a British High Commissioner. May I note it in my diary?"

"Will it be scandalously published in *The News of the World*?"

"*Octogenarian Musician Surprises Maltese Society*? No, *caro* Richard, worse luck. There is a witness who will say it was merely a matter of breakfast on a tray. Now, Elspeth, I'd like you to leave Richard and me alone because I've something to say to him."

"Aunt Mag, please."

"No, *cara,* don't worry. What you've just shared is safe with me. Now leave us in peace."

Richard placed the breakfast tray on Magdelena Cassar's lap with a flourish.

"And why, Magdelena, have you sent Elspeth away? I promise I won't pry into your confidences."

"No, Richard. These are tender times for her despite all her insouciance. I want to ask you something else because I know Elspeth will not tell me. You two have been out and about all week talking to people. Have you found out anything more about Frank?"

"A few things, but nothing conclusive. Elspeth is trying to work it out, but I think it wise if you don't ask her yet. She is the sleuth after all and wants to make sure the clues add up before she reveals all."

"There is one more thing," Magdelena said.

When Richard returned downstairs, he found Elspeth standing by the French windows in their sitting room. She was watching the rain slide down the glass and, with her finger, was tracing one of the drops down the pane. She turned as he approached.

"What did Aunt Mag talk to you about so secretly?" she asked.

"I will tell you in a moment," he said, "but there is something I want to say to you first."

He came to her and took her in his arms, holding her gently and smelling her hair. Her body responded with obvious pleasure.

"Can you stay standing up while I talk or will it hurt your tendon?" he asked.

"Not if I can lean on you a bit," she said putting her arms around his shoulders. "But, Dickie, why so serious?"

"I want to tell you about Marjorie." He felt her stiffen. "I'll have to tell you this eventually, Elspeth."

Elspeth said nothing, but he heard her swallow.

"When I married Marjorie, I thought I had the perfect diplomatic marriage. I told you this in Valletta. Everyone said we were suited to each other, and we fitted into the life we had chosen with great success. She never made demands on me and devoted her life to my career. You knew her and how exemplary a wife she was for me." He could feel Elspeth's heart beating against his chest, but she did not move. "But all the time I was married to her, I loved you at the back of my heart. I never told her, of course. I thought Marjorie and I were happy most of the time, but, until this week, I never knew what real happiness was like. No, be silent," he said, touching her lips. "I want to finish. If you remember, I asked you to marry me when I first joined the FCO and then again after Malcolm was murdered, but perhaps I was too cautious, and you politely refused me."

"I remember that both times I ran roughshod over you. For that I am sorry," she whispered to his shoulder.

"After you refused me the second time, I knew you would never consent to marry me, so for years I loved you silently. I could not believe it when you said you loved me in Cyprus because I didn't think that you would ever return my affection. I was overawed when you finally consented to marry me at Christmas, but everything seemed like a fairy tale. When you broke things off at Glenborough Castle, the fantasy was shattered."

"I do have a way of destroying things, don't I? I'm ashamed that I did it so discourteously," she mumbled.

"What you shattered was a fantasy, a dream." He held her more tightly and spoke into her ear. "What I found here with you this week is something very real. You have shown me a way of being that I never imagined possible. You have become my life, Elspeth. As you consider your answer to me this next week, remember that. I never want what we have shared between us here to go away." He lifted her face up to his and kissed her.

After a long pause, she said, "Nor do I, Dickie, but what will happen when we leave here and go back to our separate lives, our different ways of being in the world? Can we take the magic with us? I don't know if we can, and that is why I can't give you an answer yet."

They stood together quietly without speaking further. Richard wondered what Elspeth was thinking, but she did not share her thoughts with him.

Later, as they sat side by side on the sofa, she said, "You didn't tell me what Aunt Mag wanted to speak to you about at breakfast."

She was lying against his chest, her cast resting on the arm of the sofa, and was examining his hand as if she had not seen it before.

"First, we talked about Frank," he said. "She asked if we had discovered anything more about him."

"What did you say?"

"I told her we had found nothing conclusive, but I purposely didn't tell her what we learned about Frank still being alive in June nineteen forty-two."

"You were right not to say any more. If only we could find out if Frank did die later in the war or if he simply deserted.

He might still be alive today. How lucky she was to have fallen in love with my uncle. I'm certain us being here has brought back both bad and good memories for her. I worry about her. She seems to have aged a great deal, and I wonder about the visit to the doctor in Valletta. I don't remember her seeing any doctor other than the one here on Gozo."

"I suspect that your aunt has recently become bored with her life now that she doesn't travel beyond Malta, but she has found a new interest that I predict will perk her up considerably. That's the other thing we talked about."

"Not us getting married, I hope."

"No. From what she implied, she knows where our relationship is right now."

"I told her."

"Mmm," he said. "I'd figured that out. No, her new interest is the Cassar palazzo in Valletta. She wants to renovate it."

"Renovate it? Not for us, I hope."

"Not exactly."

"Not exactly what?"

"First she wants to renovate the quarters originally designed for the Cardinal, who, when he returned from Rome, had a place to stay in Valletta. She wants to give me the space to live in, but I told her I wouldn't have that."

"Good," said Elspeth and went back to examining his hand.

"I told her I would lease it."

"What?" She raised her head up and twisted around to look at him.

"I cannot stay on in Sliema in Marjorie's cousin's house. The terms of the lease that Magdelena and I agreed on are fair to us both, and I need a place for you to come and stay when you are in Malta."

"Like the Cardinal?"

"I won't demand celibacy from you as the Roman Catholic Church expected of him, if that is what you are asking."

"Beast!" she said.

He removed her hand from his because he did not want her to be distracted. "I want a place to stay in Valletta, and the palazzo would be ideal."

"Will the High Commission pick up the tab?" she asked.

"I won't ask them. I want the palazzo to be our home. But, talking of money, I am going to make some new financial arrangements. I've decided to put Marjorie's money in trust for Fergus, Marjorie's nephew, and for my brother's son and daughter. Marjorie, after all, was their aunt and would approve of me doing so. She loved them as much as she was capable of loving at all. I've invested my money carefully over the years, and caution has paid off over time. I have more than enough of my own to support the two of us comfortably. Should I have said that? I suspect you are going to say you won't live off my money, or something to that effect."

"Something to that effect," she said. "You must be learning to read my mind. I'd better be careful what I think in future."

"Elspeth, you make it impossible for a man to make love to you!"

"Do I?" she said with mock concern. "I had thought differently over the last few days."

22

The rain had stopped by midday. Richard and Elspeth brought in the food left for all of them in the kitchen to the Great Room, to where they found Magdelena among a mass of books spread out on the table where she usually ate her meals when not entertaining guests. The cutlery that Teresa had set out had been swept aside, and Magdelena had ripped some strips from an old musical score, which she was using for bookmarks.

"I knew," she said, as they appeared with the tray, "that I could find drawings showing what the palazzo looked like a hundred years ago. Elspeth, *cara,* Richard did tell you about our project, didn't he? I plan to go into Valletta on Monday to meet an architect I know who has based his work on restoration of several palazzi here in Malta. My ever-so-great-grandfather, after all, was the architect who designed many of the grand palaces after the Great Siege in the sixteenth century."

Magdelena's vitality had come back. Her dark eyes shone, and she threw one of her shawls flippantly over her shoulder.

Elspeth laughed. "Aunt Mag, should I be jealous that you shared this with Richard and not with me?"

"Of course, *cara,* because I'll take a great deal of Richard's time to advise me. Now, let's have lunch and tell me your plans. Richard, you said you are leaving early tomorrow morning. Will you come back for the weekend? And you, Elspeth?"

"I'll be staying on for a few more days, but at some point I need to return to London," she said.

Richard looked at her with surprise. Elspeth had not mentioned leaving Gozo.

"I need to return to the head clinic for final confirmation that the concussion I had in Perthshire hasn't cause further harm to my brain after the injury in Singapore.'"

"And your tendon, cara?"

"It's less painful every day. They said I'll be able to shed this thing on my foot soon after I get back to London. I think I'll pitch it into the Thames with the greatest of delight once it comes off."

"And then?" Magdelena asked.

"And then I shall see. I haven't made plans yet."

"I'll be having dinner with friends in Victoria this evening," Magdelena said at the end of lunch, "but you don't need to worry about me. They are coming to fetch me at six, so I must go and have my rest. Richard, I must say goodbye to you now, as I won't see you until you return to Malta next week. By then I should have a report for you on the progress at the palazzo and my meeting with the architect. Ring me when you are back in Ta'Xbiex."

Magdelena rose as gracefully as she must have done many times in the concert halls of Europe, came round and kissed Richard on the cheek and made her exit, brushing Elspeth's face with her fingertips as she did so.

*

"You aunt is very special, isn't she?" Richard said as they sat sipping coffee in the garden after lunch. The sky had cleared, and the afternoon was pleasantly warm.

"Most definitely. I owe so much of what I am today to her. I'm so glad you've given her a new interest in life."

"Elspeth, you didn't mention that you would be returning to London. Why so suddenly? At the clinic they said you needn't go back for a fortnight."

"I needed an excuse. Forgive me for not telling you. After all our discoveries here, I think the truth about Frank may lie in England, and not Malta. There are a few more things I need to find out here before I leave, but, after that, I want to see what more I can find in London. Does it matter, dear Dickie, where I am when you are in Brussels?"

"As I recall we have an appointment at the end of the week. I want to be at the right place to meet you then."

She touched his cheek. "I'll make sure you know."

"It's our last afternoon here together," he said taking the hand she had raised to his face and lifting it to his lips. "What is my lady's pleasure?"

"I want to go to the local parish church," she said.

"I hadn't realised you were religious. Am I wrong?"

She laughed. "Not to pray," she said. "To talk to the priest. Didn't you tell me that the piano tuner's widow said we might find records of Magdelena's children's baptism in the church records? I could go on my own while you are in Brussels, but I would prefer if you came with me to help me manage the car ride and any steps. I also thought we might find the priest there as he could be preparing for Saturday evening mass."

The taxi deposited them at the plain-fronted church in San Lawrenz, and they made their way into the Baroque interior, with a long, vaulted nave, a large dome at the crossing and a resplendent red and gold interior. They found the priest kneeing in front of the large, dark altarpiece. Richard and Elspeth had decided, for Magdelena's sake, to represent themselves honestly. They introduced themselves and told him their connection to Magdelena Cassar.

"Sir Richard, it is a pleasure to meet you and have you visit our humble church," he said as he led them up the centre aisle of the nave, lined with glass chandeliers, gilded red pilasters and ornate half-domed side chapels.

"And *Sinjura* Duff, I knew Frederick Duff toward the end of his life. Although I was never able to bring him into the fold of the Church, *Sinjura* Cassar insisted we say a mass for his soul after he died. Now, what may I do for you both?"

Elspeth assumed the straightforward manner she used when questioning people professionally. "Father, are there any records left of the baptisms or rites for the dead that were performed here during the war?" Elspeth almost fabricated a reason for wanting to know, but then decided against it.

"I've always been interested in what happened here at that time," the priest said. "Although the deaths here in Gozo weren't as extensive as those on the island of Malta, the carnage was terrible. Yes, I have those records because I've been compiling the history of the war in San Lawrenz. Is there anything you are looking for particularly?"

"Yes," said Elspeth, "my . . ." and then she stopped short of saying 'aunt', not knowing if the priest knew about the real relationship between Magdelena and Frederick. "I want to find out about *Sinjura* Cassar's father and children who died in the bombings in nineteen forty-two."

"I knew about her father, but not about the children," he said. "A funeral mass was said for her father as well as the others killed in the raid in April that year. Do you know the children's names?"

"She called her son Robin, a short form of Robert, and her daughter was named Marija."

"But do you know their surname? Robert and Marija are common names here in Gozo."

"It was an English name. Their father was called Frank Wells. *Sinjura* Cassar told me the children were baptized here in early August nineteen thirty-nine, shortly after they were born. They were twins."

"Several small children were included in the mass for *Sinjura* Cassar's father and the others. Come to my office at the Parish Centre on Monday morning. That will give me time to pull out the relevant documents. You will forgive me now as I must attend to the preparation for Saturday evening mass. Again, it was a great pleasure to see you in our church, High Commissioner. *Sinjura* Duff, I hope you will visit us every time you are in Gozo. *Sinjura* Cassar always looks forward to your visits, although I suppose you, like Frederick Duff, are not Roman Catholic."

"No, father, I'm not" she said.

"Bless you both," he said, making the sign of the cross over them. "Now I must leave you."

As they made their way back to the farmhouse in the same taxi, which had waited for them, Elspeth said, "Do you suppose he blessed us because of our heretical status? The odd thing is I do feel blessed here, although I'm more a non-believer than a heretic. Does that bother you, Dickie? I never thought to ask you about religion."

"My mother, my father, and Marjorie were all Scottish Episcopalians. I have never been much of a churchgoer and only went to please them."

"That puts my mind at rest. I should dislike it if you considered our love a sin against God. How can anything so wonderful be wrong? But come, let's have some tea and sit in the garden while it still has sunshine. Then we can decide if we want to spend our last evening together here, contemplating the nature of our sins or doing something much more pleasurable about it."

They chose the more delightful option.

*

Richard ordered a taxi for seven in the morning as he had to return to Sliema to pack for the week in Brussels and go to the High Commission to gather his papers for the conference before his midday flight. Elspeth chose not to go with him.

"For the next few days, I want to remember you as you were here," she said. "Once you have put on your official face, I may want to run away again."

They said their private good-byes before emerging into the cool morning

"Keep well, Dickie," she whispered into his ear as he prepared to leave the room. Then she put her lips to his. "Come back to me," she said, "please."

"After this last week, are you worried that I might not?" he said, perplexed.

"It never crossed my mind," she said archly, but he wondered why she chose to be so flippant at that moment. Was it to cover her ambivalence about the status of their relationship? She still had not agreed to marry him.

Their parting words at the farmhouse gate were less demonstrative and said with only a gentle kiss.

"I'll ring you, if I can, but it may not be 'til tomorrow and, even then, it will late. Do you mind? I am always so cursedly in demand at these meetings, if not from one group then from another."

"I'll make sure the line is free," she said, expressionlessly. He chuckled.

"Elspeth," he whispered, taking her hand as he departed, "please agree to marry me."

"I promise I'll give you my answer in London," she said.

*

Richard's departure had a curious effect on Elspeth. For eight days, they had spent almost every moment together. He had never bored her, often amazed her and had filled her with laughter and love in more ways than she could have ever imagined. The pompous, cautious, stiff Richard Munro had metamorphosed into a passionate and diverting lover. If I had not bolted from Glenborough Castle, she thought, would I ever have discovered this new person? Would I have married Sir Richard Munro and settled in as Lady Munro, wife of the High Commissioner? Would we soon have separate bedrooms and speak politely and dispassionately over breakfast? She thought that, if so, their marriage would quickly fail. She had consented to marry him earlier because she found his company agreeable, and he had courted her kindly and lovingly and supported her in moments of distress. She had accepted him then and told him she loved him almost by default.

Now, instead of chastising herself for fleeing from Glenborough Castle, she was filled with relief that she had had the courage to pull back and look again at her relationship with him, although in retrospect she might have left the castle less precipitously and more appropriately. Had she not bolted, their time in Gozo might never have happened. She might never have experienced all the ways they had learned to love each other, emotionally as well as physically. Would she have ever known the fire that went through her when he came to her or the pleasure of lying close to him at night, simply listening to his breathing or the rhythm of his heart? In the end, she might not marry Richard, but, after the last eight days, she knew she would always love him. She was also certain they could not sustain what they had found on Gozo in the real world, but, if they were fortunate, they might be able to recapture it for brief periods in the future.

She also knew in that moment she was overwhelmingly filled with joy.

23

Once he left Gozo, Richard's mind turned to the week ahead. From Gozo he rang his housekeeper in Sliema, who was waiting for him as his taxi came into Triq Il-Torre and drew up in front of his soon-to-be-erstwhile residence. She had prepared morning coffee, which he drank while packing his case. His PA, Margaret, had his briefcase ready in his office at the High Commission, and she ran through the items contained in it. She had ordered a car and told him that the delegate from the Maltese government to the conference would join him at Luqa, Malta's international airport. On the flight to Rome, where they had to change planes for Brussels, he and the Maltese delegate discussed the agenda and some of the more contentious items that might be raised at the meeting. In Rome, they met the Italian delegate, and, when they reached Brussels, the three of them shared a taxi to the hotel. Dinner was served promptly at eight, and he barely had time to shower and change his clothes before rushing to the dining room. The opening meal was always the first session of the week-long conference, but as the committee met four times a year, there were no official opening ceremonies. After dinner, he was cornered by the French delegate, and with several further interruptions, he did not get to bed until three. By then he had been up for almost twenty hours and fell asleep immediately. He was too tired to think of Elspeth and their time together, other than fleetingly. The morning meeting began at nine with breakfast, also a working session. The only time he recalled Elspeth that day was during a discussion of woman's clothing, owing to the French delegate's impassioned tirade about headscarves in classrooms and burqas in airports, but Richard soon shifted his mind back to business.

*

Magdelena spent Sunday morning attending mass. She returned in time for lunch and invited Elspeth to join her in the Great Room.

"Father Lucca told me that you and Richard visited him yesterday," she said. "He was most impressed that Richard came. He said you were interested my father's funeral."

Elspeth nodded but was uncomfortable telling Magdelena why. She hunted for a politic answer but wanted to answer truthfully.

"I'm still trying to find out Frank's real identity, not the one he gave you in Budapest and if he actually was in the Secret Service. I don't mean for that to sound confusing, but Frank's real history still puzzles me. I asked Father Lucca about the funeral because I wanted to see the church records kept at that time. I'm looking for something, I'm not sure what, but I'll know what it is when I find it."

"Is there anything else I can tell you, *cara*? After all, Frank was my husband."

"Do you mind talking about him again, Aunt Mag?"

"No," Magdelena said. "I've lived long and loved deeply since Frank disappeared. I had the twins for a short time and your uncle for a long one. I've always felt I had all I needed in life even though Frank chose to abandon me."

"Tell me then again about the time when Uncle Frederick came to interrogate you about Frank in the summer of nineteen forty-two."

"You must think that important, *cara*. You have asked me twice before."

"I know I have, but I can't grasp what there is about that interview that continues to bother me. You said that you and Uncle Frederick became lovers soon after the bombing in April. Do you remember the exact date when he came to ask you about Frank, the time you said he became so formal? I want to know more about that specific day, everything you can possibly recall that you might not have already told me."

Magdelena at first shook her head. "Exactly? I recall it was during the summer, late June perhaps."

*

The area in the tent in which they sat was hot and, because the power shortages had increased, the overhead fan was still. Magdelena had bought a red cotton scarf with a fringe from a friend in exchange for a half dozen eggs laid by her new hens, and she had wrapped it around her shoulders, knowing Frederick was coming. She ignored the summer heat in favour of the little fashion that she could muster as her clothes underneath were now shabbier than ever and she could not replace them. Soon it was so warm that she took off the scarf and draped it decoratively over the back of her chair. When Frederick came in, Magdelena could see the fatigue in his eyes. He was dressed in his summer uniform, a khaki shirt with epaulettes bearing the insignia of his rank, red tabs on his collar, knee-length shorts and matching socks. He carried his baton and hat under his arm, which made him look frighteningly official. She noticed that he had injured his hand and rose to rush to him, to touch his wound and make it well. He stood stiffly and cleared his throat. A young sergeant came in behind him.

Despite the tiredness in his face, Frederick seemed elated. "We have beaten Rommel back from Cairo," he told her. "Soon Malta may be saved and the Nazis driven out of Africa."

She had never seen him so excited about the fighting before, but he seemed edgy throughout the interview that followed. Magdelena answered his questions as accurately as she could, but his voice was so distant and aloof that she had started to cry. The sergeant said nothing. Frederick dismissed him, asking him to go the mess area to get her a cup of tea. Frederick then came to her. She could smell the sweat on his uniform and, embracing him, she could hear his breathing. It had been ten days since she had seen him, and she had missed him desperately.

"It will be over soon," he whispered to her, "and then we can be together—forever." He told her that Frank had disappeared and could not be found, although they had searched for him both on Malta and Gozo. She had not thought to ask when Frank had disappeared because it no longer mattered to her.

*

"Are you sure he said that the Germans had been beaten back from Cairo. I wish Richard were here; he would know when that had happened, and we would have the correct date."

"Is the date that important?" Magdelena asked.

"It may be."

"Can you tell me why?"

"Not yet because I haven't quite put everything together, but the date is significant."

"Do you think Frank is dead?"

"He most likely died during the war, but I have no proof."

"Do you think you can find any?"

"I hope so," Elspeth said. "I'm still working on it."

"Then I shall be content," Magdelena said.

"There is one other thing. May I see the papers you showed me last week, the ones you had gathered together for me relating to Frank and the twins."

"They're in the table drawer under the small Canaletto," Magdelena said. "Please take them if they will help you."

Elspeth retired to the guest quarters with the red-roped folder. The sitting room there was cool for April as the rain had returned. She poked the logs laid in the fireplace and set them alight. She cursed the inconvenience of her cast, which did not allow her to spread the papers out on the coffee table in front of the sofa and view them conveniently, but she saw a card table in the corner and opened it in front of the fire. Memories of the day before with Richard in this room flooded over her, but she tried to put them from her mind.

The documents were old and brittle and the paper of poor quality. The first was a marriage certificate from St. Stephen's Roman Catholic Church in London, on an illegible day in April nineteen thirty-eight. On that day Magdelena Marija Cassar, spinster of the parish of Valletta, Malta, had married Francesco Roberto Wells, bachelor, but no parish was given for him. Witnesses were Manwel Cassar and Joseph Butts. Elspeth assumed the latter was the church's sexton. The priest had also signed the certificate.

Elspeth had not paid attention to the entire contents of the file when Magdelena had first shown it to her, but an old passport fell out when she had tipped the papers on to the card table. The heavy blue document was unmistakable to anyone from Britain before its entry into the European Union. She opened the passport, now smelling of mould, and saw the face of the man that matched the father of Magdelena's twins shown in the one photograph Aunt Mag had recovered from the attic. His features were dark, almost glowering, and not clearly discernible. Was this intentional? The passport was made out in the name of Francesco Roberto Wells, born on December fourteenth nineteen thirteen, in Milan, Italy. It had been issued by the British Embassy in Rome on March twenty-third nineteen thirty-six. She looked down at Frank's signature and found it illegible. Magdelena had not mentioned this passport, and Elspeth had not seen it as it was buried beneath other papers in the folder. Why Magdelena did still have it in her possession? Frank may have left it with her when he was at the farmhouse on one of his visits, but for what reason?

Next, she found the baptismal certificates for the twins. Robert Francis and Marija Magdelena, born in the parish of San Lawrenz, Gozo, in the British Crown Colony of Malta, on July thirty-first nineteen thirty-nine and christened three days later. Elspeth wondered if her birthday being on the same day of the year explained the unspoken bond between her and Magdelena Cassar. Only the priest had signed the baptismal records, but, folded in the creases, Elspeth found a browning photograph of two small Churchill-look-alike babies, obviously only days old. Elspeth thought of her own children, both born in Cedars-Sinai Hospital in Los Angeles and christened, at Alistair's insistence, with great ceremony at the most opulent Episcopal Church in Pasadena, whose name she could not remember. Several well-known Hollywood stars had attended, and they outshone her children at both ceremonies. For Elspeth that life was now as foreign to her as Frank and Magdelena's in nineteen thirty-nine in San Lawrenz.

Next, she found another copy of Manwel Cassar's obituary, this one from *The Times* of London. After reading the piece, Elspeth realised that Magdelena had either played down her father's fame in the world of chamber music or she had merely accepted it as a part of her early life.

Elspeth picked up the photographs in the file. Several were of the twins and one of an older man, undoubtedly Manwel Cassar, at his cello. Elspeth touched these lovingly. Before Frederick Duff had entered Magdelena Cassar's life, these were her most cherished beings, and they had been wiped irrevocably from her life in late April nineteen forty-two.

The fire had started to die down, and Elspeth rose to coax it back to life. She wished the pieces of paper on the card table had given her new insight, but they had not. She gathered the documents, put them back in the roped file and tied the red string in a careful bow.

She glanced at her watch, and, although she did not know his exact itinerary, she expected Richard would be changing planes in Rome at that moment. Rome? Wait, Frank's passport had been issued in Rome in March nineteen thirty-six, not in London. She was certain Mussolini was in power, but what had been happening there politically? What were Britain's relations with Italy then? She needed to verify this.

As she hobbled into the bedroom where she had left her computer case, she was grateful that Teresa had insisted on having wireless Internet access at the farmhouse to keep pace with the international culinary world. She brought her case into the sitting room and pulled out her laptop. The notes that she had scribbled out the previous morning fell to her feet. Elspeth stuck out her cast at uncomfortable angle and retrieved them. She had almost forgotten their existence. Opening them, she looked at her first question, written in large letters. *WHY DIDN'T F TELL M MORE ABOUT FW'S DISAPPEARANCE?* Why didn't Frederick tell Magdelena more about Frank Wells' disappearance?

She spent the rest of the afternoon googling Mussolini in April nineteen thirty-six, the date Frank's passport was issued, and also Rommel's advance toward Cairo in June nineteen forty-two, which Frederick had mentioned in his interview with Magdelena. As with most internet searches, she discovered more than she wanted to know.

She dined with her aunt, and they played a Brahms duet together afterwards, Elspeth badly. "*Cara*, you must practice. If you do, you will find enjoyment all your life in the act of creating music," her aunt said. They did not discuss Frank.

That night Elspeth lay contemplating the yawning emptiness of the bed beside her and thought of Richard. She spent a long time considering their last week together and wondered if Frederick and Magdelena had shared such passions as well. She no longer thought of them as her aunt and uncle but two people who had woven their own lives together and grabbed any happiness they could find, particularly during the difficult time in the war.

24

After Elspeth left the room, Magdelena sat at her piano without touching the keys. Was Elspeth right in her presumption that Frank had died in the war? Elspeth had said she wanted proof, but even her suggestion implied that Elspeth and Richard had uncovered something that she, Magdelena, did not know. In retrospect, why had she asked Elspeth to find out about Frank? Now she wished she had not. Did she really want to know the truth? She had lived for sixty-five years without it. She had used the complication of ownership of the farmhouse as an excuse, but had she opened a Pandora's box that would have better stayed closed? No Maltese court would uphold the ownership of her home by a husband who had disappeared in late nineteen forty-one. She knew that in her head.

She tried to think of happier things. She had watched Richard and Elspeth over the last week and saw them unfold to each other. *Cara,* she thought, perhaps this time you will see you can not only trust him but also allow yourself to love him without being afraid that he will hurt you. And Richard, *caro,* yes, she is every wonderful thing you have discovered and opened yourself to. Take her as she is, flaws and all, but know, she, like her uncle, has an infinite capacity for loving but a fierce streak of independence with which you must learn to cope. As you give yourself to her, she will give back three times over, and you must allow for that. Magdelena thought of Frederick and sighed deeply, holding him as closely in her thoughts as if he sat there beside her turning the pages, as he had so often done.

*

Elspeth woke the next morning, grateful for a full night's uninterrupted sleep although regretting the reason for it. She found her dressing gown, wrapped it round her and headed for the kitchen. Hearing the familiar sound of Teresa pounding a ball of dough on the kitchen table, she slipped into the room and watched the old woman at work. What had life been like for Teresa? The horror of what the German soldiers had done to her must never have gone away, but Teresa was softly cooing a Sicilian love song as she kneaded the embryonic bread. She had found happiness with Giulio, Elspeth thought, which must have eased the terrors of war.

"Teresa," Elspeth said.

"*Signora* Elspetta, I do not hear you. The coffee is ready; I serve you a cup." Teresa did not mention Richard's departure.

"What was that you were singing?"

"Singing?" Teresa said. "A song my mother sing to me when I am a child. A simple song about a woman who want a bird to carry her longing and loneliness to her lover."

"And you still sing it even today?"

"It is a silly song. I have no idea why it always come to my mind. Perhaps it make me think of my mother, who is killed during the war."

Elspeth took the mug of coffee that Teresa offered her and blew across the top of it. She sat sipping it in comfortable silence. Teresa went back to her dough.

"I find the recipe for the bread on the *Cooks Illustrated* website," Teresa said. "*Signora* Magdelena always is happy when I try something new, but I always ask Giulio to taste it first, in case it is terrible. I hear some recipes are put on the Web without having a test in a kitchen." She rolled the dough once more and hit it with a joyous smash. "Come back this afternoon, and you give me your opinion about this bread too."

Elspeth had known Teresa most of her life and trusted her honesty. "Teresa, is my aunt well?

Teresa mounded the dough in a large bowl and put a wet cloth over it, before answering.

"*Signora* Elspetta, before you come with Sir Richard, she seem to lose interest in living. Giulio and I are worried. But when you come and when she see you two together, she change. Forgive me if I am too forward, but she sometimes look at the two of you in the garden from the upstairs windows and smile, and I think she is far away. I think she remember *Signor* Frederick."

"I need to return to London in the next few days. Do you think that will be bad for her?"

Teresa laughed. "No, *signora* Elspetta, she change this week. What a mess she make with all the books she pull out from the bookcases. She not let me put them back. You and Sir Richard give her new life. *Grazie, signora* Elspetta, thank you. Now you come back before teatime and try the bread before I serve it upstairs. It has walnuts and pine nuts in a multigrain flour and olive oil dough."

Elspeth asked for another cup of coffee, leaving Teresa to her preparations and told her that she would join her aunt for breakfast upstairs. Elspeth ran a hot bath, gingerly removed the Velcro straps from her cast and sank into the warmth of the water. Something Teresa had said tickled her brain, but she could not think what. Then she sighed, thinking of Richard and wondered how his meeting was proceeding in Brussels.

*

Richard was striking his gavel at the same moment and asking the Algerian delegate to refrain from angry discourse.

*

"Aunt Mag, I've booked a flight to London for tomorrow morning," Elspeth said over the fresh fruit that she had ladled into a bowl from the sideboard.

"And Richard?" Magdelena asked. "Will he join you there on Thursday? Isn't that a week?"

"No, his last session ends Friday at noon. He can't meet me 'til after then."

"Have you told him when you will be in London?"

Elspeth screwed her head upward and stared at the ceiling, the way she always had as a child when she did not want to face making a decision.

"I've not heard from him since he left," she said with slow and pained dignity. "But I shall email him and give him my flight schedule when I go back downstairs."

"And what are your going to tell him on Friday, *cara*?"

Elspeth raised her eyebrows, looked down her chiselled nose, closed her eyes and swallowed painfully. "I don't know, Aunt Mag, I really don't know. How much can I ask of him, do you think?"

"Ask from your heart, *cara,* and, if that is what you want, how can he refuse you?"

Elspeth had one more day in Gozo to follow up on the information she and Richard had uncovered. Elspeth asked Giulio to drive her to the Parish Centre on the town square, where she kept her appointment with Father Lucca. The priest greeted her with obvious pleasure.

"*Sinjura* Duff," he said with a gracious smile. "What a pleasure it was to meet the High Commissioner. *Sinjura* Cassar has mentioned that you and he are to be married."

In her role in the Kennington Organisation, Elspeth had developed a skill in answering questions without really doing so. "Father, my aunt has many ambitions for me, many of them not fulfilled."

"You call *Sinjura* Cassar your aunt?"

"I don't know how much you know about her."

"I am her confessor."

"She has always been an aunt to me, although I've known about the irregularities of her relationship with my uncle since I was young. But, Father, let me tell you why I'm here. I hope you will keep my confidence, although you are not my confessor."

"If you ask, *sinjura*."

"My aunt was married in London before the war to a man who called himself Francesco Roberto Wells. Is there any way that I can find evidence that he was a Roman Catholic? I don't know if the Church keeps such records beyond the local parish church where holy sacraments are performed."

"We keep records here of our local baptisms, confirmations, marriages and funerals, but you must go to his diocese or to the Vatican to find out what you need."

"Do you keep detailed records of the baptisms?"

"Of course, *sinjura*. They are the written verification that a child has been received by God."

"I've seen the baptismal certificates issued for Magdelena Cassar and her husband's children. Would you have the original documentation here? Or was it destroyed during the war?"

"As I mentioned to you and Sir Richard, our files were stored carefully at this centre during the war, and our church suffered only slight damage. I can retrieve them for you, if you wish."

He left Elspeth alone in his office and returned twenty minutes later with a thick book with the dates '1938-1945' inscribed on the spine. He had marked two pages for Elspeth's convenience.

Elspeth read through the record of baptisms in nineteen thirty-nine which were listed on the first marked page. Robert Francis and Marija Magdelena, son and daughter of Frank. Robt. Welles and his wife Magdelena Marija, née Cassar, of the parish of San Lawrenz, twins born on the thirty-first of July nineteen thirty-nine. She traced the names with her fingers and said, "That confirms what I already know."

Then she turned to the second page, which recorded the funerals of Manwel Cassar and the two young children. They were just three of several on that day. She tried to keep tears from her eyes.

Responding to the questioning look of Father Lucca, she said, "I think I've found what I came for. How sad for my aunt, to lose her father, and also her children when they were so small."

"War is a terrible thing. Do you have children, *sinjura*?"

"I've been blessed with a daughter and a son, both of whom are still very much alive and well. One lives in England and the other in California. I shall recommend they come and meet you when they next visit my aunt. Thank you, Father, you have been most kind."

Elspeth needed a quiet place to think, preferably away from the farmhouse, and regretted her limited mobility, she asked Giulio. Because the sky was clear and the breeze minimal, she decided to go down to the sea and asked Giulio to drive her. She thought of a spot where Aunt Mag and Uncle Frederick used to take her as a child, which had always been precious to her, a place on the western shore of Gozo called Dwejra Point. Young Elspeth loved to explore the pools in the rocky shore and gaze up at the towering cliffs. She was fascinated particularly by the massive stone arch that jutted into the sea, framing a high opening called the Azure Window. Every time she visited, Elspeth wondered how many millennia of erosion caused by the force of the sea had created this impressive, natural monument, and how many more years it would survive further battering of the waves and the wind. The overwhelming structure represented Elspeth's happy days on Gozo as well as the times she had come here to drown her grief. This seemed the perfect place to come to mull over her current concerns.

Guido had laid out a blanket for her on a stone outcrop and helped her take a seat. She asked him to leave her there for an hour. He retreated to the Mercedes on the far edge of the nearby car park but did not leave her altogether.

She sat and composed her mind. She thought of Magdelena and Frederick once more and how much they had dared to face in their lives. Magdelena, always a devout Roman Catholic, had flaunted her Church's tenets to be with Frederick. Had she not achieved international fame on her own, and not come from a prominent Maltese family, she probably would have been ostracised by her own community. She had not let this stop her from living with Frederick for over fifty years at a time when this was not done. What had Magdelena said? That she and Frederick had become lovers almost immediately, and she did not care because Frank Wells was no longer a husband to her? Elspeth wondered how much of a husband Frank had ever been and how much he had used Magdelena for his own purposes.

Frank was still a mystery. The certificate of marriage between Frank and Magdelena listed no parish for him. Was this merely an oversight or did he want to hide something? Or, if Frank really was a Roman Catholic, he might not have wanted to lie to the priest at Saint Stephen's in London and therefore had purposely not given his real parish. How much more had he fabricated when telling Magdelena and her father about himself, and why did he feel it necessary to do so? Or was he just a manipulating scoundrel?

Elspeth's mind went back to the Marsalforn. The old man had said, "It is better not to ask about this person." At the time, Elspeth had construed this to mean that Frank was an unsavoury person, but could that be wrong? After all, Aunt Mag was initially attracted to him, so much so that that she had married him. Suppose Frank was doing secret work, as he said, and that the ex-soldier in Marsalforn knew this. His sister had confirmed that when Frank was taken to hospital after the fight, he was nursed away from the others to protect him from being seen, and that a Royal Navy Commander had come to ask that Frank's eventual recovery be not revealed to anyone, no matter how high up in the Government or the Armed Forces. Why?

Who had Frank attacked during the fight? Or was it the other way round? The old *sinjura* had said that the uniformed soldier in the fight was a British Army officer. Elspeth shied away from thinking it might be her uncle, but it was a strong possibility, particularly since the officer was tall and red-headed, and Uncle Frederick had an injured hand when he interviewed Aunt Mag in late June. Much could be explained if Uncle Frederick had been the target of Frank Wells' assault. If Frank wanted to remain unnoticed, would he have risked exposure in a public fight with an officer? Did Frank attack Uncle Frederick because of his relationship with Aunt Mag? Elspeth might never know, but every assumption she made earlier now seemed specious and made Uncle Frederick's presence in Marsalforn a credible alternative.

A tour bus turned into the car park above her, disturbing Elspeth's solitude, and she signalled to Giulio that she was ready to leave. He came across the rocks and helped her up and back to the Mercedes.

Elspeth was quiet at lunch, and Magdelena did not question her.

During their dessert, her aunt spoke. "*Cara,* I shall miss you. When do you leave?"

"I'll have to leave here early for my morning flight. I've an appointment at the head clinic and later with my doctor to check how well my tendon is healing."

"How soon will you return to Gozo?"

"I'm not sure. I think that will depend on what I tell Richard."

25

Tired from his all-day meeting, Richard returned to his hotel room and for the first time since leaving Malta turned his mind fully to Elspeth. He had loved her for forty years, but in the last few days he realised he had always loved an idea and not a person. He thought back over their new relationship. When they first made love together in Cyprus, their lovemaking was polite and tentative, impassioned but somehow correct, if love affairs can be correct. At Christmas, when he had proposed to her and she'd agreed to marry him, he found her responses heartfelt but always slightly aloof, as if she loved him but still held him apart. She was affectionate and attentive, but he always felt that she was slightly distracted, as if their impending marriage would be pleasant and diverting but not completely engaging. When she had stormed out of Glenborough Castle, everything changed. He felt shocked, betrayed by the disruption to the order in his life, and disoriented, but for the first time he began to have a sense of who Elspeth was deep inside, much as Magdelena had warned him. Then the last eight days had happened. Their love, and his love for her, had changed. They had celebrated their love in ways he never knew possible, and he knew that was true for her as well. Sometimes they laughed together in intimate moments; often they teased. Other times they just touched affectionately. During the night, they would caress each other, sometimes casually, often erotically. They had learned a tender familiarity and that now lived within him subliminally, not always reaching the surface of his consciousness but creating a new dimension in his being that tingled inside him every moment, even when he was otherwise distracted. A fortnight earlier he would not have recognised what was now becoming a necessary part of him, sensations that she had opened inside him day by day and that he never wanted to lose.

Elspeth was right in her assumption that he had originally thought she could take Marjorie's place, but he knew that was no longer possible. He also knew that if she refused to marry him, he would remain her lover, despite all the implications that might have on his career or earlier sensibilities because he simply could not live without her.

His bedside clock read 02:10. He tossed over and then over again. He missed her lying beside him, occasionally waking and turning to him. She would fall back to sleep immediately, but he would lie there, holding her and feeling love flow down through him. She would wake in the morning without mentioning the tenderness they had shared throughout the night, but silently, with a chuckle, she would respond to his love for her as if it was a natural part of their very beings. He could not give this up.

Should he ring her at this late hour? He took up the pillow but it offered no comfort. In the end, he floundered around for his mobile and dialled her number.

"Hello Dickie," she said sleepily, her voice so loving that his heart turned. "I miss you being here." He imagined her lying on the bed they had shared in Gozo and smiled.

"How are the meetings going?" she asked, with a yawn. He knew he had awakened her.

"Long and often rancorous. But, as chair, I'm insisting they don't go beyond Friday noon. I can get the two o'clock plane to Rome and be in Malta for a late dinner. Will you come into Valletta to meet me?"

"I'm so glad you called. I'm flying to London tomorrow. Will you come there instead?"

"My most precious one, I would come to Timbuktu on Friday if you told me you would be waiting there for me. But why the sudden change in venue?"

"I'm developing a theory about Frank Wells, and I think I can only verify the truth of it in London. The Internet and Gozo have their limitations."

"Then I can see you Friday afternoon. How brilliant," he said. "I think a flight leaves Brussels that will get me into Gatwick at three. With any luck, I should be at your flat by five, depending on weekend traffic."

"Five o'clock then, Friday. I'll put you down for then," she said with mock efficiency as if writing it in her diary.

She was silent for a long moment, and he said, "Elspeth, are you there?"

"Dickie, there's something I've wanted to tell you, and I knew you were too polite to ask. There weren't any others," she said.

"Other what?" he said, wondering if he would ever get used to dealing with the un-prefaced thoughts that sometimes popped into Elspeth's head.

"Men in my life, except Alistair, of course, but we were married, so you can't count that, and we did have two children. Then he fell out of love with me and turned his attention elsewhere."

"I'm sorry, I didn't know there was another woman involved. You didn't tell me"

"There wasn't. He fell in love with himself, or at least his own image. I knew it was over when he gave me a pair of antique duelling swords for my birthday—ones from the court of Louis XV that he had particularly coveted. I left him and the swords behind the next week. I put a large note on the box they were in, saying "They win!" Rather childish, don't you think? As you've often said, I can sometimes be impulsive, but it had been coming a long time."

"And Malcolm?"

"I never made love with Malcolm, although I did think about it at the time. Looking back, I'm glad my girlish prudery prevailed even in the love-in era of the late sixties."

"I'm glad too, but you've never asked me if there were other women in my life," he said.

"I don't think I will. I'm just going to trust you," she said.

"You can," he said. "I always loved you too much to find any other interest outside of my marriage with Marjorie."

"I'm happy then too," she said, "Good night, darling Dickie."

"Good night, Elspeth, sweetest love," he responded. "Do you really love me?"

"I hae a bit of affection for ye, wee Richard, but mostly I do long for yer body."

Richard laughed himself to sleep.

The next morning members at the conference remarked that Sir Richard was more conciliatory than usual and that he seemed to pay less attention than usual to what was going on.

26

Upon her return to London, Elspeth entered her flat with comfortable familiarity but also was aware of what had happened to her since she and Richard had left a week before. They had stayed together here many times over the last five months. She remembered their tentative lovemaking during those times, sometimes in her bed and sometimes in the guest room. She smiled at the memory of the last week, which had nothing tentative about it, except for her not committing to marry him.

The flat was cold, and she adjusted the thermostat. She had called ahead to make sure there would be food waiting for her, but the space round her seemed empty. She touched the back of the sofa where she and Richard frequently sat together and where only ten days ago they had sipped after-dinner coffee. She saw a book he had placed on the coffee table and opened it at the page he had marked when she had drawn him to her and suggested it was time for bed.

The light on her answerphone was blinking. She pressed the button, hoping it would be Richard but knowing he would ring her on her mobile.

A familiar voice filled the emptiness. "Elspeth, ducks," Pamela Crumm's voice said. "When you are back, call me at home." The recorded time of the call was earlier that day.

Pamela was her closest friend but also her employer, a tricky balance that they managed with delicacy. Elspeth looked at her watch and saw it was after six. She doubted Pamela would be home this early, but that gave Elspeth an excuse to leave a message. Pamela, however, answered her phone instantly. Her voice, which was as grand as she was small, was business-like.

"Pamela Crumm here."

"Hello, Pamela," Elspeth said, not needing to identify herself, "I hadn't expected to reach you directly."

"This evening I'm home but am working with the manager of Eric's new hotel in Boston. He has taken over four very handsome houses on Beacon Hill, and his conversion of them into a Kennington hotel is another of his strokes of genius. Even the City Historical Preservation Commission approved. Now I'm trying to get the staff sorted out. And how are you, my friend? Have you and Richard set the date?"

"No," Elspeth said simply. She avoided saying 'not yet' as she had in Malta.

Pamela Crumm, despite her small, bent frame, had a mind as acute as they come. "No? Do I sense some trouble?"

"Not trouble; indecision rather. I'd rather not talk about it."

"I'm sorry, ducks. You know Richard is right for you, but I will say no more. How is the tendon?"

"Certainly much less painful and definitely on the mend. I should have this cast off shortly, I think. I see the doctor soon."

Elspeth heard a phone ringing in the background, and Pamela said she had to go but would call back. Elspeth went to the refrigerator and found the bottle of wine she had partially shared with Richard the night before they left for Glenborough Castle, and she poured the rest into a glass, hoping it was still drinkable. She turned on a CD of Erik Satie's piano music played by her aunt and sat staring into space without directing her thoughts. Suddenly, in a moment of inspiration, she knew what the third option could be, but would it actually work for her? She found it frightening. Was Richard likely to agree? She had no idea if he would. Her heart beat rapidly, and she swallowed deeply. She knew she could not reach him by mobile, and besides she wanted to talk to him in person. A decision like this could not be conveyed across the beams of a satellite. Waiting would also give her time to rethink, to be sure, but she was so certain that she laughed at her earlier ambivalence.

The ringing of her home phone brought her out of her thoughts.

"All right, ducks, now do you want to talk?"

"Pamela, I want to come and speak to Eric tomorrow, after my appointment at the head clinic. I'm planning on coming back to work next week. I will still have this horrid cast, but surely there is something I can do that is necessary and won't require walking any distance."

"He's been ranting on about the date of your return to work. I think he already has an assignment for you. Let me check his schedule." Elspeth could imagine Pamela tapping at her laptop as she had seen her friend doing so many times before. "Half past one is clear. Will that do?'

"I'll see you then," Elspeth said. She put down the handset and leaned back against the wall, blowing out her breath.

Only two and a half weeks had passed since Elspeth had last been in Eric Kennington's offices, but it seemed much longer. As usual, she had dressed with great care, wearing a ruby-coloured silk blouse, a simple scarf that even she found extravagantly expensive, and a fawn woollen jacket because the day was cool for early May. Pamela was waiting by the lift as Elspeth came up to the twentieth floor.

"I told him that you didn't want to discuss your plans with Richard, and he has sworn to be discreet. I hope that's all right," Pamela said.

"Thanks for that. What is his mood like today?"

"He's delighted you're coming back. We both had our doubts that you would."

*

Eric Kennington strode across his office to meet Elspeth and, seeing her uneasy gait, grinned at her.

"Not your usual elegant footwear, Elspeth. I understand you had a bit of run in with the braes in Scotland. What did the specialist say?" Eric Kennington had been in close attendance when Elspeth had been injured so badly in the head by one of the employees at the Kennington Singapore a year before. She was many months recuperating after almost four weeks in hospital.

"He said I suffered a simple concussion when I fell, and there was no recurring damage, thank heavens. Except for this wretched cast, I'm quite well."

Eric beamed at her. "Pamela tells me you want to resume your job."

"I've a few things to attend to before I come back full time," she said. "Will next Wednesday do? I originally thought I would be back on Monday."

"I suppose it will have to. You did ask for three weeks' holiday and two more days won't make any difference. I already have your next assignment in mind. You will be in London to begin with, probably for two months, and then I'll be sending you to Provence for a short while."

"Provence in July, when the lavender will be in bloom. How delightful, although knowing you, Eric, I probably will have little time to look at it. Now tell me what the assignment is."

"A visit by some celebrities to a colleague's resort. They want complete privacy, and your job will be to ensure they get it. My friend doesn't have anyone like you to help him."

After she left the Kennington Organisation offices in the City, Elspeth hailed a taxi and directed it to Myddledon Street in Clerkenwell, the location of Family Records Centre for England and Wales. Having committed herself to returning work on the following Wednesday, and, expecting Richard on Friday afternoon, she had only two days left on her own to pursue her latest theory about Frank Wells.

Elspeth had learned how to shift from Queen's English to Standard American English when she lived in Hollywood, an asset she thought would be useful in her current quest. As she approached the desk marked 'Enquiries', she became a convincing Californian. Hoping that the young woman behind the desk would not be able to determine Elspeth's exact age, which was slightly too old for someone who had a grandfather Frank's age, she said she had come from America and wondered how she might trace her grandfather, Frank Wells, who was born in nineteen thirteen in either England or Italy. This was a long shot because Aunt Mag was convinced he had been born in Milan, not England. She had kept his passport, but that could be easily be forged if Frank had indeed been in the Secret Service. The young woman told Elspeth that that she would need to know which was the country of his birth because the records for England and Wales were kept in a separate index from those in foreign countries.

"I'm not sure," she said. "His mother and father were on the musical stage, and travelled all over the UK and on the Continent. My grandfather could have been born anywhere in England or perhaps in Italy. Is there any way I can find the record of his birth without knowing where he was born or the exact date of his birth?"

"You could start with Foreign Births," the young woman suggested. "the files are not comprehensive but they are shorter." She led Elspeth to a computer sitting on a desk in a room nearby and gave her instructions on how to do a search for relatives on it.

Frank Wells' birth was untraceable in Italy in either nineteen thirteen or nineteen fourteen. Elspeth resorted to the larger index of births in England and Wales. Recalling the name that he put on the twins' baptismal record and the suggestion of the woman in the FCO archives, next she tried variations of both his surname and given name. She worked through the files slowly, trying to miss nothing.

Shortly before closing time, her back and eyes aching from viewing the screen, Elspeth found what she was looking for. A 'Franklyn Robert Welles' was born in Dorchester, Dorset, on December fifteenth, nineteen thirteen. His mother was listed as Giovanna Leonetti Welles from Milan, Italy, and his father as Robert Alfred Welles from Lyme Regis. The names and places were close enough that Elspeth was sure she had discovered what she was after.

Given this first hint as to the real identity of 'Frank Wells', she now had enough knowledge to trace him further. With luck, tomorrow she could track down Franklyn Robert Welles, where he had been and what he was doing from nineteen thirty-six onwards.

Excited by what she had found, Elspeth returned to her flat. She wished Richard would call so that she could tell him about her discovery, but her answerphone displayed a large red zero, and she had no saved messages in the voicemail on her mobile. They had required it to be turned off at the Family Records Centre, but in the taxi back to Kensington, she had checked and found only one item, a text from her daughter in East Sussex asking her if she would be in London on next Tuesday and could they have lunch together. Dear Lizzie, she thought, soon I will be able to tell you my future plans. She texted back, "I'll let you know. Love, Mum."

She found a bottle of wine in the kitchen cupboard, poured herself a glass and retreated to the sofa and her laptop. Two hours later her mobile rang. Richard was on the other end.

"Ms Duff," he said stiffly. "My PA has made the following booking for me on Friday." He gave her the flight number and time of arrival in London. "Will you make the arrangements for my accommodation in London for the weekend?"

Elspeth suspected that he was with someone and could not talk freely. "I'll have the sheets changed, make sure your pillow is to the left of mine and your pyjamas are laid out'" she said. "And after that, I make no promises about keeping the bed neat. Oh, Dickie, darling, I've . . ."

He did not let her finish. "Thank you, Ms Duff, that will be suitable." He disconnected the call abruptly. Elspeth grinned widely at his deception.

With only one full day left before Richard arrived, Elspeth made plans to go to Dorchester to see if she could find any trace of Frank Wells, or more correctly Franklyn Robert Welles, or any member of his family. She was not sure what she would find in Dorset, but she had found seven families on the Internet with the surname Welles wo lived there. Once again cursing her cast, which made walking difficult and driving impossible, she decided to take the train to Dorchester and hire a car with a local driver. She found some clothes that she had bought the last time she had visited her retreat in Marin County, north of San Francisco, and decided that they looked sufficiently Californian for her once again to assume the role of an American searching for English relatives.

By four o'clock she was regretting her choice of the day's activity because she hadn't as yet found any link between Franklyn Robert Welles and the Welles families current living in Dorchester, and her head and foot were both throbbing. She was planning one more stop before declaring her search unfruitful. She asked her driver to recommend a place for tea, preferably one where some of the older locals might congregate. He recommended the Rose and Thistle Tea Shop on the high street, which was near the last Welles residence on her list, one she had not yet visited.

After being seated, Elspeth laid her list of names and addresses down on the table and put Frank's photograph over it to see if it would attract any attention. An unkempt, heavily made-up waitress came over to take her order.

"Look at that! Where'd you get that photograph? He looks like one of our regular's father, only younger."

Elspeth looked up eagerly. "How can I contact your customer?"

"She comes in just about every day about now," the waitress said.

"I'm from America," Elspeth lied. "Doing ancestral searches. I'd love to meet her?"

"She lives round the corner from here. Wait a tick, and I'll betcha she'll be here. Always comes in Thursdays."

Ten minutes later, at the waitress's signal, Elspeth looked up from her tea and saw a woman of about forty, which would have made her too young to be Frank's daughter. She was carrying several parcels.

"This lady here's waitin' for you. She's an American," the waitress said, addressing the woman.

Elspeth rose and invited the woman to her table. The waitress brought more tea and some sorry-looking scones without being asked.

Elspeth drew the photograph from the top of her stack of papers. "Do you know who this is?" Elspeth asked. "I think his name was Frank Wells, and I've come all the way from California to find out where he might be now. He would be in his nineties today. This picture was taken about nineteen forty."

"Frank, you don't mean Franklyn Welles?" she said, taking the photograph from Elspeth. "Then it could be my grandfather. He was killed during the war, when my father, his son, was ten years old. I've only seen photographs of him. But tell me, why do you have one of him, and why are you here?"

Elspeth knew that to claim that Frank Wells was her grandfather, as she had at the Family Records Centre, was no longer an option, and therefore she improvised. "I work for a company in California that does genealogical research into families in the UK, but this case is a bit different. Frank Wells was a wartime friend of the father of one of my colleagues. Frank's friend has something that belonged to Frank and wants to return it to him, if he is alive, or to his family, if not. Since I travel to England frequently, my colleague asked me to see if I could find any of Frank's relatives. Is there any way I could contact your father to see if this picture is really one of his father?"

"Mum and Dad are up in London. They'll be back after the weekend. Could you come back then?"

"Gosh," said Elspeth, inwardly shuddering at her slang, "I've got to leave London and get back to the US. Is there any way I could meet them in London? I'm staying there until Saturday morning."

"I can try them on my mobile. They're visiting friends in Notting Hill."

"You know what?" Elspeth said, "I've got a cell phone that actually works here, but sometimes it's not real clear. If you reach them, ask them to call me. Here's my number. Tell'em I'll buy'em some lunch at a nice restaurant—and their friends, too." Neither the Blair School for Girls nor Girton College, Cambridge would have been pleased at her accent, grammar, or syntax. Elspeth gave her biggest smile.

"If this is your grandfather, I'd be real happy."

As she left the teashop, Elspeth heard the woman speak into her mobile.

"What do you suppose she has that she wants to give us, Dad? Something belonging to Grandfather. What do you think it is? You could add it to his war medals."

On the train back to Waterloo Station, Elspeth's mind was racing. Frank Wells, who now appeared to be Franklyn Robert Welles, had a son born ten years before Frank died in the war. By all accounts, that meant that Frank had married Magdelena when he already had a family in England. Was Frank's wife still alive at the time? If so, had he married to Aunt Mag illegally? On their marriage certificate the priest had listed

Frank's name as Francesco Roberto Wells of no parish. The photograph that Elspeth had now appeared to be that of Franklyn Robert Welles, born in Dorchester in December nineteen thirteen. Was Frank married to two people at the same time? At the very least he was a consummate liar, but was he also a bigamist? Aunt Mag had married Francesco Roberto Wells, not Franklyn Robert Welles, and therefore Francesco Roberto Wells did not exist, and Aunt Mag's marriage to him would be invalid. Elspeth wondered what the legal ramifications of it might be, but this might solve the problem of Aunt Mag's ownership of the farmhouse in Gozo. But how did it solve the mystery of why Frank had gone through a sham wedding with Aunt Mag, and, what he was really doing in Malta during the war. How could Elspeth tell Aunt Mag the truth about Frank, but she knew she would not feel comfortable until she did so. What would Aunt Mag's reaction be? Relief or grief, or anger, or all three?

Elspeth was no longer certain she should have so eagerly taken on Aunt Mag's request to find Frank. Telling guests bad news at Kennington hotels was far easier than confronting someone as close to her as Aunt Mag. Now she felt responsible for concluding her delicate task, which she was sure would distress her aunt, particularly if Uncle Frederick had been the officer who had beaten up Frank Wells so severely in Marsalforn.

Her mobile rang as she was attempting to walk through the crowds at Waterloo Station and reach the taxi stand. Her tendon hurt, and she was desperate to be back at her flat. She answered impatiently. Frank's son was on the line.

"Mr Welles, how great of you to call me. Why don't your wife and you and your friends meet me at. . ." Her mind raced for a place and all she could think of was "the Kennington

Mayfair at one o'clock tomorrow afternoon for lunch. Here's the address. You'll recognise me because I have a cast on my foot. I'll reserve a table in advance and let'em know you're coming. Will your friends come too do you think?"

Receiving a negative reply, she ended the call. She hoped having lunch with Mr and Mrs Welles would not attract the attention of the guests or staff of the hotel, many of whom knew her. She did not want to have to explain her American persona to them.

27

Despite her easy banter with Richard about placing his pillow next to hers, Elspeth did not sleep well, thinking of what she would say to him the next day. She knew the entire course of her future life depended on his acceptance of her third option. What had Aunt Mag said? *Ask from your heart, cara, and if that is what you want, how can he refuse you?*

The words came back to her again and again. Would he accept her terms? Her whole being ached. Please, Dickie, do accept them, she said to his strategically placed pillow. This third option can work, for me at least. Please let it work for you. Please.

Elspeth dressed simply for her meeting with Robert Welles and his wife. As she entered Lord Kennington's flagship hotel, its sophisticated grandeur struck her once again, although she had solved numerous problems here during her career with the Kennington Organisation and was familiar with all the ins and outs of the establishment. She wondered how Mr and Mrs Welles would react to it.

Elspeth took the precaution of making her presence known to the manager and to ask for a private table in the dining room, where she could talk to the Welles without being approached by anyone who might know her. She instructed the maître d' to bring the Welles to the table, where she took a seat facing the doorway to wait for them.

Robert Welles looked at the photograph Elspeth handed him.

"Yes, that's my father," he said. "Or at least as I remember him. He was away from home much of the time when I was a boy, but he would come to Dorset when he could. We lived in Lyme Regis then but moved inland during the war. My mum always said my father was involved in secret work that involved going undercover in Italy. He spoke fluent Italian, as my grandmother was Italian, and he was proficient in German and French as well."

"Do you know when your father died?" Elspeth asked.

"He died in the war. I don't know exactly when but I think in nineteen forty-two. He never came home after Mussolini declared war in nineteen forty."

"Was he in the British Army?"

Robert Welles nodded. "He had an army rank, sergeant as I remember, but I never saw him in uniform. But ten years after the war, they sent my family two medals, one the Order of the Star of Italian Solidarity given by the Italians and a Commendation from the British Government, both awarded to him for bravery. I was never sure if having a hero in the family made up for losing him. My mother married again, so I did have a father of sorts, but he never was like my real father to me. After I became an adult, I dropped my stepfather's surname and took back the name Welles."

"Tell me about him, anything you can remember. I think the father of my colleague in California would like to know all the details."

"It will be a ten-year-old's recollection. When I was a young child, he would always bring me something from London, usually toys or sweets, when he did come home. I always looked forward to that. He would carry me about on his shoulders or swing me round until I was completely dizzy. I thought he was the most wonderful father in the world."

"Did your mother mind that he was away so much of the time?"

"She did. I remember her going to mass every day, praying for his safe return. But why are you asking all this, Mrs Duff? My daughter said your co-worker's father was my father's friend during the war. Why would he be interested in my father's life before the war or in my childhood?"

Elspeth was prepared for this question, as she expected it would arise when she started asking questions about things that two wartime friends might not have shared together.

"Your father's friend is well over ninety, but his mind is very sharp. He said Frank talked about his family often. I think this person would want to know if Frank's son remembered his father. You obviously do. Will you answer one more question? What did you parents call you when you were a child?"

"Robin," Robert Welles said, frowning.

"Yes, that would agree with what my colleague's father told him," she said, although these two people were purely fictitious. "Since you're Frank's son, I'd like to give you this."

Elspeth had committed herself to producing something to give to Robert Welles that might have been sent from someone who knew his father in the war. Earlier she had rung a British colleague of her ex-husband, who was one of the leading fight and weapons choreographers in the film industry in

Hollywood. Elspeth had gone to the man's offices in London that morning and requested a gun of Second World War vintage that might have been used in Italy in the nineteen forties. From him she had obtained a small but deadly looking Beretta, a non-operative replica from his collection, and a cloth to put it in that looked as if it had been used on a battlefield. Elspeth hoped Robert Welles would accept it as genuine.

Robert Welles unwrapped the small pistol and turned it over in his hands. "Was this my father's?" he asked.

"I guess it was. Musta been. His friend said so," Elspeth said, skirting the truth.

"Is it licensed?"

Elspeth shook her head. "I brought it from the States," she lied, "so it wouldn't be registered here. Besides, I'm not real sure it works."

"You cannot know how much this means to me," Robert said. "I'll put it beside his photograph and his medals."

*

"Imagine after all this time, Robin," his wife said to him later, "that there is someone still alive who knew your father. But two things strike me as a bit odd. First, Mrs Duff never gave the name of your father's friend or let us know where we could write to thank him for his gift, and, second, how do you suppose she got the gun into the UK from the States, even if she said it doesn't still work? Don't they have all sorts of restrictions on things like guns entering the country under our new anti-terrorism laws?"

Robert Welles, still replete from roast lamb and the signature Kennington gooseberry pie, said, "Anyone who has enough money to stay at the Kennington Mayfair has enough money to arrange that sort of thing. You know people from California spend money as if it were water. But I'm glad to have my father's gun. It's a good thing we brought the car up to London. I wouldn't want to take it on public transport, even the train."

*

Elspeth returned to her flat at half past three. Richard was due at five, which gave her time to note down what she had learned from Robert Welles. She took out her laptop and typed furiously, but soon she knew her mind was no longer with Franklyn Robert Welles but with Richard's approaching arrival.

Ask from your heart and if that is what you want, how can he refuse you? she whispered and went up to the loft bedroom to prepare for his arrival.

28

Elspeth dressed with special care, choosing things she knew Richard had admired in the past or had given her, but her hand shook as she fastened the buttons on her silk blouse and put on a pair of gold earrings. As satisfied as she was going to be, she turned from the mirror and made her way down to the sitting room. If Richard reached the flat at five as he said he would, she had ten minutes to compose herself. A moment later the clock on her mantelpiece showed nine minutes remained until his arrival; and then, after an eternity, eight. She felt like a little girl waiting for a party, Was she doing the right thing? She was certain she was, but how would Richard react? She swallowed, hard, and tried to still her heart.

He rang the buzzer precisely as the hour chimed, although she knew he had a key. Perhaps he had not taken it with him to Belgium, since their original plan had been to meet in Gozo. She tried to slow her steps to the door but could not. She fumbled with the latch.

And then she was in his arms, holding him for a long time without words. Finally, he whispered to her, "Am I to hope?"

Elspeth led him to the sofa and sat beside him. She took his hand.

"I know my hand is shaking," she said. "But what I have to say is the most important thing I've ever said to anyone in my life." She took a deep breath. "Dickie, I love you. You already know that." Then she paused, "And I want to marry you. I want to marry you with no more hesitation on my part, only hopes."

Richard's eyes were so filled with joy that Elspeth reached up to touch his cheek, her hand still trembling.

She swallowed. "But I need to ask for several conditions that will make the marriage work for me."

He smiled. "What are they, my dearest Elspeth?" he said, his voice hoarse.

"One reason I've always been so independent," she said, "is that I don't know how to ask for things for myself, but with me my asking you now, I'm making myself more vulnerable than I ever thought I could be. I know there always is the good chance you may not want to accept my terms."

She put her hand to his lips. "No, don't speak, or I may I lose my courage," she said

"I've never seen you lose courage before, even in the face of a murderer," he said.

"I may now, because," she swallowed again, ". . . because these are the most difficult things I ever dared to ask for. There are three things I need."

He took her hand to calm it and waited.

"First, I want to keep my job, full-time."

He started to speak.

"Hush," she said, pressing his lips with her fingers again. "I know now I can't take on Marjorie's role, and I cannot go to Malta to moulder away in that job. This will mean we will be apart frequently, but I hope it will be sweeter when we are together."

"Yes, I've already supposed you would ask that," he said.

"Then, next, I want to keep my own name."

He looked surprised. "I hadn't expected that."

"You earned your title, Dickie, and I wasn't a part of you doing that. Besides, I find titles awkward and taking one on would be difficult, both in my work and for me personally. But more importantly, I cannot give up who I am, and somehow that means keeping my own name."

"I promise you never will have to use my name unless you choose to," he said.

"And finally, I want you to love me all the rest of my life the way you loved me in Gozo."

Having said this, she closed her eyes and turned her head from him.

He put his hand to her face and turned it back.

"Thank you, Elspeth, for your candour. Yes, my most precious one, I can accept all your terms with a full heart. Now, I've three conditions of my own."

She looked up at him, startled. "You have?" She had not considered that he might ask things of her as well.

"First, I want you to accept that I don't want you to replace Marjorie, and you are never to suggest that again. On occasion, I may ask you to act as my wife, publicly and officially," and then, with a grin, he said, "but I promise I will always introduce you by your own name if that is what you prefer."

She nodded and said, "Thank you, and I assure you I will always try to act decorously when I'm in your diplomatic surroundings, and not embarrass you the way I did in Victoria when we were having lunch."

He chuckled but then became serious. "My second condition is that I want you to feel free to ask me for anything you want. I may not always be able to give it to you, but you must ask."

She bit her lip and nodded again. "That may be harder, but I will try."

"And finally, I want to promise that you will love me all my life without any fears that our marriage won't work for us. You know I have wanted to marry you since I was nineteen, or rather I wanted to marry the person I thought you were or would become. Now I want to marry the person I got to know during our week in Gozo, a person I love more dearly than I thought possible. I expect our marriage will be highly unorthodox, Elspeth Duff, but I cannot imagine it being anything but splendid."

His last condition did not need her verbal reply.

Much later he said. "I had thought, if you did agree to marry me, that we should have the wedding in Gozo at Magdelena's farmhouse. Do you think she would agree that?"

Elspeth smiled, calm now, and happy to such an extent that she did not think she could breathe. "If we were not married in San Lawrenz, she would never forgive us. Let's make it soon, Dickie. We've waited long enough."

"I had thought in three weeks. Is that too long?"

"Not at all. I think we may need that much time to make the arrangements, although now I want it to be tomorrow. Do you mind if we invite our families to the wedding? I foolishly eloped the first time, but this time I would rather to be with those near and dear to me to declare my love and commitment to you."

"Ask whomever you like. I probably won't remember a single one afterwards because I will only be looking at you."

"Oh, Dickie, one other thing. I'd like to return to work on Wednesday."

"I see. Would you have done the same thing if I had not accepted your conditions?" he asked.

"I always assumed you would accept them if you loved me enough," she said raising her eyebrows. Her face broke into a wide grin.

"I don't believe it a minute." he cried and took her now steady hands in his. "I have something for you. I didn't want to give it to you until I was sure you would marry me."

"Did you doubt it, really?"

"Yes, often, but I never stopped hoping you would, so I bought you this."

He took a small box from his pocket and opened it. Inside was a ruby and diamond ring. "We can go and choose out our wedding rings tomorrow, but I wanted to give you this first, and if you aren't happy with it, we can choose another."

He took out the ring and put it on her third finger.

"It's perfect, Dickie," she said.

29

Across the breakfast table the next morning Elspeth related what she had learned about Frank Wells.

"What am I to say to Aunt Mag?" she asked.

"I think you'll have to tell her the truth," he said.

Elspeth grimaced. "Everything?"

"Yes, my dear, or at least enough to allow her to come to grips with Frank's past. I don't think it will surprise her, although it may sadden her. Perhaps our news will help alleviate her long-held doubts. But, Elspeth, what made you search for Frank Wells' place of birth in England as well as Italy?"

"Two things: the name Frank put on the twin's certificates of baptism, and the speculation of your raven-haired beauty."

"My raven-haired beauty? Do you mean the woman in the basement of the FCO? Somehow I'd forgotten about her."

"Good, because I've no intention of sharing you with anyone."

"But what did she say to make you come back to England?" he asked.

"She said something like 'maybe he is just plain Frank Wells from Birmingham', when you asked her to trace Francesco Roberto Wells. From the very beginning, Frank was a mixture of fact and fiction, so why couldn't his name be too. If Frank was working undercover, as now appears to be the case, what was his real name? I couldn't quite put things together until after you'd left for Brussels, because we were otherwise . . . um . . .engaged much of the time." She cocked her head and looked at him, her lips twitching. "But after you left, I asked to see the papers Magdelena had shown me when she first asked me to find out whether Frank was dead or not. The papers seemed to be in order: their marriage certificate from Saint Stephen's in London, Frank's passport issued in Rome, and the baptismal record of the twins. But then I looked more closely. On the marriage certificate, Francesco Roberto Wells had given no parish. His passport stated that he had been born in Milan, but that may not have been true. Last Monday morning in Gozo I was drinking coffee in the kitchen and listening to Teresa hum a song from her childhood, a Sicilian love song. Earlier you had asked Aunt Mag if Frank was at all musical. She said she had always been disappointed that he was not, that all he could do was whistle tunes from the London music halls. But if Frank had grown up in Italy, wouldn't he have been more likely to whistle Italian popular songs?

"Then I examined the baptismal certificate more closely. At first I thought there was a mistake. Frank's name was abbreviated and then misspelt, Frank. Robt. Welles. A Gozitan priest might have made this mistake, but I think Frank did it himself intentionally. Frank. Robt. Welles was the name given for the man who fathered the twins, but was it his real name? And, incidentally, were the twins a mistake? I learned yesterday that Frank's mother was Italian, and that his real wife went regularly to mass, meaning his family was Roman Catholic, so at the very least he was raised in that faith. If Francesco Roberto Wells never existed, then Aunt Mag was not legally married to him, was she? Perhaps Frank's Catholic upbringing could justify him hiding the truth on the marriage certificate but not on the baptismal records of his children as he probably wanted them to be recognised in the eyes of the Church. The British Government must have spent a great deal of money setting up a cover story to show he was a likely Fascist sympathiser and arranging for him to be domiciled in Malta, using his marriage to Aunt Mag for a reason for being there. But when the children came along, Frank must have felt some compelling need to record his correct name, even in abbreviated form, as he was presenting his children to God. Not being a Roman Catholic and living in two thousand and six and not in nineteen thirty-nine, I can't comprehend how his mind might have worked, but it must have been something like that. Therefore, all I needed was proof that Frank Robert Wells did exist under one name or the other, that he was truly English, and that he had lied to Aunt Mag about his origins."

"I think your conclusions are spot on," Richard said.

"That Frank had been set up by the Secret Service begins to make sense of other details, several of which seemed incongruous. I assume they sent out the false conscription notices to make it seem he had avoided active service and had given him the box of Italian chocolates, implying that he had been in Italy."

"Do you think Magdelena will be upset by this?"

"On the contrary, I think she will feel relieved to know that she was not in an adulterous relationship with my uncle for all those years, but merely living out of wedlock with him. Is that a deadly sin too? Or is it against the Ten Commandments? I'm never too sure what they all are."

"Wasn't Jean, his wife, still alive, making a second marriage impossible and his relationship with Magdelena adulterous?" Richard asked.

"Jean died shortly after I was born. Uncle Frederick and Aunt Mag lived together decades after that," Elspeth said. "Not knowing whether Frank was dead or not, Aunt Mag continued thinking she was still married to him. Do you think your Uncle Frederick knew Frank was dead?"

"I think he must have," Richard said.

"Then why didn't he tell Aunt Mag?" she asked. "For the last week, when my thoughts weren't elsewhere," she said, clearing her throat, "I've been asking myself that. Do you remember the morning I was scribbling so madly by the window and ignoring you?"

He pulled a face. "Vividly. I found it quite unacceptable."

"Mmm," she said. "I'll try to do better in the future. Nevertheless, the one thing I wrote first, and in large letters, was 'Why didn't Frederick tell Magdelena the truth about Frank Wells?'. I think I understand now. It had to be Uncle Frederick who beat up Frank in Marsalforn, possibly in a fight over his relationship with Aunt Mag, leaving him close to death. This gave the Secret Service a chance to list Frank as missing, presumed dead. I want to tell Aunt Mag what I've discovered as quickly as possible, although I don't know if I should include my assumptions about Uncle Frederick. Would you mind terribly if I went to Malta with you tomorrow afternoon so I could tell her in person? I'm sure you could come and stay at the farmhouse until I return on Tuesday to start work on Wednesday morning. We'll also need ask her about the wedding plans and enlist her help. She'll be overjoyed."

"I should be delighted to accompany the fairest lady in the world to Malta tomorrow and spend two more nights of sinful passion with her," he said laughing. "And now I think we have some telephone calls to make to share our news."

They rang Magdelena Cassar first.

Magdelena was playing a Chopin waltz on their arrival. She rose from her piano and flew to them as they came in the room, her shawls flying, beads clacking, and face beaming.

"So you two have finally come to your senses! I will never understand why it took both of you so long to see what was obvious to everyone else in the world. And to arrange for the ceremony here in Gozo. How delightful! How wonderful! Tell me your plans."

They talked through dinner about Elspeth and Richard's news, but Elspeth was distracted, mulling over what she would say to Magdelena about Frank.

After coffee was served, Elspeth took her courage in both hands. "Aunt Mag, I came to Gozo with Richard not only to tell you our news and make plans for the wedding but also because I've learned the truth about Frank. I thought it best, if you agree, to tell you what I discovered in Richard's presence as it was he asking for someone's help at the FCO that led me to the truth." Elspeth's voice broke. "This will not be an easy task, but Richard and I have discussed it, and we decided that you should know everything we have found out."

Magdelena's face stiffened. "Then he is dead, as you thought?"

"Yes, Aunt Mag. As I had speculated, he died during the war, but as a hero, not a traitor. Both the Crown and the Italian government awarded him medals posthumously for his bravery behind enemy lines. He died in September nineteen forty-two in Rome, while organizing a plot to overthrow the Fascist government. Richard contacted someone at the Imperial War Museum who confirmed this."

"And the truth?"

"Aunt Mag, I'm so sorry. Frank's real name was Franklyn Robert Welles. He was a Sergeant in the British Army, seconded to the Secret Service, probably in nineteen thirty-six, when they issued him a false passport, the one I found in your red-roped envelope. He told you the truth about his work but not his real name or his true background. When he met you, he was already married. Therefore, your marriage to him was invalid, both because he did not give his true name at the time of your marriage, and because he already had a wife. I met his son, who confirmed this."

Elspeth went over and knelt by the chair where her aunt was sitting and took hold of her hands.

Magdelena Cassar drew her body up and looked out toward her balcony. "Then he lied to me the whole time."

"Yes, but he had a reason. His mother was from Milan, and he spoke her language as if he had been raised in Italy. To the Fascists, he would have appeared to be a prime candidate for recruitment to work against the Allies. I expect the 'secret work' he told you he was doing was to portray himself in such a way that he would come to the attention of the Fascists as a sympathiser."

"But why would he choose to deceive *me*?" Magdelena's face was filled with grief.

"I don't know why you were specifically chosen, Aunt Mag. Even in nineteen thirty-six, the wiser heads in London were preparing for war, despite all the efforts to appease Hitler and Mussolini. The British powers-that-be obviously wanted Frank to have a legitimate reason to be in Malta. From here he could launch his campaign into Italy, posing as an Italian collaborator. When a person who styled himself 'Francesco Roberto Wells' exchanged his vows with you in London, the plans must already have been in place. He had a perfect excuse to live in Malta if his wife were Maltese, and it was easy for him to slip in and out of Sicily, possibly in a smuggler's boat, just as Uncle Frederick suggested."

Elspeth took Magdelena's hands more tightly in hers. "I have no way of knowing how Frank felt when the twins were born, but I think they were probably not part of the British Government's plan, and therefore their birth and existence were something he had to deal with personally. Frank's family was Roman Catholic, and I assume he remained so into adulthood. He must have agonized about bringing children in the world who were not born within the sanctity of marriage."

Magdelena sat without moving. Finally, she lifted her head and said, "You said he died in September nineteen forty-two. He left here in December nineteen forty-one. Was he in Italy all the time after that?"

"Not the whole time, Aunt Mag. I am sorry. Until August nineteen forty-two he was here in Gozo."

"Did he know about the death of the children and my father?"

"Probably."

"Why didn't he come to the funeral? Wouldn't any father do that?"

"I think because he was ordered not to."

"By whom?"

Elspeth inwardly twisted in pain and looked up at Richard, who was standing beside her. "We think by the British Secret Service, but we can't be sure," he said.

Magdelena seemed to diminish slightly. "Did Frederick know Frank was still here?"

"Yes, I think so."

"And why didn't he tell me?"

"Aunt Mag, before this last week, I didn't understand what a powerful force love can be."

"Are you suggesting that Frederick didn't tell me because he loved me? If he truly loved me, wouldn't he tell me the truth?"

"There was a reason he didn't, Aunt Mag. Uncle Frederick didn't tell you the truth because, for the rest of his life, I believe he thought that he had killed Frank."

"Killed Frank? You just told me Frank died in Rome."

"He did, but that information was classified until recently, and Uncle Frederick probably never knew. He and Frank had a terrible fist fight in Marsalforn in June nineteen forty-two. Uncle Frederick was already in love with you and probably aware that Frank had no intention of returning to you. In our conversation with him, Brigadier Fenech assumed that Uncle Frederick was doing counter-intelligence work in Malta during the war. When Uncle Frederick and Frank met in June, one or the other started a fight that ended with Frank being terribly wounded, almost to the point of death. Didn't you tell me that Uncle Frederick had a bandaged hand and seemed stiff when he came to interrogate you about Frank, and then told you Frank could be a traitor? If you remember, I asked you about this several times."

Magdelena nodded in acknowledgement but did not speak.

Elspeth looked up again at Richard, whose eyes were filled with concern as he returned her glance.

"I'm certain that Uncle Frederick never knew that Frank survived the fight. He must have always believed that he had murdered Frank, although Frank recovered under the care of an army nursing sister who was sworn to protect his identity, even from the highest authorities. That is why Uncle Frederick never told you about meeting Frank in Marsalforn, and why, even after Jean died, he had to uphold the fiction that Frank might still be alive. How devastating this must have been for him, even right up to his death. He must have felt that he couldn't share his perceived misdeed with you and still keep your love."

Magdelena rose and wiping tears from her eyes went to her piano. She began to play Sibelius' *Valse Triste*.

"*Cara*," she said as she finished playing, "These things were long ago. Now we must celebrate your happiness and make plans for the wedding."

"We would like to be married here at the farmhouse," Richard said. "In a civil ceremony."

Magdelena smiled. "Unfortunately, *caro*, that will not be possible. Several people have asked me the same thing before. I would love to celebrate the wedding here, but Gozitan law does not allow weddings in farmhouses, even one as grand as mine. You must be married in a public place."

Elspeth was dismayed. "But, Aunt Mag, why? I so wanted the wedding to be here."

Magdelena sighed. "I did too, but, knowing the law, I wanted to find someone I know who could officially marry you. Before you arrived, I called a friend at the Public Registry Office in Victoria, and he once again confirmed that we could not have the wedding here at the farmhouse as such celebrations are specifically forbidden in Gozitan civil marriages regulations. I am not one to criticise the government. I find it much easier that way, but, as you know, San Lawrenz has a grand hotel, where I go sometimes with friends. The ceremony can be held there and it can be brief as you wish. Afterwards we can return here to the farmhouse for the wedding celebration. I am already planning the menu for our luncheon. Teresa will be delighted."

Part 3

Elspeth and Richard

30

Elspeth returned to work Wednesday as promised. Pamela Crumm was waiting for her on the twentieth floor at express lift door.

"Come into my office, ducks, before he comes out and devours you. I told him that you have decided to marry Sir Richard after all. I think he's a bit jealous."

Pamela loved romantic details, but Elspeth decided not to share any with her other than to say, "We have decided to be married in Gozo three weeks on Saturday, and have the reception at my Aunt Magdelena's farmhouse afterwards."

"Not in Perthshire?"

"No, Richard's brother David, his wife, and most of my family will be coming. Pamela, I know you wouldn't ask to be invited, but I want you and Eric to come as well."

Pamela's eyes, magnified by her large round glasses, beamed. "Richard won't mind?" she asked.

"I would mind if you weren't there, dear friend, and his lordship as well," Elspeth said, tossing her head toward Lord Kennington's office. "You have both been so much a part of my life over the last eight years that I think of you as my closest friends as well as my employers. You won't tell Eric that last bit, will you?"

Elspeth did not mention Richard's comment about him being oblivious to all who would be at the wedding other than her.

"Of course not," Pamela replied. "It would swell Eric's head even more if he knew how you felt. I shall be delighted to come. Tell me who will be there from your family and Richard's as well."

"My mother and father from Scotland, of course. My son Peter and daughter Lizzie with her husband Denis, Biddy Baillie Shaw, whom you know, and my cousin Johnnie Tay, although he and his wife are separated and she won't attend. Johnnie is Richard's oldest friend and he will be the best man and look after the rings. My Aunt Magdelena Cassar is on Gozo already. Finally you, and Eric, if he will come.

"Let me buzz him and tell him you're here. I think he would be delighted if you asked him personally."

Pamela pressed a button on her telephone console and put him on speaker.

"How many?" Lord Kennington said.

"How many what?" Pamela asked.

"How many people will be at Elspeth's wedding?"

"She told me there will be thirteen, including the bride and groom, but she wants to come in and ask you if you will be the fourteen for luck." Elspeth was amazed how quickly Pamela had tallied the guests.

"I'd be absolutely delighted," he said. "Send her in. I'll call René Le Grand at the Kennington Valletta to book rooms for us all, with my compliments. I only needed the count. Thank you. Now when is this to be? I'm already free whether I am or not."

"How did you know it would be in Malta?" Pamela asked.

"I haven't built my hotel business on lack of intelligence, Pamela. Of course they will be married in Malta. Isn't Sir Richard our High Commissioner there?"

Pamela switched off the intercom, and they burst into giggles.

"Dear Eric." Elspeth said. "He never changes, does he?"

31

Eric, Lord Kennington had been discreet in choosing the rooms for his guests at the Kennington Valletta, particularly for the bride-and groom-to-be. Having been a hotelier for many years, he knew that on the night before their wedding, couples, particularly those embarking on a second marriage, should be given two options, either to sleep separately or to share a room. Consequently, he had chosen adjoining rooms with a connecting door for Elspeth and Richard.

Elspeth had made choices too. Shunning her usual silk pyjamas, which she normally wore when staying with Richard in the past, on a whim she had bought a very low-cut satin and lace nightgown when she was having her wedding outfit made. As she slipped into it, she looked at herself in the mirror. You silly woman, she said to the glass, do you think this extravagantly expensive negligee will stay on long enough for Richard to notice it? Almost shyly, she knocked on the connecting door.

Richard later admitted that his heart was pounding as he opened the door. He drew her tightly into his arms, kissing her hair and then her mouth and finally, drawing back, he looked at her. His smile recorded his appreciation.

"Elspeth, are you trying to seduce me?"

Her grin was wider than his. "Yes, that was the general idea. After all, this is our last night of unwedded bliss together, and I wanted to make it as rapturous as possible."

"Oh, Elspeth, Elspeth, Elspeth! How can you entice me so!" he whispered to her.

*

The next morning she propped herself up on her elbow and said, "Dickie, I shall miss our lovemaking outside the sanction of church or state. It's more exciting this way."

"Elspeth, you are both wicked and sinful."

"I try," she said. "What shall we do when we become respectable later today?"

"We won't change a thing," he said.

She wondered if he would have said the same words five weeks before when she had rejected their agreement to be married at Glenborough Castle.

"Good," she said. "I hadn't planned to."

Later she said, "Eric has decided that it would be 'proper' for us to go to Gozo separately. The women will go ahead, which is just as well, because we need to dress before the men arrive. Aunt Mag has reserved a room at the hotel where we can change."

"In the grandest of traditions, the ladies are to proceed together to the island of Gozo in preparation of the wedding of one of their clan. Your mother, Biddy, Lizzie and you all look so alike, I shall have trouble knowing which one I am supposed to marry."

Elspeth threw a pillow at him. "Fiend," she said. "If you can't pick me out, I shall marry Eric Kennington."

"I thought he was already married."

"He is, but, if you choose another, bigamy is definitely in order."

They both leaned back and laughed in a most merry way.

*

As the launch Lord Kennington had hired for the ladies cut through the waves, Elspeth's daughter Lizzie took her cousin Biddy aside.

"Biddy, why is Mummy marrying Sir Richard? If there ever was a stuffed shirt, he is one. When he came to LA when Peter and I were young, we choked up with trepidation. He was so distant, and Lady Marjorie terrified us."

"Lizzie," Biddy said, "did you look at Richard last night?"

"He seems quite besotted with my mother, I must admit."

"Did you look at her?"

"Mummy?"

"Yes."

"Well, I just kept wondering what she saw in him."

"Did you look at her, not as your mum but as a woman?"

"No, I suppose not. She is my mother after all."

"Lizzie, she is as besotted with him as he is with her."

"How can that be?"

"Love doesn't stop at twenty."

Lizzie blushed. "But they. . ."

"Are too old? I predict that they will have a wonderful life together for many years to come." Biddy smiled at Elspeth's daughter. "I don't expect your mother has ever shared much of her past life with you, but she has never enjoyed the happiness that she has with Richard now."

Lizzie looked puzzled.

"Your mother has always believed that one should plunge ahead without considering the long-term consequences. More than one person has called her impetuous, but she has always had, how can I say it, complications with the men in her life?"

"Men, not just my father?"

Biddy took Lizzie's hand. "Someday I'll tell you the story of Malcolm Buchanan, but not now. Today is your mother and Richard's day. Celebrate it, Lizzie. They both deserve it."

*

The staff of the grand hotel near San Lawrenz greeted the wedding party with practiced grace and showed the ladies to the suite Magdelena Cassar had booked for them. She had arranged also arranged for a separate room for the men on another floor. The women's suite looked out over the swimming pool and the grounds, which were carefully groomed and tree filled, in contrast to the barren landscape of most of Gozo. Elspeth was too absorbed in the day to compare the hotel to those run by Lord Kennington. All that mattered were her family and friends and the ritual ahead.

"Mummy," Lizzie said as they shed their everyday clothes and began to dress for the ceremony, "do you really love Sir Richard as much as Biddy says you do?"

As she looked in the mirror, Elspeth regarded her daughter. "Lizzie, I love him with all my heart. Does that surprise you?"

"It does a bit. When he came to California with Lady Marjorie, Peter and I used to shake with fear that we would not behave well enough to meet their aristocratic standards. We always thought them just too, too proper. When Peter and I spoke after you told us you were going to marry Sir Richard, we wondered why."

Elspeth put her hand to her daughter's face. "Because we can all change. I don't think you will find Richard as stiff as he used to be."

"Change? Has he really changed?"

"A great deal, and I have as well. Dear Lizzie, I hope you and Denis have as much love for each other as I have for

Richard. You may not understand, but please just accept that what I am doing is right for me—and for Richard as well."

Lizzie looked at her mother and smiled. "I've never seen you looked so radiant, Mummy."

"No, I never have felt so before, or as certain of what I am doing," Elspeth said.

"Then I'm delighted for you and wish you both a brilliant life together. I've brought something for you—something new—but I hope you enjoy it even after today." She produced a small, light blue box. Elspeth undid the white ribbon and drew out a simple gold brooch.

"Something new? Darling, what a lovely piece. I shall cherish it always. Help me pin it on. As for the rest, Magdelena gave me an antique Maltese lace handkerchief to tuck into my pocket."

"Something old, something new. And something borrowed?"

"These earrings. Richard's brother's wife, Susan, lent them to me. They belong in the Dunsmuir jewellery collection and were worn by Richard's great grandmother when the family entertained Queen Victoria and Prince Albert at Dunsmuir House, Richard's family home in Aberdeenshire."

"Something blue? Of course, your blouse. Mum, you look marvellous."

Elspeth smiled, cherishing this moment of closeness. She loved her daughter but always felt somehow apart from her. Perhaps it was for the best, as they often sparred even in good times together.

"Help me finish dressing, Lizzie. I want to look my best."

Elspeth had selected her clothes carefully. She did not want to appear the blushing bride, and consequently asked her dressmaker to create her something appropriate for a second marriage and the warm, late May weather in Gozo. She had chosen a light, cream-coloured Thai silk long-lined, short-sleeved jacket, with touches of blue stitchery at the buttonholes, a knee length skirt to match, and a simple cobalt blue silk top underneath. Teresa had pressed the outfit, and Giulio had delivered it to the hotel.

Richard and Elspeth wanted the marriage ceremony to be simple and had decided that everyone should wear a single white rose, including themselves. Lizzie helped her mother pin it on her jacket so that it was straight. Elspeth reciprocated.

Elspeth smiled at her reflection. "Here we go," she said to it and blew out her breath. "The men should be waiting for us below."

Luckily, the weather held and they were able to have the ceremony outside in a shady spot in a circle of olive trees. According to Richard and Elspeth's wishes, the attendees stood together under the trees, Richard and Elspeth in the middle. Richard took Elspeth's hands in his and his eyes never strayed from hers, but at one point Elspeth looked up and saw Lord Kennington beaming even more widely than her father.

Their vows were simple and the ceremony brief. Elspeth recited the words that she and Richard had chosen, partly taken from *The Book of Common Prayer* and partly an expression of their love and commitment to each other.

Facing Richard, Elspeth began solemnly. "In front of my family and friends, I declare my love for you, Richard, and do take you as my wedded husband, forsaking all others, to love and cherish you all the days of my life until death do us part." The word 'obey' had been judicially dropped.

Richard followed her with similar wording.

Afterwards the Gozitan 'marriage officiator', Magdelena's friend, declared Richard and Elspeth to be husband and wife,

When they returned to the farmhouse, Father Lucca was waiting and came forward. He was unable to marry them because they were not of the Roman Catholic faith, but he gave their union God's blessing.

Elspeth felt blessed indeed.

*

As they finished the wedding breakfast which Teresa and Giulio presented with great pomp, James Duff, Elspeth's father, raised his glass to Richard.

"To you, Richard. A year and a half ago you came to me and asked if you had my permission to address my daughter on the subject of marriage. The language was so Victorian that it made me smile. I told you only one person could answer that, and that person was Elspeth herself. You apparently have won her heart and her hand, and her mother and I welcome you into our family with all the joy in the world. And to you, Elspeth. You have been the most precious thing in our lives. All your life you have been fiercely independent and have always known your own mind, but we feel you have now made the best decision of your life. Love Richard as I've always loved your mother, and you will always be happy."

Johnnie Tay came next and saluted his good friend and his cousin Elspeth.

"Dickie, you sly old fox. You finally landed her. Forty years must be a record. And you, Elspeth, why did it take you so long?"

Everyone laughed.

Eric Kennington stood up and delivered a toast of his own.

"Richard, my congratulations. You have stolen the heart of my best employee. Elspeth, if you hadn't set your heart on Richard, he might have had competition from me!"

Denis Foxworthy, Lizzie's husband, stood next. "Richard, we ask you to treat my mother-in-law as she deserves. She is a fine person and an excellent grandmother to our twins. And, Elspeth, why didn't you tell us this was going on? Heavens, you surprised us both when you announced you were going to marry Richard."

Peter Craig, Elspeth's son, rose from his place and stood silently looking at his mother, his head tilted slightly to one side. "Mom," he finally said, grinning, "I always suspected you had hidden depths. Richard, I'm so glad you've discovered them."

David, Lord Dunsmuir, Richard's brother, was the last to propose his toast. "Elspeth," he said, "why has Richard kept you from us for so long? We also welcome you into our family. And, to you, Richard," he said raising his glass "We are honoured to welcome her into the Munro family. Don't keep her a secret longer."

*

After the ceremony and the wedding lunch, Elspeth and Richard said goodbye to family and friends. The launch Lord Kennington had hired was waiting for them at Mgarr. Giulio escorted them both to the boat and bade them goodbye. Tears in his eyes, he threw a rose to them as the launch pulled away from the dock. They waved back.

"I wonder if he was remembering his wedding to Teresa in war-torn Sicily? How different this must be," Elspeth said.

"Mmm," Richard replied.

Elspeth was not sure to what he was referring, but she was too filled with the moment to ask.

When they arrived back at the Kennington Valletta to prepare for their departure to London, Richard said, "Do you know that since we both emerged from our rooms this morning, which I hope they all noticed was done discreetly and separately, I've not been alone with you. My dearest wife, how are you feeling?" He kissed her through his words.

"Must I say?" she said, basking in his closeness.

"Yes."

"I've been feeling, er, ah, em, flushed all day after last night."

"Is that a proper thing for a bride to say on her wedding day?"

"I hadn't noticed that we were particularly proper last night."

He was no longer shocked at her joking about their lovemaking. "Did you even notice that we got married today?"

"Luckily my mind has the ability to think of two things at once," she said, kissing him. "I'm so glad we are finally married. Oh, Dickie, I do love you so. Who would have ever thought this day would come?"

"I'd hoped it would for the last forty years," he said dryly.

He remembered his marriage to Marjorie. It had been over a month before she consented to the privileges of marriage with him and then only tensing herself with the physicality of it. He had made love to Elspeth more in the last seven months than he had in his thirty years of marriage to Marjorie.

Richard was a man who acted prudently in all things, except perhaps in his four-decade pursuit of Elspeth. Lord Kennington had insisted that Richard and Elspeth return to London in his private jet. Dusk was falling when they arrived at the airfield where he kept his plane. Lord Kennington's personal Jaguar and his driver was waiting for them.

"I want to make certain that we are properly married," he said after they arrived at Elspeth's flat in Kensington.

"Aren't we?"

"After the complication of Frank's wedding to Magdelena, I want our union recorded in the UK. Before I left London, I rang the Archbishop of Canterbury and asked him to issue us a special licence. He was delighted to oblige, and when he came to Malta several years ago, I took him out on my yacht for a day's sailing. Now we can be married under the official rites of the Anglican church, which should please your parents. My housekeeper, Mrs Brown, and her husband have agreed to meet us at Kensington Church in the morning and act as our witnesses. By the way, the Archbishop sent you greetings and said he was hoping to meet you soon."

For the first time, Elspeth realised how many consequential people Richard had personally entertained over the course of his career, many more than she had done working for Lord Kennington, or during her time in Hollywood.

They were duly married for a second time, which Richard assured her would avoid any complications in the future. After the brief ceremony, Richard took her hand, and they walked back to the flat through the springtime gardens that lined their path.

"Well, my twice-wed wife, I am truly satisfied now. No one can doubt that we are indeed man and wife," he said as they neared her flat.

"No one at all," she replied, first looking sternly and then with a radiant smile. "Oh, Dickie, this is such an enchanted time for me."

*

Pamela Crumm later placed a short notice in both *The Times* and the *Times of Malta*:

> *On May 31st, 2006, The Honourable Sir Richard Munro, KCMG, Her Majesty's High Commissioner to the Republic of Malta, and Mrs Elspeth Duff of Kensington and Loch Rannoch, Perthshire, were married on the island of Gozo, Malta, in the presence of those dearest to them.*

She did not mention a second wedding in Kensington. Elspeth had carefully avoided giving Pamela the details.

Epilogue

In the British Airways First Class lounge at Heathrow, Elspeth stood with her back to the wall and surveyed the passengers awaiting their various flights. The monitor above the bar showed that Elspeth and Richard's flight to San Francisco was on schedule. They would arrive in time to meet their hired car, and the driver would meet them and take them to Elspeth's retreat in western Marin County. They planned to spend the next three weeks there and hoped to savour its seclusion to the fullest. Elspeth looked down at the diamond and ruby ring that Richard had given her, now banded by her wedding ring. Her heart was bursting with happiness.

Richard returned to where she was standing and offered her a tall glass of orange juice. She accepted it and raised her eyes to his, which sparkled back at her.

"I've spotted a colleague," Richard said. "He's rather high up in the FCO. Do you mind if I introduce you?"

Elspeth knew this would not be the last time such a thing would occur when they were in public together. "Not at all," she said. "They all will have to meet me eventually, I suppose."

"I promised to keep a low profile for us, and I plan to meet that commitment, but I can't ignore him."

"Oh, Dickie, I don't want to seem standoffish. Please go ahead."

Richard's colleague saw them and waved. Richard took Elspeth gently by the arm and led her over to where the man was seated.

"Elspeth, meet Sir Colin Swift. We served together in Africa many years ago."

Elspeth suspected that members of the diplomatic community would immediately compare her with Lady Marjorie, but she had not expected to face this ordeal so soon. She straightened her back, adjusted her stylish jacket and pinned a smile on her face. She hoped she would act appropriately but knew she had much to learn about the ways of the diplomatic community.

Sir Colin was older than Richard and not as trim. Years of responsibility had not treated him as well as they had Richard. Sir Colin wrestled his rotund form from his chair.

"Colin, meet my new wife." Richard said and then, after a pause, "Elspeth Duff."

Sir Colin extended a hand. "I heard you getting married again, Richard. Congratulations to you both. And best wishes to you, Lady Munro."

"Call me Elspeth, please." She grinned. "As yet I'm not used to being addressed as Lady Munro."

She looked at Richard as she spoke. He nodded approvingly in response. She had cleared the first hurdle.

After a brief conversation of banalities, the attendant in the lounge approached them and told them that their flight had been called and she would escort them to the plane. As they passed the line of queuing passengers at the gate, one was overheard saying, "They look so happy, one would almost assume they were newly-weds except, of course, for their ages."

Elspeth contained her merriment until they were seated. "Are we that obvious?" she asked, grinning.

"We must be," he answered.

Author's Notes and Appreciation

Writing a series of books has many delights but also presents challenges. Elspeth and Richard's story may seem resolved at the end of *A Gamble in Gozo*, but in the next book in the series, readers will find that the course of true love . . . you can fill in the rest. As I developed the plot for *A Gamble in Gozo*, I realised I would have to end with the wedding, although at first I intended to omit it. The mystery of Frank Wells was resolved, but I thought Elspeth and Richard's relationship needed closure—at least temporarily. Therefore, I included snippets about the wedding, which were not part of the original book.

I visited Malta and Gozo for a second time in May 2017 to confirm information for *A Gamble in Gozo*. Despite the heatwave while I was there, I walked extensively around the village of San Lawrenz and the surrounding countryside and visited Marsalforn and Victoria to verify small details. Sadly, I discovered that the Azure Window, shown on the cover, had totally collapsed into the sea on March 8th, 2017 during a storm.

Many people helped me during the writing of this book.

Ian Crew again needs to be thanked first as he is my constant supporter and helps me with all the details that writing and publishing a book involves.

Jerene DeLaney, a friend and former nurse, gave me medical advice on how to treat a damaged Achilles' tendon.

Mary of Peter's Minibus Service on Gozo gave me a plethora of information when I visited Malta in 2004 while researching for my first book in the Elspeth Duff mystery series, *A Murder in Malta,* and I used much of that information here. I thanked her in my first book, but I want to thank her again. I went back to my photographs and notebook and found answers to many of the questions that I had asked her when I visited Gozo for the first time, and which were relevant to *A Gamble in Gozo.*

Appreciation also to goes the many people I met in Gozo in 2017, including Stefano Grotto of Grotto's Paradise B&B, where I stayed, who showed me around Marsalforn and other places which appear in future books, Neville Galea, Assistant Principal, DG (Operations), Public Registry, Ministry of Gozo, who led me through the requirements of a civil wedding on Gozo, the staff of the 'grand hotel' near San Lawrenz, who allowed me to tour their extensive grounds, and Carmen, the librarian at the Nicholas Monsarrat Library in San Lawrenz, and several older patrons of the library, who all gave me information on the village today and what had happened there during the Second World War.

Special gratitude goes to my friend, Jocelyn Jenner in Scotland, who with the help of her husband read my final drafts and corrected mistakes and my British English and whose eagle eyes I admire immensely, since this is not a great skill of mine. Others who read the final draft of the book include Patricia McCairen, and Bev Mar, who spotted typographical errors.

For readers interested in what happened in Malta and Gozo during the Second World War, I recommend the historical novel *The Kappillan of Malta* by Nicholas Monsarrat, who wrote the epic tale while living in San Lawrenz. In the War Bookshop in Valletta, I also found a copy of *Wartime Gozo 1940-1943, An Account of the Bleak Years,* by Charles Bezzina, which provided me with many details I had not found in other sources. Of note, there was an air raid on San Lawrenz on July 28th, 1942, in which four people were killed. Their names are inscribed on the outside wall of the Parish Church in San Lawrenz. The air raid in *A Gamble in Gozo* is fictitious, but the island of Gozo was heavily bombed in nineteen in 1941 and 1942 with much destruction of the buildings there, and many civilian deaths. There also are numerous other non-fiction sources that recount the events in Malta and Gozo during the Second World War, many of which can be found on the Internet.

Read on for an excerpt from the sixth book in the Elspeth Duff series, *A Deception in Denmark.*

From *A Deception in Denmark:*

Exhaustion overcame Fabia Alberti. Her role as *Madama Butterfly* always had that effect. Was it the weighty wig or the heavy emotions she portrayed in the last act of the opera? She sat at her dressing table and slowly removed her stage makeup. The scars still slightly showed despite the many skin grafts she had endured after the car crash. She was noted for her beauty on stage but, once the grease paint was wiped off, she found a face that reflected her duplicity. Would she ever forget what she had done and accept her life as it was now? No one had questioned her confusion in the ambulance when she had uttered Fabia's name rather than her own, and she had been careful ever since never to correct her mistake. Did she need to continue being so cautious after all this time?

She had never gone back to New York because there they might uncover her deceit. She justified this by saying her career was in Europe, and she needed to establish herself before considering a return to her home city. The Alberti family wealth meant she could continue living in luxury but, if she told the truth about what happened ten years before, all that would end. No, it was best to stay quiet.

A gentle tap came at her dressing room door.

"Come in," she called, anticipating her companion who also served as her dresser.

"Fabia, it's me. Diana. I've brought the flowers thrown at the curtain call, and a massive bouquet of roses with a card left at the stage door desk."

"Diana, be a love. Put the roses is a vase, please. The others can go to the nursing home."

Fabia rose and took the card Diana handed her. She tore open the small envelope and read the contents.

Madama Butterfly,

Unlike Pinkerton, I would not desert such a beautiful lady. Will you have a late supper with me at the hotel?

With all my love,
Robbie

"They're from Robbie," Fabia said. Her heart glowed at his continued attention. Initially she did not want to be drawn into a relationship with him, but his British good manners and handsome face attracted her more than any other man she had ever met.

"Fabia, be cautious of him. He's too smooth," Diana said.

"He's delightful. I love his posh British accent and gentlemanly courtesies. Did you know he comes from an old family in Scotland who own a castle?"

"Don't be fooled by that. You have no proof."

"It's nothing serious, Diana. I find his attention diverting."

"Just be careful," Diana said.

"Diana, don't bully me."

"I don't want to bully, Fabia. My main concern is for your safety."

Another knock came at the door.

"That must be Robbie. Will you let him in, please."

The person who entered was not Robert MacArthur but an older woman who carried herself proudly. Her salt-and-pepper hair with a distinctive white streak at her forehead was pulled up in a fashionable top knot, and her clothes shouted high fashion. Fabia turned toward the woman and felt her heart stop. She took a deep breath. No, it can't be, not after all this time, she thought, panicking.

"Hello, Jill," the woman said.

Fabia turned to Diana. "Leave us alone please," she said.

Diana, looking puzzled, turned from arranging the flowers and frowned at Fabia.

"Leave us alone, Diana," Fabia said again through clenched teeth. "You can take away the other flowers later."

"Call me if you need me, Fabia."

Fabia did not respond but indicated with a flick of her head that she wanted Diana gone.

Once alone with the woman, Fabia turned to her. "How did you find me?" she said.

"I was in Copenhagen and saw Fabia's name on a poster in a store window on Strøget. I had heard she was making a success here in Europe, so I came to hear her sing. I didn't expect it would be you, Jill. Both of you were good, but your voice had, has, more depth. I taught you both the same techniques, but I always thought you and not the real Fabia would be successful in the world of opera."

"You always did favour me over Fabia."

"Only because of the quality of your voice, which was so much better than hers."

"You won't let on, will you, Eve?"

"Why did you take her name?"

"They asked me for a name after the accident. I said 'Fabia' because I thought they were asking for her name, not mine."

"Why didn't you tell them afterwards who you really were? Was it the Alberti money? Is that why you never came back to New York?'

Fabia turned away from her accuser, who had guessed correctly.

"Only you would have known the difference. Everyone said we looked alike and we played on that when we were children. People often asked if we were twins."

"You look like Fabia now."

Fabia laughed weakly. "The result of plastic surgery after the accident. I gave the doctors photographs of Fabia when they were reconstructing my face."

"But you couldn't change your voice. You spoke alike but you did not sing alike."

"Only you would know, Eve. I've made Fabia's name famous and with the Alberti money was able to launch my career."

"Does Fabia's brother know?"

"As you said, I've never been back to New York. Matthew probably wouldn't recognise the difference. There was fifteen years between them. He was away at prep school when Fabia was born, and he had little contact with her when she was growing up."

"I saw in *The New York Times* that both of Fabia's parents are dead."

"They died six months apart."

"So they never saw you after the accident?"

"No. They were the only other people who might have known, but even they called us 'the twins'."

"You took Fabia's part of the estate, I assume," Eve said.

"She would have shared it with me. I'm preserving her name."

Fabia was beginning to feel defensive. What right did Eve Gardiner have to barge into her dressing room and try to destroy her career? Other than Fabia's parents, Eve was the only person in the world who would be able to see through the deception.

"You won't reveal my secret, will you, Eve? Please don't."

"Jill, I always have been an honest person, and I've never liked fraudsters. That's exactly what you are. I'll leave you tonight, but I need time to consider my next move. Did you seriously think you could get away with this forever?"

Ann Crew is a former architect and now a full-time mystery author who, when not writing, spends time travelling the world, gathering material for future Elspeth Duff mysteries. She currently lives near Vancouver, British Columbia.

Visit *anncrew.com* or *elspethduffmysteries.com* for more information on the author and the book series.